If th
coul

We'd be speechless! In a recent shocking "confession,"
cantankerous family patriarch Caine Stockwell aired
enough dirty laundry to fill a laundromat. Twice over.
Mr. Mean-old-moneybags rose up from his sick bed
muttering about dear Madelyn. Of course his children's
ears perked at the mention of their mother, but whoa—
what came next! To think mommy dearest hadn't
drowned after all, but has been living in a secret love
nest for decades—with Caine's twin brother, Brandon!
Well, the new generation of Stockwells is reeling—
and on a truth quest. Of course *we* know the real
scuttlebutt.... You, on the other hand, will have to
read on to get the down-and-dirty!

And as if Caine's ravings weren't enough to blast
his son Rafe Stockwell's ordered world into a billion
pieces, the bachelor lawman just discovered his
ex-girlfriend is seven months pregnant. Yep, the
same former flame who told him to take a hike
exactly seven months ago. Coincidence? We
think not....

The lovely Kate Stockwell
nabs the man who got away in
Her Unforgettable Fiancé
by Allison Leigh, SE #1381,
available March 2001,
only from Silhouette
Special Edition.

Dear Reader,

What if...? These two little words serve as the springboard for each romance novel that bestselling author Joan Elliott Pickart writes. "I always go back to that age-old question. My ideas come straight from imagination," she says. And with more than thirty Silhouette novels to her credit, the depth of Joan's imagination seems bottomless! Joan started by taking a class to learn how to write a romance and "felt that this was where I belonged," she recalls. This month Joan delivers *Her Little Secret,* the next from THE BABY BET, where you'll discover what if...a sheriff and a lovely nursery owner decide to foil town matchmakers and "act" like lovers....

And don't miss the other compelling "what ifs" in this month's Silhouette Special Edition lineup. What if a U.S. Marshal knee-deep in his father's murder investigation discovers his former love is expecting his child? Read *Seven Months and Counting...* by Myrna Temte, the next installment in the STOCKWELLS OF TEXAS series. What if an army ranger, who believes dangerous missions are no place for a woman, learns the only person who can help rescue his sister is a female? Lindsay McKenna brings you this exciting story in *Man with a Mission,* the next book in her MORGAN'S MERCENARIES: MAVERICK HEARTS series. What happens if a dutiful daughter falls in love with the one man her family forbids? Look for Christine Flynn's *Forbidden Love.* What if a single dad falls for a pampered beauty who is not at all accustomed to small-town happily-ever-after? Find out in Nora Roberts's *Considering Kate,* the next in THE STANISLASKIS. And what if the girl-next-door transforms herself to get a man's attention—but is noticed by someone else? Make sure to pick up Barbara McMahon's *Starting with a Kiss.*

What if... Two words with endless possibilities. If you've got your own "what if" scenario, start writing. Silhouette Special Edition would love to read about it.

Happy reading!

Karen Taylor Richman,
Senior Editor

Please address questions and book requests to:
Silhouette Reader Service
U.S.: 3010 Walden Ave., P.O. Box 1325, Buffalo, NY 14269
Canadian: P.O. Box 609, Fort Erie, Ont. L2A 5X3

Seven Months and Counting...

MYRNA TEMTE

SPECIAL EDITION™

Published by Silhouette Books

America's Publisher of Contemporary Romance

Special thanks and acknowledgment are given to Myrna Temte for her
contribution to the Stockwells of Texas miniseries.

This book is dedicated to Mary Buckham.
You know why.

My thanks to the following people for their help with research:
Kristine Fisher, R.N., Health Education Coordinator
for Parenting and Pediatric Programs at Community Health,
Education and Resources, Spokane, Washington;
Belinda Bass; Deb Bryson; Laurie Schnebly; Jackie Bielowiez;
and RaeAnne Thayne.

 SILHOUETTE BOOKS

ISBN 0-373-24375-8

SEVEN MONTHS AND COUNTING...

Books by Myrna Temte

Silhouette Special Edition

Wendy Wyoming #483
Powder River Reunion #572
The Last Good Man Alive #643
*For Pete's Sake #739
*Silent Sam's Salvation #745
*Heartbreak Hank #751
The Forever Night #816
Room for Annie #861
A Lawman for Kelly #1075
†Pale Rider #1124
A Father's Vow #1172
†Urban Cowboy #1181
†Wrangler #1238
†The Gal Who Took the West #1257
†Wyoming Wildcat #1287
Seven Months and Counting... #1375

*Cowboy Country
†Hearts of Wyoming

Silhouette Books

Montana Mavericks
Sleeping with the Enemy

MYRNA TEMTE

grew up in Montana and attended college in Wyoming, where she met and married her husband. Marriage didn't necessarily mean settling down for the Temtes—they have lived in six different states, including Washington, where they currently reside. "Moving so much is difficult," the author says, "but it is also wonderful stimulation for a writer."

Though always a "readaholic," Myrna never dreamed of becoming an author. But while spending time at home to care for her first child, she began to seek an outlet from the neverending duties of housekeeping and child-rearing. She started reading romances and soon became hooked, both as a reader and a writer. Now Myrna appreciates the best of all possible worlds—a loving family and a challenging career that lets her set her own hours and turn her imagination loose.

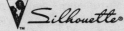

Chapter One

Good God, she was pregnant!

Deputy U.S. Marshal Rafe Stockwell came to an abrupt halt inside the doorway to the offices of Carlyle & Carlyle in Grandview, Texas. Crushing the brim of the pearl-gray Stetson hat he carried in his left hand, he rocked back on his boot heels and stared at his former lover, Ms. Caroline Carlyle, Attorney at Law. She stood beside a large, jumbled stack of boxes at the far end of the reception area, checking something off on a clipboard, her concentration so intense she didn't notice him.

It was a darn good thing, too. He needed the time to close his mouth. He couldn't believe the change in her appearance. She'd been sleek and chic when she'd dumped him three months and twenty-nine days ago. Not that he'd been counting.

Now, here she was, filling out a maternity dress and

wearing plain black flats instead of the sexy high heels he'd been used to seeing her in. And her sunshine-yellow hair had been cut into a short, trendy style that curled under just below her jawline. It looked attractive on her, but he'd loved playing with her long, silky hair so much, he felt a twinge of sadness at the thought of anyone taking scissors to it.

He'd never had a thing for pregnant ladies before, but Caroline still was one of the most beautiful women he'd ever seen. In his eyes, the pregnancy had actually enhanced her looks. It had softened her features somehow, made her seem less perfect, warmer and more approachable. An invisible hand wrapped around his heart and squeezed it hard.

He was hardly an expert on pregnant women, but the way her belly was hanging right out there, he wondered just how far along she was. Five months? Six? Maybe even seven?

She flipped the top page on her clipboard, then heaved a dispirited sigh. Rubbing the small of her back as if it ached, she closed her eyes and rolled her head from side to side. She looked tired.

An urge to protect her and take care of her surged inside Rafe. Gritting his teeth, he reminded himself that she was only a friend these days; her well-being now was another man's responsibility. Her pregnancy had nothing to do with him.

Or did it?

The hair on the back of Rafe's neck zinged a warning to his nervous system. Whoa. Wait just a damn minute.

He blinked, then focused his gaze on Caroline's belly again. *Five, six or seven months?* If any of those numbers was right, it would mean that the baby she was carrying could be—

No. No, it couldn't. She would have told him. He was sure of it. Nevertheless his heart suddenly revved faster than one of his twin brother Cord's pricey little sports cars, and the strangest sensation invaded Rafe's insides. He shut his eyes and raked his right hand through his hair, but the thought he'd always considered unthinkable echoed in his mind.

What if that baby was *his?*

He'd been mighty careful about birth control, but the only truly foolproof method was abstinence, and he sure hadn't practiced *that* with Caroline. Making love with her had been... He wasn't going to think about that just now. He needed to use his head and keep other, more unruly parts of his anatomy under control.

Besides, there was no sense jumping to any wild conclusions.

Caroline didn't have "accidents." Shoot, she was almost as much of a control freak as he was. No way would she allow herself to get pregnant without a husband around to make everything nice and socially acceptable. Rafe hadn't heard anything about her getting married, but he'd been working a lot. And, because of her father's battle with Alzheimer's disease, she might've decided to have a small, quiet wedding.

So what if she was really big? Maybe she was carrying twins. Maybe twins ran in her husband's family. The same way they did in his own.

Oh, God. What if that baby really *was* his?

"Aw, jeez," he muttered, shoving his fingers through his hair again.

Caroline started at the sound of his voice, then whipped her head around and stared at him. Her blue eyes widened in what looked like pleasure when she first caught sight of him. A heartbeat later her expression changed to one of shock, which was quickly covered by a mask of professional courtesy. She straightened her shoulders and raised her chin, presenting him with the poised image he'd come to expect from her. Nothing flustered Ms. Caroline Carlyle for long.

"Rafe, what a nice surprise," she said. "It's been a long time."

Rafe had to smile. He'd forgotten how much her proper little Boston accent tickled him. Her folks should have let her come home to Texas from that Massachusetts boarding school more often.

"It sure has, Caroline." He walked farther into the suite of offices, glancing at her belly, then shifting his attention to her face. "Well, I guess congratulations are in order."

She sidestepped a box and came toward him. Damn. Pregnant or not, with or without high heels, she still had the sexiest legs and the greatest walk in Texas.

"Thank you, Rafe." She offered him her right hand. "What can I do for you today?"

Still reeling from the possible implications of her pregnancy, Rafe could barely remember his own name, much less the original reason for his visit. He tossed his partially mangled hat onto the reception desk and shook her hand, then instinctively reached for her left hand and lifted it up beside her right one. Her fingers felt small and fragile in his.

She wore a plain gold wedding band.

Rafe swallowed hard, telling himself he felt relief that she was married. Rubbing his thumbs over the backs of her fingers, he cleared his throat and raised his gaze to meet hers. "Who's the lucky guy?"

Wariness skated across her expression, but she recovered in the next instant and smiled at him. How could she stand there looking so composed, when he felt so damn confused and about half crazy for thinking what he was thinking? Dammit, he wasn't meant for marriage and fatherhood. So why were his guts tied into painful knots at the thought of her exchanging vows with another man?

"Actually, there isn't a lucky guy." She pulled her hands from his and stepped back. "It just didn't work out."

"Are you saying the baby's father left you?" The knots in Rafe's guts gave a savage twist while he waited for her answer. When she'd ended their relationship, Caroline had told him there was someone else she wanted to spend more of her time with, but she hadn't mentioned any names. He could only hope that at one important time there had been another guy besides him. Of course, if he found out who it was, Rafe would probably have to kill him.

"He doesn't want a family," she said, glancing away for a moment. Shrugging as if that didn't bother her a bit, she added, "Fortunately, I do."

Anyone who didn't know her well would have believed that shrug was for real. Rafe didn't buy it. Caroline was as conventional as they came. She never would've willingly chosen to be a single mother. "So why the ring?"

"We live in the Bible belt," she said with a wry smile. "It saves me a lot of hassle when other people think I'm married."

"Who's the father?"

She met his gaze again. Comprehension of what he was driving at dawned in her eyes and she let out a mirthless laugh. "Oh, for pity's sake, don't worry, Rafe. My baby is no concern of yours."

"Really?" Her words failed to reassure him. He'd never known her to lie outright, but she could skate around the truth as easily as any other lawyer. She was skating hard and fast now. "When's your due date?"

"That's none of your business." Pulling herself up to her full height, she crossed her arms over her breasts.

Seeing her blue eyes flash with anger sparked his own. Years of law enforcement training and experience kicked in, however, prompting him to clamp down on his emotions. "Sure it is, Caro. Your baby needs a father. If he won't do the right thing by you on his own, I'll be glad to convince him for you."

"Oh, please." She rolled her eyes in exasperation. "If you can't make it all the way into the twenty-first century, do at least join the twentieth. Millions of women raise children alone every year and do a fine job of it. I'm more than capable of supporting myself and my child."

"Don't give me that hogwash," Rafe said, shaking his head. "You don't believe it any more than I do. Who's the father?"

"That's none of your concern."

Rafe silently counted to fifteen and moved in closer, intentionally crowding her. In spite of his training, Caroline's attitude was seriously starting to tick him off. "Wrong answer. If you're as far along as you look, I'd say the chances are excellent that baby's mine."

Her face flushed, but she didn't flinch. Her hands curved protectively around the jutting mound beneath her clothes. "She's *my* baby, Rafe Stockwell. Mine and mine alone."

"Aw, come on, sugar. You know it doesn't work quite that way." Lowering his voice, Rafe gave her the best smile he could manage. "You must've had a little help from *some*body."

"My baby's father is my business." Though she was a good five inches shorter than his six-foot, one-inch height, she still managed to give the impression she was looking down her nose at him. "I don't intend to discuss it with you or anyone else."

"Dammit, Caroline, I'm not completely ignorant. I know how long it takes to make a baby, and I can count months as well as anyone." He paused for another deep breath, but it didn't help much. "Right now I'd bet my badge we were together when that baby was conceived, and—"

"Bet whatever you choose, but—"

"Don't even *try* to tell me you were having sex with someone else at the same time you were sleeping with me. I know you better than that."

"Stop browbeating me." Hectic color suddenly faded from her cheeks, making her look wan and exhausted. "I don't need this right now."

"Hey, I'm not judging you, Caro." He reached out and cupped the side of her face with his palm, coaxing her to meet his gaze. "I'm just thinking about your well-being and the baby's."

"We're fine." She pushed his hand away and stepped back, her eyes silently warning him not to touch her again. "I know what I'm doing."

"Maybe so. But you shouldn't have to go through this by yourself. Any man who gets a woman pregnant should face up to his responsibilities and do the right thing by her and his kid."

"No, thank you," she said, shaking her head at him. "I'd rather be alone than marry someone who views me and my baby as responsibilities he has to face up to."

"Would it really be that bad?" Rafe asked.

She shot him a droll look. "Trust me. He's not, as they say, 'the marrying kind.'"

Rafe's insides froze. He'd always been honest with the women he dated, and he'd often used that very phrase—*not the marrying kind*—to explain his plans to remain single. Caroline's use of that phrase was hardly a coincidence; she made her living by using precise language. Just how dense did she think he was? So much for the Mr. Nice Guy approach.

Allowing a sharp edge into his voice, he said, "I deserve to know the truth, Caroline. Is that my baby you're carrying?"

She stuck her pert little nose in the air and spread a haughty layer of New England frost onto every syllable she spoke. "I don't intend to discuss this any further."

"You can't do—"

"I *said*, I don't intend to discuss this." She shot him a glare that made him sincerely glad she hated guns, then waved one hand toward the stacked boxes. "As you can see, I'm busy. If you have business to conduct, I'll be happy to help you. Otherwise, I need to finish my work."

Damn, frustrating woman. He studied her for a moment, noting the fierce determination lurking behind her professional veneer. He still didn't have the straight answer he craved, but he'd learned early in their affair that when dealing with Caroline, a strategic retreat sometimes was more effective than a frontal assault. He wasn't about to let this topic go for good, but at the moment, there was no sense in getting her any more riled up at him than she already was.

He needed to leave before he said something he'd regret. He'd come back at a more opportune time. Like, in about a week, when he had a firmer grip on his temper.

"All right. I'm sorry, Caroline," he said, backing off a step. "I didn't mean to upset you."

He turned around and took two strides before she stopped him. "Wait a minute, Rafe. Why did you come here today?"

"It doesn't matter." He picked up his hat from the desk, then looked over his shoulder at her. "I'll take care of it later."

"If there's some business we need to conduct, I'd rather do it now." She rubbed her right hand over her belly. "I really don't know how much longer I'll be working."

"I'll come back soon, then." Without another word, he turned around and left, feeling as if she'd taken his whole world and blasted it into a billion pieces. And wondering how in hell he was ever going to be able to put it back together.

Caroline waited until the office door shut behind Rafe and she heard the muted hum of the elevator working. Only then did she release her pent breath and grab the back of the receptionist's chair to support her wobbly legs. Pulling it closer, she collapsed onto the seat and wrapped her arms around herself, needing to still the inner shaking she'd worked so hard to hide from Rafe's too observant eyes. Had she succeeded? She didn't think so.

"Oh, Lord," she murmured, rocking back and forth. The instant she'd seen him standing there in the entryway, she'd experienced a flash of pure joy. She'd wanted to run to him, throw her arms around him and savor the warmth of his embrace.

How she'd missed seeing his handsome face and his gorgeous, midnight-blue eyes. When she'd realized those eyes were staring at her as if a pregnant woman was a horror to behold, however, she'd had to face the heartbreaking truth about her future with him one more time. She simply couldn't have one. If ever there was a man who truly needed his freedom, that man was Rafe Stockwell.

For all these months she'd managed to avoid him, his family and anyone else who knew both of them. Why on earth had he found it necessary to visit her office today? While she would love to believe that he'd missed her as much as she'd missed him and wanted to restart their relationship, she knew there must be another reason. But what could it be?

She wished he'd told her. They could have handled whatever he needed and she wouldn't have to see him again. At least not anytime soon. Unfortunately now that he'd smelled a mystery to solve, he would never let go of it until he knew the truth. And *then* what would she do?

Groaning, Caroline massaged her aching temples with her fingertips. As if sensing her distress, the baby chose that moment to practice her high kicks. Caroline cupped her right hand over a tiny foot pressing against the inside of her abdomen.

"It's all right, little one," she said. "We'll get through this somehow."

For one insane moment she considered the merits of going home, packing a couple of suitcases and simply disappearing. She could change her name and start over somewhere she'd never been before. Somewhere she and the baby could start a new life without having to worry about what anyone else wanted and needed. It sounded absolutely wonderful.

It was also impossible. She didn't want to leave her obstetrician at this stage of her pregnancy. And, even though he no longer recognized her and had round-the-clock care, she couldn't abandon her father. She also had a thriving law practice to run and clients who were depending on her to keep their legal affairs in order.

Most important, she could run away from Rafe, but she couldn't hide from him. His job with the Marshals Service involved apprehending federal fugitives. With his experience and resources, he could find anyone. The part of her that still loved Rafe would never want to hide from him anyway.

Besides being tall, dark, handsome and independently wealthy, he was extremely intelligent and a gifted raconteur with a seemingly endless supply of fascinating stories to tell. Sometimes he was charming and fun. Sometimes he was serious and withdrawn.

But always, he was passionate and so intensely masculine, he made her feel delightfully aware of her own femininity. He was a skilled and generous lover. And, behind his tough-guy facade, there was a deep well of tenderness most people never saw.

She loved nearly everything about him. At first glance, he appeared to be the perfect mate for her in every way. Unfortunately she'd discovered two important glitches in his makeup she knew she couldn't accept.

He didn't love her. And, even if he did love her, his job would always come first on his list of priorities. She'd finally understood both of those things at the same time she'd realized she was pregnant. Rafe was such an honorable man, she'd known he would insist on marrying her if he knew he'd fathered a child.

However, she'd already had one painful relationship

based on obligation rather than love with her father. She had no desire ever to have another one. From childhood, she'd vowed that if she ever married, her husband would love her, and he would be a man who valued his wife and family above everything else in his life.

Her baby would have a loving, caring father who enjoyed spending time with her and supported her in her activities, whether they were ballet recitals or soccer games.

Caroline couldn't tolerate anything less than that. For herself, or for her child. Better to be completely on their own than suffer the wounds of neglect and abandonment every time something new and exciting at work claimed Daddy's attention.

Sighing with bone-deep weariness, Caroline forced herself to stand, picked up the clipboard and went back to work. She had no time for regrets or self-pity. Sooner or later Rafe would be back, demanding the truth about her baby's father again, and she would have to be ready for him.

Her baby's future depended on it.

Cursing under his breath, Rafe jammed his hat onto his head and stepped from the air-conditioned building into the blistering summer heat, then marched down the steps and around the corner to the parking lot. His irritation grew when he spotted a shiny, silver-gray Porsche parked two spaces down from his own dusty, puke-green, government-issue sedan. Great. A surprise visit from his bossy, not to mention nosy, brother was just what he needed to round off the afternoon.

Cord climbed out of the Porsche and stood a careful six inches from the pristine finish of his latest pride and joy while he waited for Rafe.

"Don't you have anything better to do than drive around Grandview checking up on me?" Rafe asked.

"Of course I do, little brother," Cord said.

Cord's grin annoyed Rafe almost as much as his "little brother" dig. Though Cord was only eight minutes older, to hear him go on about it, a person might think he was eight years older and twenty years wiser. Most days Rafe would have ignored it.

Today wasn't most days.

Besides the shock of discovering Caroline's pregnancy, Rafe was operating on only three hours of sleep. He'd been called out in the dead of night to coordinate a special task force operation with the FBI and the Texas Rangers, and he just plain wasn't up to dealing with Cord right now.

"Then what the hell are you doing here?" Rafe asked.

Cord let out an indignant snort. "Is that any way to talk to your own flesh and blood?"

"Yeah." Rafe planted his feet wide apart and propped his hands on his hips. "If you didn't think I could handle this, you should've—"

"I never said you couldn't handle it."

"Then my question stands. For God's sake, you just announced your engagement. You should be at home with Hannah, up to your eyeballs in wedding plans."

"Give me a break, Rafe." Cord shoved his hands into the front pockets of his suit trousers and glanced over at the office building.

Rafe took one look at Cord's unusually sober expression and set aside his own irritation for the moment. Their father, Caine Stockwell, was in the advanced stages of terminal cancer. Besides supervising Caine's care, Cord carried the burden of running the family conglomerate, Stockwell International. Rafe wouldn't have traded places with Cord for anything, and when push came to shove, Cord was the best friend he had.

"What is it?" Rafe asked. "Is the old man worse?"

"He's incoherent again, but physically, he's holding his own." Cord rubbed the back of his neck. "Dammit, I just want to know the truth."

"We all do," Rafe said. At the moment, he and Cord were talking about two different truths, but Cord didn't need to know that.

"So where are Dad's files?" Cord asked. "You got them, didn't you?"

"Not yet," Rafe admitted.

"Didn't you show Caroline my power of attorney?"

"Not exactly."

Frowning at him, Cord mimicked Rafe's stance. "What happened in there?"

"We just got a little sidetracked is all," Rafe said with a shrug he hoped looked casual.

"Uh-huh." A considering expression settled over Cord's face. "I suppose you two got to talking about old times."

"Something like that," Rafe agreed.

"Uh-huh. And how is the lovely Ms. Carlyle?"

"Fine."

Cord laughed, then shook his fool head and pointed a finger at Rafe. "So that's why you're so damn cranky today."

"I'm not cranky."

"Yeah, little brother, you are. I should've guessed seeing Caroline again would make you a little... skittish."

Aw, hell. This was what he'd been dreading since he'd found Cord waiting for him. Ever since it had happened, Cord had been relentlessly curious about Rafe's breakup with Caroline. Rafe hadn't wanted to talk about it back then any more than he did now, but it was damn near impossible to hide much of anything from an identical twin. That was how it was between Cord and him, anyway. Well, the best defense was still a powerful offense.

"That's the dumbest thing you've said lately." Rafe kicked at a pebble, scuffing the toe of his black cowboy boot. "We're just friends now."

"She's one gorgeous lady," Cord observed. "And you haven't been out with anyone else since your breakup."

"I don't have a nine-to-five job," Rafe grumbled. "And I've been busy as hell at work lately."

Cord just smiled. "Too busy to find a date? In *how* long?"

Rafe silently asked for patience. Obviously Cord's engagement to Hannah Miller had left him addle-brained, starry-eyed and too damn eager to butt his nose into other people's personal lives.

"Forget about it," Rafe said. "Go home and take Hannah and the baby out somewhere for fun."

"You and Caroline were good together."

"If that were true, we'd still be together." Rafe yanked the brim of his hat lower on his forehead and folded his arms across his chest. "You go ahead and trot on down the aisle if you want. I'll even be there to cheer you on. But don't expect me to follow your lead this time, bro."

"Aw, c'mon, Rafe. Life can be good with the right woman."

"I know that." Rafe clasped Cord's shoulder and squeezed it. "I'm happy for you and Hannah, but forget about me, all right? I've seen too many law enforcement marriages fail. They just don't work.''

"Some of them do." Suddenly dead serious, Cord met and held Rafe's gaze. "I think you care more about Caroline than you want to admit. But don't be afraid of it—"

Rafe pulled his hand from Cord's shoulder and stepped away from him. "I'm not afraid of anything. Things didn't work out, but Caroline and I are still friends. End of story."

Scowling at him, Cord turned and opened the driver's side door of his car. "I'm not talking about friendship." He lowered himself into the seat and leaned out the window. "You had something special going with her. Think about it. And get those files. Now." He backed his car out of the parking space, then roared off in a wave of heat and exhaust fumes.

Rafe waved a hand in front of his face, straightened the Western-cut sports coat that had been specially tailored to hide his shoulder holster and headed for his own car, once again cursing under his breath. Cord was one hell of a sharp businessman, but when it came to Rafe's love life, Cord didn't have a clue what he was talking about.

Yeah, Rafe and Caroline had been good together. Well, better than good. He'd never known another woman who was confident enough to speak her mind, smart enough to graduate with honors from Harvard Law School and passionate enough to wear him out in bed. Somehow, they'd just clicked. If any woman could have changed his mind about marriage, it would have been Caroline.

But it wasn't meant to be.

Until today, he'd been absolutely convinced that he

had no business even thinking about marriage. Law enforcement wasn't simply a job or a career choice for him. It was a calling. He hunted down some of the worst criminals humanity produced and took them off the streets.

As long as law enforcement was his passion, he would make deadly enemies. He couldn't promise that he wouldn't go out there and get himself killed or maimed. He knew he'd never be able to give a wife and kids the attention they needed, and he'd rather pass up having a family of his own than make some unfortunate woman and a bunch of kids miserable because of his neglect. Caroline had known the score. She'd made the decision to move on with her life, and he'd respected that.

But, if he'd already fathered a child, all of his reasons for staying single didn't amount to anything more than a blast of hot air. No matter what Caroline said, her baby deserved to have two parents. Rafe intended to make sure the kid would have them.

Dammit, his whole life seemed to be tied up in a quest for the truth. The truth about what happened to his mother and his Uncle Brandon. The truth about Caroline's baby. God only knew what other truth he would need to find next.

He looked over at the office building and decided to go back inside. Getting his father's files from Caroline was straightforward legal business, which shouldn't be any problem. Getting at the complete truth regarding her baby's paternity was going to require a more thoughtful approach. Something with more finesse than his usual roll-over-'em-with-a-bulldozer mode would be good.

He would use getting his dad's files as his excuse to see Caroline again. At the same time, he would find a way to mend his fences with her. One way or another, he would regain her trust, and this time he wasn't going to push her so hard. If he had fathered her baby, he'd do whatever it took to make things right, even if it meant giving up his bachelorhood.

A Stockwell always took care of his own.

Chapter Two

Impatient to put his new plan into action, Rafe retraced his route to the sixth floor. Through the strip of windows beside the door, he saw Caroline sitting on the edge of the reception desk, her shoulders slumped, her face buried in her hands. Good Lord, was she crying? Crying women normally didn't bother him the way they bothered some guys, but Caroline was the strongest woman he'd ever met. Even the possibility that he might've reduced her to tears upset him.

She straightened her posture and jerked her head up when he opened the door, but he saw no evidence of tears. He saw no hint of welcome in her eyes, either. Only wariness. The realization made his heart contract painfully, but he crossed the room at a steady, unhurried pace.

"What are you doing here, Rafe?" she asked, her voice echoing with a bone-deep weariness he doubted

anyone who didn't know her as well as he did would
have noticed.

"I promised I'd come back soon," he said. She
opened her mouth as if to speak, but he smiled and held
up one hand to forestall any objections she might make.
"Truth is, we do have some business to conduct, and
Cord'll have my head on a platter if I go home without
taking care of it."

A smile curved her lips, as if the thought of his head
on a platter held great appeal. Pushing herself to her
feet, she gestured toward an open doorway on her left.
"All right. Let's go into my office. How is Cord, by the
way?"

"Fine." Rafe followed her into a large room with a
massive oak desk on one side and a round table with
four padded chairs on the other. In spite of the towering
bookcases and file cabinets, the room had a warm and
comfortable atmosphere. "He just got engaged yesterday."

"Oh really? Do I know her?"

"Probably not," Rafe said. "She's from Oklahoma."

Caroline settled into a high-backed burgundy leather
chair behind her desk and folded her hands together on
top of the blotter, looking every bit the seasoned professional. "What can I do for you?"

Rafe hesitated for several seconds before answering.
"I need information."

"What kind of information?" She pulled out a clean
legal pad and a pen.

"It involves some work your father may have done
for my old man. Financial records."

"Father handled a lot of financial transactions for
Caine Stockwell. Can you be more specific?"

Rafe glanced away, calculating how much he absolutely needed to reveal about this whole sordid story. Oh, what the hell. This was Caroline, not some stranger. Still he had to ask, "Is this protected by attorney-client privilege?"

"Of course it is." She scowled at him as if she found his question extremely insulting.

"I wasn't questioning your integrity." Rafe's face felt hot, but he forced himself to go on. "It's just...well, this is about some old family history. It's not real pretty."

"I practice family law." For the first time that day, her gaze was direct and, oddly enough, reassuring. "Believe me, it can't be any worse than the things I've already seen. Just tell me about it."

After another moment's hesitation, he nodded, then began. "Caine may have hired your dad to send some payments to my mother, Madelyn."

"What kind of payments?" Caroline asked, jotting notes onto her legal pad.

"Child support payments." Rafe stretched out his legs and crossed one ankle over the other.

"For what child?"

"I don't know." Rafe shifted around in his chair but couldn't get comfortable. Jeez, this was embarrassing. If he'd been trying to tell this to anyone but Caroline, he already would have left. She shot him a questioning look, but he honestly didn't know any more. To think that he might have another sibling he'd never even met out there somewhere boggled his mind.

If his mother really was still alive...well, he hadn't had time to figure out how he felt about that.

"When did the payments start?" Caroline asked.

"Twenty-nine years ago."

"When did they stop?"

"If your dad set them up on an automatic plan..." He paused and cleared his throat, "they probably haven't."

Looking up at him in surprise, Caroline paused with her pen in midair. "I thought your mother died a long time ago."

"So did I."

"I'm sorry, Rafe," she said with a frown, "but I'm afraid I don't understand."

"Join the club." Rafe gave her a grim smile. "Okay, I know this doesn't make much sense so far, so here's the lowdown as I understand it."

Unable to remain seated for one more second, he got up, shoved his hands into his pants pockets and began to pace. "For as long as I can remember, my old man told us our mother and our Uncle Brandon died in a boating accident. Now Caine's dying and out of his head with pain most of the time, and all of a sudden, he's claiming there was no accident."

"Oh, my," she murmured.

He flicked her a glance, then went on. "Allegedly, our mother and Uncle Brandon had an affair, and when she got pregnant, Dad threw them both out. He says they might still be alive, and since the baby Madelyn was carrying could have been his, he sent her support payments, using your father as a conduit. Madelyn never touched a penny of his money, so the payments are supposedly being held in some kind of trust for the baby, who is now almost thirty years old."

Caroline searched his face, for what, he didn't want to know. The sympathy in her eyes made him desperately want to leave, but he'd gone this far. He might as well finish it.

"Does your father have any idea where your mother and uncle might be now?" she asked.

"No, but before we start a search, I want to see if there's any proof to back up his story. He may be hallucinating from the drugs he's taking now. Or, he could just be making it all up to drive the rest of us crazy. But, if he's telling the truth, there should be some kind of a paper trail in your dad's files."

Caroline nodded, but her thoughtful frown told Rafe she doubted his assumptions were true. He didn't blame her. While Caine Stockwell had a well-deserved reputation for being greedy, mean and vindictive, this didn't sound like the sort of thing even he would make up. After all, it cast him in a pretty unfavorable light.

"All right." She tucked a lock of hair behind her left ear. "I'll find your father's files and get back to you as soon as I can."

Rafe stopped pacing and looked over his shoulder. "Define as soon as you can."

"I don't know."

Turning around, he raised his eyebrows at her, silently demanding an explanation. Her face turned pale and he suddenly noticed dark circles under her eyes and lines of strain around her nose and mouth. She raised one hand and massaged her temple as if she had a bad headache.

"What's wrong?" he asked.

"Nothing." She gave him a lopsided smile, but it was patently forced. "Things have gotten a bit complicated around here in the past month, but I'll have it all straightened out soon."

"Hey, this is me you're talking to," Rafe said, thumping his chest. He walked around her desk, shoved a file tray and a potted plant aside and parked his rump on the edge of the desk, right beside her chair. "What's really going on here, Caro?"

The sincere concern Caroline saw in the depths of his eyes and heard in his deep voice nearly undid her. *He* was what was going on here, and she wasn't ready for this. Had it really been necessary for him to come back so blasted soon?

She needed more time and space to collect herself before she had to deal with him again. She was still too attracted to him—too vulnerable to him. Especially now, when she felt so utterly alone.

Her eyes burned and her throat tightened, and for a moment she experienced a horrifying urge to throw herself into Rafe's arms and weep like a lost, frightened child. He wouldn't turn her away. On the contrary, he would hold her, stroke her hair and comfort her. Given the slightest invitation, he'd undoubtedly step right in, take over her life and tell her not to worry her pretty head about anything. If she had her usual strength, she would laugh out loud at such an idea.

But right now, she was tired. She was tired of being big and awkward, of having backaches, heartburn and leg cramps and having to go to the bathroom all the time. She was so tired, even her hair follicles ached. She felt as if she'd always been tired and always would be tired.

In truth, she really didn't want anyone to run her life and take care of her, but occasionally, she certainly could use someone to lean on.

Lord, what would it be like to have even a moment's respite from the constant burden of responsibilities to the baby, to her father and to this firm? She wanted that so desperately, she could almost feel the heat of Rafe's body next to hers and the strength and security of his strong arms wrapped around her. Almost smell the familiar, spicy scent of his aftershave. Almost hear his gentle, murmured assurances that everything would be all right.

If only she would ask, Rafe would give all of that to her and more without stopping to count any possible present or future cost to himself. Of course, she couldn't afford to ask Rafe for anything. She couldn't afford to let him get close to her again. If he ever learned the whole truth, she would never be able to get him completely out of her life again, and she couldn't bear that.

Furthermore, she didn't need him or any other man. She was a strong, independent woman who had been taking care of herself for as long as she could remember. Right now her hormones were in rebellion because of the baby. But, as soon as the little darling was born and everything got back to normal, she would be fine.

"Nothing's going on, Rafe," she said, feeling more confident than she had only a moment ago. He raised a doubtful eyebrow at her. Wishing she had more room to maneuver, she rolled her chair slightly away from him. "Really."

He frowned thoughtfully for a moment, then shook his head. "Then what did you mean when you said you'd *find* Caine's files? Don't you know where they are?"

"Of course I do. The most recent ones are in the file system. The older ones are in some of those boxes in the reception area. The files you want are probably in the boxes."

"But you don't know which ones?"

She hated admitting it, but it was, after all, the truth. "That's right. My father's illness has made him quite paranoid. He accuses me of stealing his money and without my knowledge, he hid most of his older files in all sorts of bizarre places. I believe I've found them all now, but I haven't been able to sort them and archive them yet.''

''Can't your secretary do that for you?''

''At the moment, I don't have a secretary.''

''Why not?''

''She quit when I checked my father into the twenty-four-hour care facility.''

''That doesn't seem very reasonable,'' Rafe said. ''I don't see why she even thought that was any of her business.''

Caroline held out her hands and shrugged. ''I think maybe she was in love with him. Whatever was going on with her, she felt that I should have kept him at home. I doubt she realized how violent he'd become, or how often he wandered away from home.''

''I'm sure sorry to hear about that,'' Rafe said. ''Clyde's always been a good man.''

The urge to weep washed over her again, stronger this time. Caroline turned her head away, drew a shaky breath and clamped her lips together until the fierce pain in her chest eased to a hollow ache. Oh, this was ridiculous. She never cried. At least not in front of anyone else. Raising her chin, she looked back at Rafe and nodded. ''Thank you. Now then, where were we?''

''You were saying the secretary quit. Nothing like support when you need it most, is there?''

Caroline shook her head in disgust. ''Yes, of course.''

''Well, what about your receptionist?'' he asked. ''Couldn't she give you a hand?''

''I stopped taking new cases because of the baby, and we really weren't that busy, so I gave her three months off to travel with her husband. She'll be back in a few weeks.''

"You mean on top of your daddy and the baby, you're running this place all by yourself?" Rafe asked, obviously appalled at the idea.

"For now."

"That's crazy. Why didn't you ask somebody for help?"

"I can handle things," she said, using a cool tone she hoped would set him back on his heels. "Let's get back to business, shall we? How soon do you need the files?"

Rafe scowled at her, telling her with his eyes that he knew exactly what she was doing and didn't plan to cooperate. "Yesterday. We're all tense about this."

"I can imagine." She tapped her pen on the legal pad for a moment. "All right, here's what I'll do. I'll hire a temp to come in and—"

Before she could finish her sentence Rafe shook his head at her and stood up. "Forget the temp, Caro. I'll help you."

Suddenly feeling dwarfed, she stood up, too. With Rafe's big frame and her protruding abdomen taking so much room, the area behind her desk shrank to the size of a business card. She looked at him expectantly, willing him to leave. He didn't, of course. "That's not necessary," she said.

"Sure it is." His gaze drifted from her face down to her abdomen and lingered there. "You've got more than enough to deal with right now. I can take an afternoon off—"

"You don't understand." Desperate to get some space, she made shooing motions at him. He obligingly stepped out of her way, waited until she passed him and followed her out of the office.

"My father did all sorts of legal work for Caine for thirty years." When they reached the main entrance, she waved a hand toward the mound of boxes. "That's only half of the pile, and God only knows how many of those contain Stockwell files. Daddy didn't label the boxes, so I really have no idea which ones might have the information you want. I'll have to go through all of them folder by folder. It could take days to find something useful. Perhaps even weeks."

Rafe frowned for a moment, then shrugged. "That's all right. It'll still go faster if I help, and you don't have to worry about a conflict of interest. I don't care what your dad's other clients might've been up to, and I swear I won't even open any of their files. I'll just look for ones with Stockwell on the label and you can take it from there."

Knowing she was going to lose this argument, she still made one more attempt to make him see reason. "What about your job? Don't you have a big case you're working on?"

"Remember Percy?" Rafe asked.

Caroline nodded, barely able to repress a shudder. When she'd been dating Rafe, Percival Jones had been the number two man on the U.S. Marshals Service's "15 Most Wanted Fugitives" list for the murder of a government witness, kidnapping, rape and a variety of drug charges. Rafe and his partner, Vic Innis, had nearly caught Percy on two occasions, but he'd escaped both times.

"We're going to get him this time," Rafe added with a smile that chilled her blood.

"I'm sure you will," she said, "but with a case like this, you'll never be able to find time to look for Caine's files."

"I'll make the time." Rafe propped his hands on his hips. "I really don't want some temp digging around in the old man's business. There are probably things in those files that would leave us wide open to blackmail."

She rolled her eyes at him, but didn't disagree. The very same thought had crossed her mind. Since it was impossible to know how long Alzheimer's disease had been affecting her father's judgment, Caroline wanted to go through all of those old files personally before they joined the firm's archives. She'd intentionally created this mess in order to force herself to take care of it before the baby arrived. She hadn't counted on feeling so exhausted, however, and she was running out of time.

One side of Rafe's mouth kicked up in an endearing grin. "C'mon, sugar, you know I'm right. Let's just keep it in the family and get it done. What do you say?"

"Oh, all right," she said, softening her grudging tone with a wry smile. "But don't say I didn't warn you. This is *not* going to be easy."

"I hear you." Rafe took off his sports jacket and folded it across the receptionist's chair, but left on the shoulder holster he wore under his left arm. Then he crossed the room to the boxes. "If you'll open your daddy's office, I'll get these off the floor and laid out so we can see what we're doing."

"It's almost closing time. You want to do it right now?"

Rafe winked at her. "The sooner the better. Let me get you a chair so you can sit down and supervise."

Caroline unlocked her father's office and pushed the door open wide. By the time she finished turning on the lights, Rafe had carried in the first box and set it on the conference table. Rafe dragged out the high-backed leather executive's chair from behind her father's desk, then found her a step stool for her feet and a cold bottle of orange juice to drink. She lowered herself into the chair, doing her best to ignore the pangs of loss she felt whenever she entered this room.

Clyde Carlyle had built a long and successful career here. She had stored his memorabilia—diplomas, civic awards, autographed photos with various dignitaries at all levels of government. Without her father's forceful presence, this office was just another room, not the mystical place that had absorbed so much of his time, energy and passion. But she still felt like an intruder whenever she crossed the threshold.

Hoping to distract herself, Caroline focused her attention on Rafe. Heedless of his white shirt, he carried in the rest of the dusty boxes as if they weighed next to nothing. She envied his strength and energy, and soon found herself visualizing the flex and play of the hard muscles under his shirt.

When they'd been lovers, she'd reveled in running her hands over his chest, shoulders, arms and back, feeling the smooth, warm texture of his skin, playing with the swirls of hair on his chest. She hadn't known a man's body could be so beautiful. Exhaling a soft sigh, she laced her fingers together on top of her abdomen and closed her eyes against the regrets she couldn't quite banish no matter how hard she tried.

"You okay, Caro?" he asked.

She opened her eyes, then nodded and struggled to her feet. "I'm fine. Just ready to go home. Are you almost finished?"

"That was the last load." He dusted off his hands and followed her back into the reception area. After putting on his sports jacket, he turned to face her. "I'll be back tomorrow afternoon, all right?"

"Certainly. I'll do what I can in the morn—" Caroline clasped one hand to the side of her abdomen. "Oh, my."

"What is it?" Rafe asked, immediately stepping closer to her, his brow furrowed with worry.

"The baby's just getting her exercise," Caroline said.

"You're sure that's all it is?"

"It happens every day." Caroline tucked her hair behind her ears, then rested her hands on her hips. "It's perfectly normal."

Rafe took another step closer and pressed his palm against the same spot on Caroline's belly. Shocked by the unexpected contact, she jerked her gaze up to meet his, but his eyes were half-closed as if he was concentrating on something only he could see. The baby rewarded him with a vigorous thump, and a smile of pure delight spread across his face.

Caroline's heart turned over. How she'd longed for someone to share her own sense of awe and wonder at the miracle taking place inside her. Rafe was absolutely the last person she would have expected to react like this. Much as she hated to admit it, his lingering touch gave her a sexual thrill that was equally unexpected, but she couldn't bring herself to move away from him.

"Wow. That was pretty hard," he said. "Does it hurt?"

"No. It's disconcerting at times, though."

"I can see why."

He looked into her eyes then, his expression warm with affection, or perhaps approval. Either one was enough to make her feel weepy again, which prompted her to shift to one side and break the physical connection. Rafe's eyes narrowed, his lips tightened and he left his hand extended toward her abdomen.

Caroline cleared her throat before he could say anything. "Well, I should be going home."

"All right. I'll see you tomorrow."

He picked up his hat from the reception desk and left the office without so much as a backward glance. Locking the door behind him this time, Caroline turned away and wrapped her arms around her midriff, scolding herself as she waddled back to her office. Dammit, she couldn't afford to feel anything for Rafe Stockwell.

Yes, she probably needed more emotional support right now, but she couldn't expect or accept it from him. So he'd smiled when he'd felt the baby move. Big deal. Most people would smile at something like that. It didn't mean he suddenly was ready and eager to take on the lifelong commitment of being a father. Which was exactly why she couldn't tell him the truth.

Rafe would do whatever he thought was right without considering his own feelings or needs, but as far as she was concerned, he could keep his precious honor and nobility. She didn't need his money to support herself or her baby, and she refused to allow her child to spend even one day of her life being treated as if she were someone's obligation.

Having spent her childhood through twelfth-grade graduation in boarding schools far from home, Caroline had grown up feeling lonely and unwanted. Her years in college and law school had been more of the same. When she'd finally come home and joined her father's law firm, their relationship had been based on business, not family ties.

Well, *her* baby's childhood would be different. *Her* baby would know nothing but acceptance, happiness and, most important of all, love. Her baby might have only one parent, but she would never doubt for one instant that she had been truly and deeply wanted. Caroline would see to that.

Chapter Three

Angry and frustrated by Caroline's stubborn reticence and don't-touch-me attitude, Rafe drove out to the Stockwell estate. Though he had his own town house in Grandview, he still maintained a suite of rooms in the family mansion. He'd been staying there since his old man's doctor had announced that, other than keeping him as comfortable as possible with pain medication, there was nothing more anyone could do for Caine.

With everything he had to think about, Rafe would much rather stay at his own place tonight, but it wasn't fair to saddle Cord with all of the responsibility for their dad's care, and Cord would want a report about what had happened at Caroline's office anyway. He wasn't going to be happy about the delay, of course, and Rafe hoped his twin wouldn't insist on personally talking to Caroline. Rafe intended to tell his brother about her pregnancy soon, but he didn't want to do it until he knew all of the important facts.

Man, he'd never forget that moment when he'd felt the baby pushing against his palm from inside Caroline's womb. His hand still tingled from that brief contact. He didn't know where the impulse to do that had come from, but he hadn't even thought about resisting it. He must be losing his mind. Outside of his own suspicions, he had no logical reason to believe he had any connection to her kid. Dammit, he really needed to know who the father was.

So why wouldn't she just tell him? There was no reason he could think of for her to hate him enough to deny him knowledge of his own child. After all, she was the one who'd broken off their relationship with virtually no warning. If anyone had a right to feel angry about the way it had ended, he did.

Heat waves shimmered off the pavement, momentarily blurring his vision. The sensation eerily mimicked the way he'd felt when he first realized he might have fathered a child. Man, oh man, he needed a drink. Maybe two.

At last, he turned into the long, paved drive leading to the Stockwell mansion. Thanks to an expensive and intricate sprinkler system, the grounds were lush and green compared to the surrounding countryside. The acres of lawn and the big oaks and sweetgum trees soothed his troubled spirits, but the sight of the sprawling, two-story building with its wings and outbuildings automatically raised his anxiety back to its original level.

There were so many memories—good and bad—tied up here. He honestly never knew what to expect when he walked through the white portico and entered the house. That was due mostly to Caine's mercurial personality, of course, but now Rafe sensed that change might well be in the air for the rest of the family regardless of what was happening with their patriarch.

Cord's recent discovery that he had a baby girl had been the first shake-up. His impending marriage to Hannah would be the second. Besides the present turmoil in his own life, Rafe had to wonder what might be going on that he didn't know about in his oldest brother Jack's or in his little sister Kate's lives.

And what if their mother was still alive? How would that affect his siblings? Could any of them forgive her for abandoning them to Caine's nonexistent mercies? Could he? And if they all had another sibling—the one Caine had supposedly made all those payments for? What then?

Unable to find any answers, Rafe parked in the circular turnaround and trotted up the front steps, then hurried to his suite, which was located next to Cord's on the second floor of the west wing. Acting on sheer force of habit, he tossed his hat onto a hook mounted on the wall, stripped off his sports coat and folded it across the back of a wing chair, then removed his shoulder holster and locked his automatic pistol in the small safe he kept in his closet for that purpose.

After a cool shower he dressed in jeans, a T-shirt and an old pair of cowboy boots. Grabbing a beer from the fridge in his sitting room, he picked up his mail and carried it to a leather recliner in front of the television, where he settled in to watch the evening news. He needed a few minutes to unwind before he reported back to Cord.

The mail was mostly junk and the news didn't hold his interest. Finding a pen on the end table, he took one of the empty envelopes, flipped it over and started doodling. First a handgun, then a sports car, then a dancing pizza like the one cavorting across the TV screen appeared in turn, and he laughed and tossed the envelope aside.

It wasn't art by any stretch of the imagination, just a funny knack he'd had for as long as he could remember. His old man had always had a fit whenever he caught Rafe drawing, calling him a sissy and worse. Rafe didn't know why Caine was so hostile about it, but he learned to hide his hobby rather than give it up. It relaxed him, it didn't hurt anybody and he no longer worried about anyone calling him a sissy. Besides, he'd been operating for a very long time under the premise that Caine didn't need to know about a whole lot of things.

His fingers still itching to put pen to paper, Rafe yanked a second empty envelope out of the pile and started another doodle that, in a series of quick, simple strokes, became the outline of Caroline's face. A little shading here, an extra line added there, and she suddenly wore the same expression as when he'd left her. Anxiety, sadness, fatigue bordering on exhaustion, they were all there in her eyes and in the tension around her nose and mouth. With all of the burdens she was carrying—the baby, her father, the law firm—no wonder she felt all of those things.

Though he didn't hold much affection for his own father, Rafe still found it extremely painful to watch Caine withering away. He didn't know how he'd ever get through it without Jack, Cord and Kate for support. In contrast, Caroline seemed to be real close to her father. As far as Rafe knew, other than the baby she was carrying, Clyde Carlyle was her only living relative.

When he died... Well, it must be at least a hundred times worse for her.

Whatever else had passed between them, Rafe had always liked Caroline. He was her friend, dammit, and he knew for a fact that she didn't have any good friends to burn. She was a strong woman, but even a strong woman needed help sometimes, and he intended to make sure she got it, whether she wanted it or not. At least until the baby was born.

He drained his beer, then decided to go downstairs to give Cord his report. Cord had moved the corporate offices of Stockwell International to the mansion when Caine had become bedridden. Rafe thought his brother had done a masterful job of taking care of business and Caine at the same time.

When Rafe stepped into the hallway, however, he heard his baby niece babbling away farther down the hallway in Cord's suite. Telling himself he was just going to make sure she was all right, he turned away from the main staircase and walked to the nursery.

He quietly turned the doorknob, pushed open the door and poked his head inside. Three-month-old Becky met his gaze with a wide, toothless grin. Waving her little arms and flailing her little legs, she chortled out loud. Rafe stepped into the room and leaned over her crib.

"Hi there, sweet potato," he said softly. "Remember me?"

Her arms and legs moved faster, and it seemed as if her entire body strained toward him, practically begging him to pick her up. Since she'd started crying the one time he'd ever held her, he resisted the invitation. She was so tiny and delicate, it terrified him even to think about handling her without Hannah around for backup.

Becky blew baby bubbles at him and kept up her

gyrations anyway, and he wondered if the kid thought he was her daddy. He and Cord had fooled enough adults in their day to make him wonder if a baby had a chance of telling them apart. Maybe she could, but he didn't think she'd get this excited over a mere uncle.

Not that it mattered. If she hadn't stolen his heart before, she had it now. Lord love a duck, if she wasn't the cutest little thing with her dark, wispy hair and her big blue eyes and that tiny shirt all covered with pink bunnies.

Until Becky had come to live at Stockwell Mansion, he'd rarely thought of babies at all. He'd assumed they were annoying little creatures who did nothing but poop, spit up and squall in restaurants and movie theaters. Now he couldn't understand why he'd never realized how appealing they could be.

If Caroline's baby looked anything like Becky... No. He wasn't going to start thinking that way. Just because he'd finally decided babies were cute, it didn't mean he'd ever be a good father. Given the statistics on abused children and his own upbringing, he knew he was more likely to make his own kids miserable than to provide a happy childhood for them. No way would Rafe Stockwell ever risk doing that to anyone.

If he was the father of Caroline's baby, he'd marry Caro to give the child his name and to fulfill his obligations, but he seriously wondered what kind of husband and father he'd be. He didn't know the first thing about happy marriages or close family relationships.

Suddenly Becky's tiny fingers grazed his lower lip, skidded off, then came back and curled over it. He smooched them and was rewarded with another delighted chortle. In the next second, her little face clouded up and her lower lip stuck out in unmistakable preparation for a crying jag.

"Aw, come on, squirt," he begged softly. "Don't do that. Smile for Uncle Rafe."

She scrunched up her little face, which had turned an alarming shade of red, opened her mouth and let out a wail loud enough to shatter the crystal all the way down in the dining room.

His heart pounding, Rafe started to reach for her, then chickened out and jerked his hands back. He cast a frantic glance toward the door on the opposite side of the room that led into the master bedroom. Where the hell was Hannah? As a nanny, she'd know what to do for the baby, whose wails were becoming full-fledged shrieks.

He desperately wanted to run from the nursery, but he couldn't just leave the kid all alone when she was screaming her guts out, could he? He walked to the other end of the crib, thumped the baby monitor and called, "Hannah? Can you hear me? Becky needs you."

Becky made a strangled little gasping sound that raised the hair on the back of Rafe's neck better than any horror movie he'd ever seen. Good God, what if she stopped breathing or something? Trying to control his shaking hands, he slipped one under her head and the other under her rump, then lifted her until he could hold her against his chest. The whole movement felt as awkward as trying to shave with the wrong hand, but it got the job done.

Becky's head bobbed around a bit, but the awful gasping sounds stopped. Rafe gently patted her back and swayed from side to side. Becky let out a sniffling sigh and snuggled into the crook of his neck. Then she poked her thumb into her mouth and sucked on it as if it was her last meal. Her soft hair caught in his five o'clock shadow and he caught the scent of something clean— maybe baby lotion or shampoo.

Holding this sweet, tiny person and knowing he'd somehow managed to comfort her when she'd been so terribly distressed was the most agonizingly wonderful sensation he'd ever experienced. He didn't dare move, could hardly bring himself to breathe for fear he'd shatter the moment and she'd start screaming again.

At last the door to the master bedroom opened and Hannah Miller, his soon-to-be sister-in-law, entered the nursery. "Hey, there, Rafe," she said with her distinctive Oklahoma twang. "I'm sorry I took so long to get in here. I was sort of tied up when she started fussin'."

Fussing? If that was just fussing, Rafe didn't want to hear what Hannah would call screaming. "Well, she seems okay now," he said. "I didn't mean to upset her. I just wanted to see her for a second."

Hannah pushed her shoulder-length brown hair behind her ears and smoothed down the front of her dress. Her face looked a little flushed. "An' I'll bet she got real excited to see you."

"You might say that. She seemed real happy at first, but I swear I didn't touch her. I don't know why she started crying like that." Becky cranked her head around this way and that, obviously searching for Hannah. Holding on for dear life to the suddenly wiggly little body, Rafe turned Becky around to make it easier for her to see her new mama.

Hannah crossed the room and stood beside him, the top of her head barely level with his shoulder. She was a slender young woman with green eyes, pretty in her own quiet way. A social worker who'd gotten too attached to her charge, Hannah was nothing like Cord's

usual beauty-queen girlfriends. Rafe was frankly surprised and impressed that his twin had had the good
sense to fall in love with her.

"Hi, baby girl," she cooed to Becky, who again had
all four limbs going at once. "You're puttin' on quite
a show, aren't you?"

Rafe hitched Becky higher against his chest. "Am I
doing this right, Hannah?"

"Why sure," she said with a grin. "Long as Becky's
happy, you're doin' just fine."

"But what do I do if she's not happy?"

"Well, there's certain things you check," Hannah
said.

"What things?"

Hannah offered an index finger to Becky. The baby's
fingers wrapped around it. Becky immediately tried to
drag it into her mouth. "First off, I usually check her
britches. Babies hate to have a wet or dirty diaper."

"Uh-huh." Rafe barely suppressed a shudder. He
doubted he had the intestinal fortitude to handle the
dirty diaper thing. "What else?"

"Once I make sure she's all dry and comfy, if she's
still fussing, I try to get her to take a bottle." She
pointed toward a small refrigerator in the kitchenette
area. "I always keep a couple of spares over there. And
there's an automatic warmer you can use."

"What if a bottle doesn't work?"

"Then I do just about what you're doing right there.
I walk her and cuddle her and try my best to figure out
what's bothering her. She's usually a very good-natured
baby, but sometimes she cries to let off steam."

"Really?" Rafe asked, surprised at that idea.

"You bet. Babies can get overstimulated to the point

where they have to bawl to tire themselves out enough to sleep. Little kids do that, too, once in a while.''

''Well, how do you know it's just that and they're not sick or in pain?''

''You don't always,'' Hannah said. ''Usually if they're hurting somewhere, their cries'll just about bust your eardrums, but if they're only all wound up, their cries'll be irritating, but not quite so sharp. Babies don't come with an owner's manual, 'cause they're all different. You have to learn about each child by experience.''

''Oh, boy,'' Rafe muttered, picturing himself sweating bullets while he frantically paced the floor with a screaming baby in his arms. He'd only been holding Becky for a minute before Hannah had arrived to rescue him. What on earth would he have done if he'd been alone with Becky for hours and hours? Jeez, he'd been right before. He wasn't father material and never would be.

Becky made smacking noises and stuck her own fingers into her mouth. Sensing another shift in the baby's mood, Rafe quickly passed her to Hannah and stepped back, crossing his arms over his chest.

Hannah patted Becky's back. ''What's this all about?'' she asked Rafe. ''You fixing to become a daddy like Cord?''

Shocked by the keenness of her insight, Rafe sputtered an immediate lie. ''No. I don't think so. I just figure I should know, uh, what to do in case Becky ever needs me. You know, like if you and Cord aren't around or you want me to baby-sit or something. Do you think maybe you could teach me some more stuff about babies later?''

''Of course I could. I'd be real happy to.'' Hannah

gave him a beatific smile that made him feel like a heel for lying to her. "Why Rafe, that's so sweet of you."

"What's so sweet of him?" Cord asked, entering the room from the same doorway Hannah had used. His silk shirt was halfway unbuttoned, his hair was mussed and he had a satisfied gleam in his eyes Rafe had seen in his own mirror often enough to know what his brother and Hannah had been doing.

"He wants to know how to take care of Becky," Hannah said. "Isn't that wonderful?"

"Yeah." Cord gently chucked his daughter under her chin, then focused his gaze on Rafe. "Real thoughtful of you, little brother. Did you find out anything at Carlyle and Carlyle?"

"I was just going down to the office to fill you in."

Cord sighed, then grudgingly nodded and turned toward the hallway door. "Okay, let's get it done before dinner. I want to spend the evening with my lady and my baby. Sounds like a song title doesn't it?"

Rafe snorted with laughter. But when Cord kissed the lady and the baby in question and they both chuckled in response and waved bye-bye at him as he sauntered out of the nursery, Rafe couldn't deny that what he felt was a definite pang of envy.

Caroline stopped at her favorite little restaurant for a chicken salad, then dutifully drove for another half hour to visit her father at Rosewood Manor. Though the nursing home for advanced stage Alzheimer's patients was well-kept and beautifully landscaped, she still cringed inside at the realization that Clyde Carlyle would live out the rest of his life behind that fence with other people seeing to his most personal needs. Lord, would the guilt of the decision to admit him here never go away?

She hadn't had any choice. Not really. Even his doctor had said as much. She'd learned everything about the disease she possibly could, hired the best caregivers money could buy, installed every security device she could find.

Unfortunately as Clyde had become increasingly confused, more determined to wander away from home and occasionally violent, her pool of attendants willing to handle his care had quickly dried up. If not for the baby, Caroline supposed she would have hung on longer, but she knew that eventually, it would have come to this anyway. And even though she visited him as often as possible, she still felt guilty.

She parked in the visitors' lot and entered the building, carrying the container of his favorite pasta salad she'd brought from the restaurant.

"Hello, Ms. Carlyle," the receptionist called out. "You're always so good about coming to see your daddy, I just knew you'd be here tonight."

"Hello, Maryanne." Caroline smiled at the plump, perpetually cheerful young woman and held up the restaurant container. "Would you mind putting this in the refrigerator for his lunch tomorrow?"

"Not at all." Maryanne accepted the container and wrote Carlyle across the top with a red marker. "I'll see that the dining hall staff gets it."

"Do you know where he is at the moment?"

Maryanne nodded. "He's in the rec center."

Doing her best to ignore the nursing-home odors, Caroline slowly walked down a long, tiled hallway to the recreation center, rubbing her lower back with one hand. Heavens, she felt like a waddling walrus these days. Would she ever get her figure and her energy back after the baby was born?

She spotted her father sitting at a small table in the farthest corner of the rec center. He looked up when she sat down at the chair adjacent to his, but he didn't speak.

"Hi, Daddy," she said, hoping against hope that he would know her this time. If he did, he didn't show it. He looked back down at a partially finished jigsaw puzzle on the table and shook his head as if he'd never seen it before.

"What's that on your puzzle?" Caroline asked.

He pointed at the black stripe on the side of what was obviously a tiger's face. "Lion."

Well, he was close, she thought with a rueful smile and an ache in her heart. Thank God he was past the stage of knowing what was happening to him. That had been the absolute worst time—seeing his fear and frustration and knowing there was nothing she could do for him. Absolutely nothing. She still couldn't do anything, of course, but at least now he wasn't afraid, because he no longer understood that this awful disease was robbing him of his mind.

"Lion," he repeated, stabbing his index finger at the loose pieces on the table.

Caroline selected one, gave it to him and gently guided his hand to the appropriate spot. He pushed the piece into place with his fingertips, then smashed it with the side of his fist, gleeful as any little boy. They repeated the process again and again, as they had done many times since her father had been diagnosed. There was a soothing rhythm to it, and since they were far enough away from everyone else to ensure a private conversation, Caroline soon found herself pouring out her heart.

"Rafe Stockwell came to see me today," she said. "It was a terrible shock for him and for me. Of course, the look on his face when he realized I was pregnant was absolutely priceless.''

Clyde stuck out his hand, silently demanding another puzzle piece. Caroline obliged him. "It was wonderful to see him again, but it hurt, too. And I know he suspects he's the baby's father. I didn't tell him anything, but he's too intelligent to think I can fool him indefinitely. Oh, Daddy, I'm so confused.''

Holding out his hand again, Clyde smiled and nodded at her. She put the next puzzle piece in the center of his palm.

"I thought it would be best for all of us if I ended our relationship," she continued. "He was always so adamant about not getting married or having a family, what else was I supposed to think? But now…well, I don't know anymore. He's really a very decent man, you know.

"It's so weird, Daddy. Here I am, almost as big as an elephant, and he's just such a hunk. Well, sometimes I think I'm a pervert to be so attracted to him when I'm seven months gone. Do you think I'm a pervert?''

Clyde grunted and smashed the next puzzle piece into place.

"I know. I know. A father doesn't want to hear about that sort of thing from his daughter," she said with a grin. "Our relationship hadn't lasted very long, but oh my, it was heaven while it did. Sheer heaven. But if he truly doesn't want to be a husband or a father…''

Unable to finish that thought, Caroline let her voice trail off and handed Clyde another piece. "I wish you hadn't made such a mess of the filing system. I don't suppose you remember anything about monthly payments from Caine to Rafe's mother, do you? Of course you don't. Now I'll have Rafe underfoot all the time, trying to find Caine's records. But maybe I'll get lucky and find them tomorrow.''

She wanted to stand up and pace, move around, go to the bathroom for the hundredth time in the past six hours. But if she left her father now, he'd probably throw a tantrum and upset the staff and the other residents. Sighing in resignation, she selected a new puzzle piece and handed it to Clyde.

''I feel overwhelmed, Daddy. There's so much to handle every day, and I don't have any help at the office or at home. And I get tired so easy. I'm whining, aren't I?'' She uttered a soft chuckle and felt warmed inside when her father chuckled too, nodding his head and smiling as if he understood and agreed with her, but he didn't mind hearing her whine.

It was getting late and he looked so normal, and it had seemed as if he was listening intently to everything she'd said, she took his hand between her palms and gently squeezed it. ''So what do you think, Daddy? Should I tell Rafe the truth?''

His blank expression said it all, even before he tipped his head to one side and asked, ''Who are you?''

Feeling as if a gaping wound had just opened up in the center of her body, Caroline released his hand as if it had caught fire, then closed her eyes and slumped back in her chair. It hurt to breathe. Her eyes stung as if someone had thrown acid into them. And that gaping wound continued to expand until she feared that if it didn't stop, she simply would vanish.

''Lion,'' Clyde said, his voice sounding peevish. He hit the puzzle with his palm three times. ''Lion.''

Caroline inhaled the deepest breath she could manage, then forced herself to open her eyes and smile at him. ''All right, Daddy. We'll finish your lion.''

Picking up another puzzle piece and handing it to him, she reminded herself that it was the disease talking. Not him. He wasn't trying to be unkind. None of what was happening to him was his fault. It was her fault for forgetting, even for an instant, that, in every way that mattered, her father was already gone.

She stayed until visiting hours ended, walked Clyde to his room and made her way back out to her car with her head up and her eyes dry. No matter what was happening, a Carlyle always maintained his or her dignity. But when she drove away from Rosewood Manor and got onto the highway that would take her home, grief formed a lump in her throat that was nearly big enough to choke her.

"Who *are* you?" she said, whacking the steering wheel with the side of her fist. "Who *are* you? Oh, that's rich, Daddy. That's incredibly, stupendously rich."

Along with grief she heard anger in her voice and immediately fought to suppress it. Grief was an appropriate response to her father's condition. Anger was not only inappropriate, it was counterproductive. It certainly wouldn't change anything.

The entire time she was growing up, going to college and law school and then becoming a partner in his law firm, she had craved his attention and approval. She gladly would have sacrificed a limb to hear him once say, "I love you."

Her father had always been too wrapped up in his work to do anything more for her than write checks to pay for her physical needs. He'd never spent the time or energy to find out who she was as a person. Now, because of Alzheimer's disease, he never would. And there was nothing she could do but learn the lessons this sad, sad relationship had to teach her.

The world contained too many men like her father. Their dedication to their work earned them all sorts of wealth, awards and respect. But their personal lives were as dry and desolate as west Texas. Wives, children and anyone else who might have a reasonable claim on their time were automatically sacrificed whenever duty called. Or whenever duty *might* call.

"And Rafe Stockwell is a member of the club," she muttered, tightening her grip on the steering wheel. "A charter member."

The baby moved inside her, a gentle turning over rather than kicking this time. Caroline patted her abdomen and thanked heaven for the important reminders this evening had given her. Rafe had been so nice to her that afternoon, she really had begun to feel confused and guilty for not telling him he was the baby's father.

Now she knew better. She wasn't doing this out of selfishness, or because he hadn't fallen all over himself wanting to marry her back when they'd been dating. It simply was the right thing to do, and she was doing it for the sake of her baby. No child of hers was ever going to suffer the hurts she had suffered from having a father who found his work more important than his family.

No way.

Chapter Four

Rafe returned to Caroline's office at four-thirty the next afternoon, feeling a sense of anticipation at seeing her again that seemed dangerously out of proportion. He couldn't stop himself from feeling it, however, so he forged ahead. "Caroline? It's me. Where are you, sugar?"

The lights were on in both her office and her father's. He checked hers first, but the room looked as if it hadn't been disturbed all day. He walked down the hallway to Clyde's office. There she was, sitting on a typing chair at the conference table in front of a box of files with a folder spread open beside it. Her hair stuck out in odd places, her face looked pale and drawn and her eyes were nearly glazed over with what he hoped was only fatigue.

"Nice you could make it, Stockwell."

"Sounds like somebody's had a bad day," Rafe said,

repressing a grin at her crabby tone. He crossed the room and stood behind her chair, leaning forward to read over her shoulder. "What's up?"

"Oh, nothing much." Sighing, she smoothed down one side of her hair. "It's just that this job is going to be at least a hundred times worse than I thought."

"Why?" He glanced down at her and felt his mouth go dry. He'd always appreciated Caroline's curves, but today she had on a pink sleeveless dress with a scooped neck that, from this vantage point, displayed more smooth, enticing cleavage than he remembered her having before. And there was a light, wonderfully sweet scent coming from her hair, or maybe it was her skin, that made him want to nuzzle her neck…and a few other places.

"These files are in such a mess, I think Daddy may have dropped some of them and shoved the loose pages in wherever he could make them fit. I've had to go through every page to be sure I'm not missing anything important."

Feeling the first warning signs of arousal, Rafe stepped back from her and hid his discomfort by turning away and walking three feet to the big window that overlooked a small park across the street. What the hell was the matter with him? He'd been around plenty of pregnant women and never felt turned on by any of them.

He'd readily admit that they could be beautiful in a maternal sort of way. He remembered thinking that very thing about Caroline yesterday, but he didn't think there'd been anything really sexual about it then. Made him feel strange to realize he was having downright carnal thoughts about her now. He turned back around and met her gaze.

She was looking at him expectantly, clearly waiting for him to respond to whatever she'd just said. For the life of him, he couldn't remember what it might've been because he was still too fascinated with the new fullness of her breasts to think straight. He'd obviously been without a woman far too long. He blurted out the first question that came to mind.

"How many boxes have you gone through?"

"I'm still on the first one." Her voice had a defeated quality to it he'd never heard from her before. "This is going to take forever, Rafe. I'm sorry."

"Hey, none of that." He hurried back to her chair and squatted down beside it, putting their eyes on the same level. "It's not your fault. It's probably just that one box."

Her eyes took on a misty sheen. "But what if it's not? What if they're all like this?"

"Then we'll just have to keep looking until we find the right papers." Brushing her cheek with his fingertips, he smiled at her. "It'll be okay."

Her chin trembled the same way little Becky's had last night, but Caroline's chin made him want to kiss it and then her luscious mouth, and then string a whole line of nibbling kisses down the side of her sweet neck and across her collarbones and then back down to her magnificent cleavage. Oh, man, he was really fixating here and it had to stop. She needed comfort, not a come-on.

He grasped her hands, drew her to her feet and gathered her into his arms for a hug. At first it was like trying to hug an ironing board, but he stroked her hair and her back, and gradually, she relaxed against him, burying her face in the hollow of his shoulder.

"It'll be okay," he repeated, rocking her back and

forth. The mound of her belly touched his lower abdomen and her breasts pressed into his chest, reawakening the arousal he'd just fought to suppress. He tried to suppress it again before she noticed it, but knew the exact instant when his efforts failed.

She stiffened first, then jerked her head up and stared at him, her eyes wide and her lips forming a nearly perfect O. He felt his neck and ears get hot and figured he was probably blushing like a green kid. God knew he was acting like one in every other way. He hadn't felt this awkward at his first dance.

"What's going on, Rafe?"

"You know damn well what's going on." Irritated and embarrassed, he set her away from him and stuck his hands into his jacket pockets. "Don't worry about it. I'm not planning to jump you."

"I wasn't worried about that," she said with a soft chuckle. "I was just...surprised."

He looked over his shoulder at her. "Why? You know you've always turned me on."

She cupped her hands on the sides of her belly. "I didn't think you'd find me very attractive like *this.*"

"Yeah? Well, go figure." He cleared his throat and shifted his weight to his opposite foot, then noticed that her face had drained of color and she was swaying. He automatically reached out to steady her. "What's wrong?"

"Nothing." She gave her head a hard shake. "I'm just a little woozy."

He guided her back onto her chair. "When's the last time you had anything to eat?"

"Around noon," she said. "But I can't eat very much at one time, so I suppose I should eat again."

"Do you have anything here in the office?"

She nodded. ''There's a refrigerator in the break room. I've got juice, yogurt and fruit in there.''

Rafe pointed a finger at her. ''Stay right there and put your head between your knees if you start to get dizzy again. I'll bring you something.''

He hurried down the hallway until he located a small room with a table and chairs, a refrigerator and a microwave oven. Grabbing a bottle of apple juice, a carton of blueberry yogurt and a plastic spoon, he jogged back to Clyde's office. Caroline's color hadn't improved much, but he was glad to see that she was still upright. He opened the juice and handed it to her, then peeled the foil lid off the yogurt.

She took a long, thirsty drink from the bottle and set it on the table, then took the yogurt and spoon from him. ''Thank you,'' she said between bites. ''I usually keep better track of time, but I got pretty involved with the files.''

''Are you sure you should even be working?''

''Of course, I should. Lots of women work right up until the baby's born,'' she said. ''It's not as if I'm on my feet all day or doing anything strenuous.''

''I don't know, Caroline,'' Rafe said, doubtfully shaking his head. ''You looked pretty bad. I really don't like the thought of you being here alone.''

''I'd be alone if I stayed home,'' she said. ''There isn't much difference.''

''But at home you could wear more comfortable clothes and lie down when you need to. You could always have your calls here forwarded to your home phone.''

She scraped the bottom of the yogurt container, ate the last bite and handed it to Rafe for disposal. ''You have a point,'' she admitted. ''And I have more of these boxes in my garage at home. If you carry some of them into the house for me, I could still keep searching.''

''Good. That's what we'll do then.'' Rafe retrieved a phone book from the bookshelf behind Clyde's desk, brought it to her and gave her his cell phone as well. ''Call the phone company right now and then we'll get you home.''

''We'll?'' she asked. ''There is no *we'll*, Rafe. And may I remind you that I don't take orders from you?''

''Excuse me, Ms. Carlyle.'' He managed to hold in an exasperated snort, but it wasn't easy. He didn't remember her being so contrary before. ''I didn't mean to give you an order. Could we just go back and change that to a suggestion?''

Her eyes narrowed in suspicion as she studied him for a long moment. ''I suppose.''

''Then here's another suggestion,'' he said. ''As soon as you've made that call, why don't we get you home?''

''Don't be ridiculous. I'm feeling better now. There's no reason I can't go on and finish this box.''

''Humor me, sugar. I'll bring this one home for you if that's what you want, but you look exhausted. If you won't think of yourself, think of the baby.''

Scowling at him, she gave him a grudging nod before flipping open the phone book. Rafe left the room and went back to her office to find her purse. He found it in her bottom desk drawer, opened it and took out her car keys, then went back to get Caroline. She was just pushing the off button on his phone.

''All done?'' he asked.

With what looked like an awful lot of effort, she got to her feet and rubbed the small of her back with both hands. She insisted on using the rest room before they left, but agreed to stay in the lobby until he started her car and gave the air conditioner a chance to start working. Rafe drove out of the parking lot directly behind her and followed her to the historic neighborhood where her father had lived.

The two-story brick house with white trim and green shutters was a far cry from the ultra-modern condo she'd lived in when he'd been dating her. The lawn looked as manicured as any golf course and the shade trees and flowering shrubs all looked healthy and well-watered in spite of the day's heat. Caroline pulled into a narrow driveway to the right of the house, and Rafe pulled in after her.

Lugging the box he'd brought from the office, he walked around to the backyard and saw Caroline drive into a detached, two-car garage that matched the house, right down to a second story, which he guessed contained an apartment. Between the garage and the house sat a swimming pool that looked mighty inviting. Caroline didn't even look at it when she passed it on her way to the back steps.

He heard a muffled yapping while she unlocked and opened the door. A small black animal ran through the opening, wiggling in a joyous dance around Caroline's feet. She cooed and talked to it in a sappy, mommy's-little-sweetums voice, but Rafe could only stand there and stare in amazement. With a spaniel's head and the long body and short legs of a dachshund, the beast was the ugliest dog he'd ever seen. When it was down on all fours, its long, droopy ears dragged on the ground.

A laugh burst out of him before he had a chance to think about the wisdom of it. Eyes flashing blue fire, Caroline turned on him. As if it knew exactly what he was laughing at, the damn little dog charged and sank its teeth deep enough in Rafe's ankle to strike bone if he hadn't been wearing the leather cowboy boots he always wore. A surprisingly deep and ferocious growl emanated from the dog's throat.

"Truman!" Caroline shouted. "Bad dog. Stop that this instant!"

Only the fear and anguish in her voice stopped Rafe from following an almost undeniable urge to swing his foot hard enough to send the little animal flying. Juggling the box to avoid dropping it, he took a short step closer to the house, hoping to dislodge Truman, but Truman hung on to his boot with maniacal determination. Caroline tossed her purse to one side and awkwardly dropped to her knees.

"Truman, no! Bad dog. Shame on you, sweetie. Let go!" She grabbed Truman's hindquarters and tried to pull him away, but his jaws held fast. "Oh, *please,* Truman. Let go."

"It's all right, Caro. He's not hurting me."

She shot him a dubious glance. "Are you sure?"

"It's pinching a little, but he's not getting through my boot."

Rafe bent down and set the box of files on the floor. When he tried to pet Truman's back and calm him down, the dog let go of the boot and bit Rafe's hand. The little varmint drew blood on two fingers, but Rafe managed to pull his hand back before Truman could inflict any more damage. Caroline gently smacked Truman's nose, then hauled him into her arms and swung his snapping teeth away from Rafe.

Using his good hand, Rafe fished his handkerchief out of his hip pocket and blotted up the blood. "Is he always this friendly?"

"I don't know. I haven't had much company since I got him. He's all right with the lady next door."

"You haven't had him around any men?"

Caroline petted and shushed the still writhing dog, who obviously still wanted to attack Rafe. "Just the gardener and the pool service man. I never let Truman out when they're here."

Rafe smiled inwardly. She hadn't had any other men around for a while, huh? Though he probably shouldn't be so pleased to hear that, he was, and now he was even more certain that he was Caroline's baby's father. Striving for a casual tone, he asked, "How long have you had him?"

"Nearly four months." She continued trying to soothe the beast. "Calm down, now, Truman. Be a good boy."

Rafe's sense of certainty and satisfaction grew. That would have been just about the time she'd dumped him. He didn't know whether to be pleased that she'd missed him enough to need a new companion or insulted that she'd replaced him with that vicious little ankle-biter. "Tell me he's had his shots."

"Of course he has," Caroline said, her voice calm now that Truman finally had stopped fighting her. She climbed to her feet and turned back around to face Rafe. The dog bared his teeth in what looked amazingly like a sneer. "He's a wonderful little guy, Rafe. Really. I think he's just being protective."

"Where did you get him?" Rafe set her purse on top of the box and picked up both, then followed Caroline into her kitchen. He put the box on the seat of a straight-backed wooden chair that looked as if it might have been one of the house's original furnishings.

Caroline rubbed her cheek against the top of Truman's head. "At the animal shelter."

The surprises just kept coming with her, Rafe

thought. In his experience, women like Caroline rarely had pets and didn't go to animal shelters to find one. If they did have a dog, it was usually some snotty, carefully researched and ridiculously expensive little pure-bred with bows in its fur.

"Didn't they have any better-looking dogs than that?" he asked.

Scowling, Caroline cuddled Truman closer against her breasts. "That was why I chose him."

"You intentionally chose an ugly dog?" He tried, but just couldn't keep a hint of laughter out of his voice.

Caroline rolled her eyes at him, then continued. "I saw him on television first. On one of those pet-of-the-day segments they have on the local news. They said he only had a few days left before they...well, you know what they do with homeless dogs."

Rafe nodded.

"It's terrible," she said fervently. "And poor little Truman looked so odd, I just knew nobody else would adopt him. So I did."

"Why don't you set him down and we'll see what he does?" Rafe suggested.

"I think I'd better hold him for a little while longer," she said, eyeing Truman with a doubtful expression.

"All right, but let's get you off your feet."

She led him through a large, formal dining room and an equally formal living room, both of which had an air of disuse about them. Branching off from the living room, however, was a homey, inviting family room complete with an overstuffed sofa with an afghan draped over the back, a pair of blue recliners and an entertainment center. Still holding Truman, she lowered herself into one of the recliners with a sigh of relief.

The dog curled up in her lap, but kept his beady black

eyes on Rafe as if he expected the man to do something bad. Rafe stared right back at him, feeling a flash of jealousy at Truman's blatantly territorial behavior. Telling himself it was ridiculous and irrational to feel that way about a dog did nothing to ease Rafe's irritation. He knew how to battle a human rival, but he'd better tread carefully with this canine one.

Truman had obviously wormed his way into Caroline's affections. Carefully avoiding the dog's teeth, Rafe leaned down and reached for the foot rest lever. Caroline stopped him. "It's too uncomfortable to lean back like that. Then I can't get out of the chair."

She pointed at a small footstool by the sofa instead. He brought it to her and helped her raise her feet enough to use it.

"Oh, that feels better," she murmured, closing her eyes as if to savor the moment.

"Rest a while then," Rafe said. "If you don't mind I'll bring in some of those boxes from your garage and get started."

"That's fine," she said. "Use the dining room table."

He made his way back through the house, pausing to strip off his jacket and shoulder holster in the dining room and hang them over a chair. Rolling up his shirtsleeves, he went out to the garage to bring in the boxes and felt his jaw drop in dismay at the number he found stacked in front of her car.

Man, this really *could* take forever, he thought. What the hell had possessed Clyde Carlyle to do this? It was absolutely the last thing Caroline needed to deal with right now. Snorting in disgust, Rafe lifted the first one and hauled it back into the house. A quick peek in the family room told him Caroline was already sound asleep.

Figuring this was as good a time as any, he snooped through the kitchen for something good to feed Caroline. Since she obviously hadn't shopped for groceries lately, he called a restaurant he knew she liked and placed an order for delivery in an hour. A colorful calendar hanging on a bulletin board above the phone caught his attention.

There was a notation for "First Lamaze class" in one of the squares in two weeks. Didn't she need a coach or a partner for that? He wondered if she had one yet. She didn't have any close girlfriends in town, and if, as he suspected, he was the baby's father, she might need him. He wouldn't mind if she needed him for something. Maybe she could use a little repair work done around the house.

Quietly wandering from room to room, he noted a burned-out lightbulb in the kitchen that would be impossible for her to reach without a ladder; she was in no condition to be using one of those. The nursery wore a fresh coat of soft yellow paint and a colorful strip of goofy clowns midway between the floor and ceiling on all four walls. It was a warm, inviting room, but it looked as if Caroline had run out of time, energy or both before it was finished.

The room was half-filled with baby things, but the crib needed to be assembled, the shelves needed to be mounted on the wall and a couple of bright, cartoon-character pictures needed to be hung. He wasn't exactly a qualified handyman, but he could manage that much.

A fat white teddy bear sat in a big oak rocking chair. He picked it up, stroked the soft fur and felt a hollow ache blossom in the center of his chest. From the number of shopping bags filled with little blankets, clothes and God only knew what else, he had no doubt that Caroline's baby would have everything any child could ever need.

But, if it was his baby too, he wished he'd been included in those shopping trips. Not that he didn't like what she'd bought. He didn't particularly like to shop, either, but this wasn't like buying a shirt or a pair of jeans for himself. This was for his child, and he hated being shut out of so many important decisions. If the baby was his, he'd let Caroline be the main parent, but maybe he could be sort of a part-time father.

For a second he imagined he could hear his old man's derisive laughter, his harsh voice demanding, "Yeah? And what makes you think you'll be any damn better at it than I was? Hell, I was just like my daddy was, and you'll be just like me."

Rafe shook his head hard and dropped the teddy bear back into the rocker as if it had suddenly sprouted needles all over it. Caine's voice went silent, but the taint of those shaming words lingered. Rafe didn't know what he'd ever done to earn his old man's unending dislike, but he'd lived with it for as long as he could remember.

Still, the thought wouldn't leave him—what if his old man was right? His blood ran cold at the possibility, then colder yet as another thought occurred to him. Was that why Caroline wouldn't tell him he was her baby's father? Because she thought he'd abuse their child? Did she see Caine's meanness in him?

Rafe knew he had his fair share of the Stockwell temper. Once in a while Cord lost his, but Rafe ruthlessly clamped down on his. He had to in order to do his job, and he hated feeling out of control. But he couldn't deny that it was still there inside him.

Cursing under his breath, he left the room and went back downstairs, reminding himself of all the reasons he'd planned to stay single. He'd take care of Caroline and the baby, but he wasn't going to get involved with them. He was more suited to chasing down thugs like Percy Jones than he was to being a husband or a father. As long as he remembered that, everything would work out fine.

The question was, how long could he remember it?

Caroline awoke with a growling stomach, a full bladder and Truman curled up in her lap. Truman jumped to the floor when she started to get up. He raced off like a dog on a mission, but she was too intent on getting to the half bath off the family room to think about it—until she heard Rafe yell from the direction of the kitchen.

Remembering Truman's earlier attack she started to go after him, but nature wasn't just calling; she was demanding, and Caroline had no choice but to obey. Rafe was a grown man who routinely confronted armed and violent felons. Surely he could defend himself against one little dog.

She hurried nevertheless, and when she neared the kitchen, she heard Rafe utter a soft chuckle that eased her anxiety. Then she heard Truman growl.

"Yeah, you're one tough dude, all right," Rafe said, "but I'm bigger, meaner and uglier than you are, bud."

Truman's growl came again, more intense and nasty sounding than she'd ever heard it before.

"I don't think Caroline's going to like that," Rafe said, chuckling some more.

Caroline stepped through the doorway, took one look at the man and dog playing tug-of-war with a dish towel and laughed out loud. Without letting go of the towel, Truman shifted his gaze toward her and wagged his tail in greeting. Caroline moved closer to Rafe.

"Have you two made up?"

"I don't think so," Rafe said with a grin. "I just gave him something to bite besides me. Sorry about your dish towel."

"I don't mind. I don't normally use a dish towel, but he loves to play like that."

"Our old dog, Slider, used to like it, too."

"I didn't know you had a dog."

His grin stretched into a smile. "There are a lot of things you don't know about me."

"Such as?"

He handed her his end of the dish towel, walked to the stove and opened the oven door. "I'm about to put dinner on the table."

Her mouth watered at the heavenly aroma of chicken fettuccine wafting into the room. "You cooked?"

"No." He held up his right index finger and said solemnly, "I ordered. It's amazing what you can get delivered these days."

"Isn't it, though?" She pulled Truman across the kitchen, still growling and shaking his head with his teeth clamped into the towel. She filled his food dish and set it on the plastic place mat she'd put down to protect the floor from spills.

"It's ready whenever you are," he said. "Since I piled boxes on the dining room table, I thought we'd just eat out here."

She turned toward the breakfast nook and found the table already set, complete with dinner salads, a fruit plate and a small bouquet of flowers from the garden stuck haphazardly into a water glass. "It looks wonderful, Rafe."

The nook had a padded bench that curved around three sides of the table in the shape of a U. Reaching the bench was awkward for her now, but Rafe seated her with the grace and charm of a true southern gentleman. Then he brought the rest of the food to the table and sat across from her. Neither of them talked much, but simply having his company improved her appetite and enhanced her enjoyment of the meal. Lord, but she'd missed him.

So much had happened since she'd broken up with him, she hadn't had a chance to appreciate what a big hole he'd left in her life. He was the one person she'd ever felt completely at ease with, and he seemed to feel equally at ease with her.

"I noticed a Lamaze class on your calendar," he said, interrupting her thoughts.

"Oh, I've decided not to go to that."

"Why? Don't you need it for when you're in labor?"

"I'll be fine." She took a crusty roll from her bread plate and pulled a chunk out of it. "Dad's secretary volunteered to be my partner, but she suddenly wasn't able to make the dates."

"Because you admitted Clyde to the nursing home?"

Caroline nodded. "She thinks I'm not showing him enough respect."

"She's wrong, sugar. You do know that, don't you?"

"With my head, I do. My heart hasn't caught up yet though."

"Well, let it. Whether or not you were expecting his grandchild, Clyde wouldn't want you taking care of him. I know he wouldn't."

"You really think so?"

"Of course. He'd be mortified to have you bathing him and doing other things like that for him."

"I thought that, too, but then I wondered if I was simply trying to justify doing what I wanted to do."

"You're not. And I'll be happy to step in as your Lamaze partner," Rafe offered, his voice as calm and his gaze as level as if he'd just offered to take out the trash.

Though everything he'd done for her today had touched her deeply, she was too afraid of her own feelings for him to accept. "I don't think that's a very good idea."

"Why not? It's not like I've never seen your body."

"Well, you haven't seen it like this," she retorted. "And frankly, I don't want you to."

"Now, don't go all shy on me."

Bristling at his patronizing tone, she yanked her napkin off her lap and tossed it beside her plate. "You really don't want to do this. You're only offering because you think you might be the baby's father."

"Am I?" he asked, gazing straight into her eyes.

"I told you, I'm not answering that question. Now, thanks for dinner and for bringing in the boxes for me, but I can take it from here." She started to slide out of the booth, but Rafe reached across the table and took her right hand in his left one and held her in place.

"Hold on, Caroline. I know you're a strong and independent woman, but there's no reason you have to go through this all by yourself. Whether or not the baby is mine, I'm still your friend. Right now you need some help, and I'm going to see that you get it."

There was such a dear, concerned light in those incredible dark blue eyes of his, she felt her throat and chest tightening with emotions she couldn't share. She looked down at their joined hands and said in a thick voice, "Don't, Rafe."

"Don't what? Don't care about what's best for you and that baby? Sorry, honey. No can do."

"Don't be kind to me," she said.

"What's wrong with a little kindness?"

"My hormones are all confused right now, and you'll make me cry all over you."

"Wouldn't be the first time I've been cried on." He gave her a lopsided smile. "I won't melt."

"Well, I might. I never cry."

"I know you don't like to, but you're only human. Everybody needs a hand now and then, so why don't you just relax and accept that I'm going to be here for you?"

Because I don't believe you'll be here when I really need you. The words were so clear in her mind, she was afraid she'd blurted them out, and now she'd have to have a big argument with him over that. But he simply continued to gaze at her with his question still hanging in the air.

"I don't know, Rafe."

"Just let me be your Lamaze partner and we'll go from there. I'll do a good job."

She knew he would, of course. Whatever he did, Rafe did well because he put out the effort necessary to succeed.

"No strings attached, I promise," he added, holding up his free hand as if he was taking an oath in court.

Oh, dear. She *was* going to cry if she didn't get him off this subject and out of her house. And she really didn't want to go through labor by herself.

Maybe if she let Rafe be a part of the baby's birth, he would be content to leave her in peace and go on

with his life. Besides, if she really didn't believe he
would be there for her in the long run, it made no sense
to worry about something that was extremely likely to
be a short-term problem.

"All right," she said. "You can be my partner until
the baby's born, but then we go our separate ways.
Agreed?"

"Yeah, whatever."

Rafe helped her out of the booth, cleared the table
and loaded the dishes into the dishwasher. She was
about to invite him to have a glass of iced tea with her
on the patio when his cell phone rang. He raced to the
dining room and came back a moment later strapping
on his shoulder holster and carrying his sport coat
draped over his arm.

"I hate to cut the evening short, but Vic just got a
new lead on Percy. I'll meet you here tomorrow."

He leaned down and gently kissed her forehead, then
disappeared out the back door with Truman barking in-
sults after him. She squatted halfway down, scooped the
little dog into her arms. Since she'd known from experience that this would happen sometime, it didn't
make sense for her to feel let down.

But she did, dammit. And that was exactly the reason
she'd broken up with Rafe in the first place. Why was
it so blasted impossible to remember that when she was
with him?

"You're the only male I can really trust to be here,
aren't you?" she murmured, nuzzling Truman's silky
ears. "Don't let me forget that, will you?"

Truman licked her face and snuggled against her
neck, as if telling her he was willing to do anything she
wanted. She loved him for it, of course. But a silly,
immature part of her wished for equal devotion from
Rafe.

Chapter Five

"Where the hell have you been?" Rafe demanded from the back steps of Caroline's house.

Even with his hat pulled low over his eyes she still could see that his face was flushed. With a fist on each hip and his elbows sticking straight out at his sides, he looked like some old-fashioned, outraged father confronting a wayward daughter who'd missed her curfew by several hours. Just what every pregnant woman needed after a long, miserable morning.

"Why, hello, Rafe," she drawled, putting so much syrup into her voice she nearly gagged. "It's nice to see you, too."

Trudging from the garage toward the back door, she carried her purse and the small sack from the pharmacy in one hand and her keys in the other. Her back hurt, her ribs hurt and it felt as if every inch of skin touched by clothing was either chafing or covered with prickly heat. She paused beside the pool to rest for a moment, trying to figure out a way to lure that big jerk close enough to push him into the water with his clothes, his boots and his damn, beloved hat on.

"You *said* you'd be here at noon, and it's not easy for me to get extra time off. If you had to go somewhere, couldn't you have left me a note? I should've gone back to work an hour ago."

"A whole hour? You poor baby." She bribed herself into moving again with the promise of a long, cool shower, a fresh dusting of talcum powder and a nap. She hoped Truman would bite Rafe again.

"What's that supposed to mean?" Rafe asked.

"It means stop whining before you give me a headache," she muttered.

"I don't whine."

"Really? What do you call it then?" She stuck her key into the lock and opened the back door. Truman ran out to greet her, doing his usual jumping, wiggling and yipping ritual until she managed to set aside her things and give him the attention he demanded. Once he was satisfied, he immediately turned on Rafe with a warning growl and raised hackles.

Before Caroline could call him off, Rafe pulled a dog biscuit out of his pants pocket and tossed it at Truman's feet. Truman sniffed at it, then turned up his nose, obviously unimpressed with this blatant bribe. Barking as if he meant business, he ran toward Rafe.

"Truman, no!" Caroline shouted. Irritated as she was at Rafe, she really didn't want Truman to bite him again. She didn't want her dog to bite anyone. She just wanted to cool off and get some rest.

Rafe stood perfectly still, his hands poised to strike, his weight distributed evenly on the balls of his feet.

His body radiated a leashed, but potent energy that attracted her and worried her at the same time. She didn't believe he would hurt Truman, but she couldn't imagine what he intended to do either.

Truman lunged at Rafe's right foot. Sidestepping, Rafe reached down, clamped a hand around the dog's muzzle and held his mouth shut. Truman tried to shake his head, pull it back, roll over and break the man's hold, but he was no match for Rafe's superior size and strength. Rafe patiently waited until Truman wore himself out enough to sit still. While she knew her pet's behavior toward Rafe needed a serious adjustment, Caroline still felt Truman's distress as if it were her own.

"He's all right, Caroline," Rafe said, his voice soothing as he squatted down in front of Truman. Stroking the dog's head and back with his free hand, Rafe held Truman's gaze with his own. "We're not going to play this game every time I come here, Truman. You can bark at me if you want, but you've got no call to bite me. Understand?"

Truman tried to pull his head free again, and this time, Rafe cautiously released him. The dog trotted away until he was safely out of Rafe's reach, then turned around and cut loose with a deafening barrage of barking. Rafe pointed his index finger at him and said in a loud firm tone, "Truman, no."

The little dog yipped and raced out of the room, but he stopped barking. Shaking her head in amazement, Caroline stared after him before turning her attention back to Rafe. "Did you win that one?"

"I may have won the battle, but I don't think the war's over yet. That's one feisty little mutt you've got there."

Caroline supposed she should smile at that, but some-

how, she just couldn't. In return for a daily bowl of
food, clean water to drink and a place to sleep, Truman
had given her his complete loyalty, trust and a whole-
hearted affection she'd never received from any of the
people she'd spent her entire life trying to please. Beside
that, all of the logical reasons for correcting him meant
nothing. She felt like a traitor.

Turning away, she picked up her prescription. Before
she could carry it to the sink, however, Rafe put his
hand on her arm and held her in place. She tried to pull
it away, but, like Truman, she was no match for his size
and strength. The thought infuriated her on Truman's
behalf as well as her own.

"Let me go, Rafe," she said as calmly as she could
manage.

His eyebrows swooped into a scowling V in the center of his forehead. "I didn't hurt him, Caroline."

"I never said you did." She yanked on her arm again,
and this time, he released it.

"You wanted me to let him bite me?" Rafe demanded.

"Of course not." She carried the prescription bottle
out to the sink. Taking a glass from the cupboard, she
filled it with water and rummaged through a drawer for
a measuring spoon.

"Then why are you so angry?"

"I didn't say I was angry."

"You didn't have to. For God's sake, I can read body
language as well as any lawyer." He watched her fill
the spoon and stick it into her mouth. "What are you
taking?"

"Medicine."

"Medicine for what?"

"Don't worry, it's been fully approved by my doctor."

"Doctor? When did you see a doctor?"

She made a show of looking at her watch. "About an hour ago. That's where I was while you were waiting for me."

Rafe paled, then crossed the kitchen in three long strides. "Are you all right? The baby?"

"We're both fine," she assured him.

"What happened?"

"I was having chest pains, so I went to the doctor's office."

Rafe's face lost even more color. "Chest pains?"

"It wasn't a pleasant visit, believe me," Caroline said. "And then it took forever to get my prescription."

He shook his head as if to clear out the confusion. "Wait a minute. You were having chest pains, so you *drove* yourself to the doctor's office? You could have been having a heart attack. Why didn't you call me? Or an ambulance?"

"There wasn't time."

He muttered a word she was just as glad she couldn't make out. He took a deep breath, then pinched the bridge of his nose between his thumb and middle finger.

"All right," he said, using a slow, deliberate tone that made her want to kick him. "We'll come back to that one later. It obviously wasn't serious enough to admit you into the hospital, so would you mind telling me what was wrong?"

His question brought back the pain she had just endured, the doctor's infuriatingly patronizing attitude, as if she were simply another in a long line of hysterical, first-time mothers whose ignorance about pregnancy was a waste of his precious time. She'd felt incredibly stupid.

Almost as stupid as she felt now, trying to explain any of this to Rafe.

He wouldn't understand the depths of her fear any more than the doctor had. Now that she thought about it, just why did she have a male doctor in the first place? He'd never been pregnant and never would be. He didn't even have the same body parts she did. So where did he get the unmitigated nerve to treat her concerns like so much trivia?

"Caroline, what was wrong?"

"It turned out that it wasn't any big deal," she snapped.

Rafe stared at her for a long moment, took another deep breath, used that same slow, deliberate tone. "You could have been having a heart attack, but it wasn't any big deal?"

She tossed the spoon into the sink, creating a satisfying clatter and banged the glass down on the counter. "No. It was a bad case of heartburn."

"Just heartburn? You put me through all of this over heartburn?"

"I didn't put *you* through anything. And it wasn't *just* heartburn. It was acid reflux. The baby takes up so much room now, she presses against my stomach and forces the acid up into my throat. It's quite painful."

"Then you had no business driving. Why the hell didn't you call for help?"

"I've been handling my own emergencies since I left home for boarding school." Shaking her head, she uttered a soft, bitter laugh. "It never occurred to me that there was anyone I *could* call."

Shocked and hurt that she could say that to him after

he'd made such a point of offering his help, Rafe couldn't think of an intelligent response. He was one of the good guys, not some bum who didn't know how to keep his word. If he made a promise, he damn well kept it, and Caroline should know that much about him. So why didn't she? His expression must have revealed how dumbfounded he felt, because she laughed again and said, "What? You don't believe me?"

Her casual cynicism angered him, but he did his level best not to let her see it. "I told you I was going to be here for you. Did you think I didn't mean it?"

"I thought you meant it when you said it."

"But?" he prompted when she fell silent.

"But that's such an indefinite concept." She shifted her gaze to some point beyond his left shoulder. "I mean, how exactly, do you define 'being there' for someone? I honestly didn't think you'd appreciate having me call you before nine o'clock in the morning."

"I get emergency phone calls all the time. That's my job."

"Exactly. It's your job and it's all right when they call you at weird hours because you get paid for it. But I'm not part of that, and I certainly don't expect that kind of service from you or anyone else."

"Service?" Deeply offended, Rafe stalked across the kitchen until he stood within a foot of her. "Service is what you get from the gardener or the guy who delivers pizza. I think our friendship means more than that. Believe me when I say that if you need me, day or night, call me and I'll come running."

"Of course you will." She shook her head and gave him a tight smile. "If you're not off on a big stakeout or halfway across the country handling some crisis with that Special Operations Group you work with."

Wanting to shake some sense into her, he curled his fingers into fists and held his arms close to his sides, telling himself that he should know better than to argue with a lawyer. "Give me a break."

"That's not a criticism of you or your work," she said. "It's simply...reality."

"Well, hell, Caroline. I might be out doing something like that, but I might be five minutes away, too. You could at least try calling my cell phone, or—"

"Why waste the time? The only person you can ever really count on in this world is yourself."

Rafe fell back a step, feeling as disoriented as if she'd punched him in the face. In fact, he would've preferred a physical assault to the verbal one she'd just delivered. He didn't know what was making her act so blasted cantankerous, but he knew he couldn't hang around and find out. He needed a few minutes alone to rein in his emotions or he'd risk saying something they'd both regret.

Turning around, he walked straight across the room and on out the back door. Standing on the top step, he heard Caroline muttering back in the kitchen.

"Oh, right. When the going gets rough, a man always walks away."

Rafe gritted his teeth and inhaled long, loud breaths. Though the idea was tempting, he wasn't about to go back in there and start arguing with her again. Not until he had his head on straight.

Dang woman. He had the distinct impression that he'd played right into her hands, somehow. It was almost as if she'd intentionally been trying to push him away. But why would she do that?

There was no logical reason as far as he could see, but then, women in general, and pregnant women in particular, weren't exactly known for being logical. In that respect, however, Caroline was different from the other women he knew. She usually was logical. In her profession, she had to be.

So what really was going on here?

He'd managed to drop by her house every day during the past week and a half, and he thought they'd gotten along pretty well together. Digging through those boxes was slow, frustrating work. So far they'd only found one section of Stockwell files, none of which contained any useful information, but he and Caroline had begun to find a more comfortable footing with each other. Until today, he would've said that they were making real progress in reestablishing the bond they'd once shared.

But now? Shoot, he didn't have clue one about what to do next. He only knew that he couldn't take off and leave her, or himself, in such a lousy state of mind.

Excruciatingly aware that Rafe was still standing out on her back steps, Caroline poured herself a glass of iced herbal tea and settled onto the padded bench at the breakfast nook. She should be working on the files, but she couldn't bring herself to do it just yet. If she was completely honest with herself, she'd admit that she wanted to go outside and try to resolve her argument with him.

But she wasn't quite ready to be that honest. Ever since she'd agreed to let him help search for his father's files, Rafe had been nothing but kind, thoughtful and patient with her and with Truman. Just knowing he might be dropping by had brightened her days and taken her mind off the physical discomforts of being seven months pregnant.

They'd gotten along surprisingly well, and he'd helped around the house so much. While she supposed he still wanted to know if he was the baby's father, he hadn't asked her about it once. Gradually she'd stopped feeling threatened by his presence and started wishing there could be more than a friendship between them.

If she didn't watch herself, however, she'd start hoping that would happen, which was a far more dangerous prospect than wishing. Once it took root, hope was terribly difficult to kill. When a person's hopes were destroyed, it hurt a thousand times worse than any unfulfilled wish.

The back door opened, ending her reverie. The sound of Rafe's footsteps set her nerves on edge. She sat up straighter and raised her chin, meeting his gaze head-on. His midnight-blue eyes intently studied her face for a long moment, making her feel as if he could see into the deepest, most secret parts of her heart. Thank heaven she'd had so much practice in masking her emotions under pressure.

"I'm sorry," he said, his voice sounding rough and abrupt.

Rafe was a proud man, and an apology, no matter how blunt, surprised her more than anything else he might have said. "Sorry for what?"

"For stomping out of here the way I did." He tucked his hands into his pants pockets and kept his elbows close to his sides. "It was rude and I shouldn't have done it."

"Why did you do it then?"

"Because I was angry and was coming too close to losing my temper. I work hard at not doing that, but sometimes the only thing that helps is for me just to back away until I cool off."

"Apology accepted," she said.

"Good. That makes the next one a little easier."

"Next one?"

"Yeah. I'm sorry for upsetting you, too. You were always so good about letting me know if your plans had changed, I was worried that you weren't home when you'd said you'd be. Guess that's why I overreacted a little when you finally showed up."

A little? He thought shouting, "Where the hell have you been?" constituted a *little* overreaction? But in light of his seemingly sincere apology, it wasn't worth it to argue the point. "All right. I accept that apology, too."

"There's one more thing." A grin tugged at one side of his mouth, but his demeanor remained serious. "What really made me angry was having my integrity questioned."

"I didn't do that," Caroline protested.

"Yeah, you did, sugar. I don't know where you got this notion that you can't ever count on anyone but yourself, but—"

"I got it from practical experience and it happens to be the truth."

"Sometimes things turn out that way, but not always." He sat on the opposite end of the padded bench and leaned toward her, bracing one forearm on the tabletop. "Once in a while, circumstances prevent me from doing something I really want to do, but have I ever given you any reason not to believe that I'll do whatever I can to keep my word to you or to anyone else?"

She cast her mind back over the duration of their relationship, trying to come up with something. "Not so far," she finally admitted. "But we only dated for a short time. Who knows what might happen?"

"So, it's early days yet, and the jury's still out?" When she nodded, he let out a deep, rumbling chuckle that made her smile in spite of herself. "You're price-less, counselor. You know that, don't you?"

"Maybe."

"There's no maybe about it." He stood up, walked over to where she sat and hunkered down beside her. Sliding his fingers into her hair at the side of her head, he stroked her cheek with his thumb. "Always so cautious, so precise, so…cute."

"I'm not cute," she murmured, though why she should protest when he was looking at her with a blatant hunger in his eyes that gave her delicious goose bumps, she didn't know. Her heartbeat stuttered and her lips tingled, making her realize she wanted him to kiss her. Really kiss her the way he had back when they were lovers.

As if she'd spoken her desire out loud, he slid his other hand into her hair and tipped her head back, aligning her mouth with his. The spicy scent of his aftershave filled her nostrils, drawing her closer to him and awakening desires she hadn't felt since the last time she'd made love with him. And then his mouth brushed over hers, paused and brushed back across it from the opposite direction. She parted her lips for him, but he pulled back, leaving her aching for more.

"I've got to go," he said, his voice little more than a hoarse whisper. "Next time you could use some help or just some moral support, will you think about calling me?"

Fearing her own throat was too tight for any sound to come out, she nodded slowly. A warm, approving smile started at his mouth and spread to his eyes. Straightening to his full height, he dug his keys out of his jacket pocket.

"Thanks. It's a good start. Is there anything I can do for you before I take off?"

Kiss me again. Take me to bed. Make love to me. Shocked at her thoughts, Caroline shook her head. "Thank you for asking, but I'm fine."

"All right. You've had quite a day already. Why don't you take it real easy and I'll bring some supper when I come back this evening?"

"You're coming back?"

"Of course I am," he said. "Why wouldn't I?"

"We've just had an argument."

"So what? We made up, didn't we?"

Caroline nodded. "I suppose we did."

"Then it's over. What would you like for supper?"

"Something light. I'm not supposed to eat big meals anymore."

He gave her a nod, then left. Truman scurried into the kitchen, stood up on his hind legs and rested his front paws on her thigh, looking to her for reassurance or maybe a doggie treat. She gently scratched around his ears, but her thoughts remained with Rafe.

What was he up to? Since when had anyone meant enough to him to warrant not only one apology, but two? And why did he care so much about whether or not she trusted him to "be there for her"?

She'd never thought of him as being particularly hard-hearted, but she *had* thought him to be more emotionally detached, more like her father than he'd acted just now. Had she misjudged him? Was he capable of setting his work aside for his family? She wasn't at all sure, but it was something worth watching.

After a sharing a huge chicken Caesar salad with Caroline that evening and digging through files for two and a half hours, Rafe drove back to Stockwell Mansion. When he arrived, he hurried up the big staircase to his room, put away his gun and jacket and washed his face and hands, then walked down the hallway to the nursery. He could hardly wait to see Becky.

Who would've thought he could be so eager to hold a baby? The guys at the office would never believe it if he told them about it. Entering the nursery, he saw Hannah getting Becky ready for bed.

Glad to have found Hannah without Cord around, Rafe crossed the room to the changing table where his tiny, naked niece lay on her back with her feet in the air, playing with her toes. The instant she saw him, she energetically flapped her arms and legs and gurgled at him. Hannah smiled at him.

"Hello, there, Uncle Rafe," she said. "You ready for another baby lesson?"

"What did you have in mind?" he asked.

"I think it's high time you learned how to put on a diaper."

Rafe grimaced. "I don't know, Hannah."

"Fiddlesticks. She's all sweet and clean from her bath. It doesn't get any easier than this."

"All right." He moved around to the other side of the changing table rolling up his sleeves another notch. Hannah slowly took him through the steps of diaper changing. He watched her intently, and tried to repeat the process by himself, but little Becky thrashed and wiggled so much, it was all he could do to hold her still long enough to get the job done.

After destroying the tapes on three disposable diapers, he looked at Hannah. "Where's the duct tape?"

She sputtered with laughter. "I can't believe you said that. You don't put duct tape on a baby."

"Well, maybe you should. It'd work a lot better than those flimsy little things." He finally got the flimsy little things to work, however.

"Nice work, Rafe," Hannah said.

The diaper looked crooked and way too loose to him, but he thanked Hannah for the compliment. He picked up Becky and cradled her in his arms, feeling pretty ridiculous when she started rooting around on his chest in search of a nipple. Laughing softly, Hannah took a bottle of formula from the refrigerator and set it in an electric bottle warmer.

"You look real natural holding a baby," she said with a grin.

"Thanks." Rafe grinned back at her. "By any chance would you be interested in teaching me about pregnant women, too?"

Hannah's face turned pale and the laughter in her eyes changed to sadness in a heartbeat. Rafe felt as bad as if he'd just kicked a kitten. This sure seemed to be his day for upsetting women. "Hannah, did I say something wrong? You know I wouldn't hurt you on purpose."

"Of course not," she murmured, swiping at her eyes with her fingertips. "I...well, I had a baby once, but she died. It still hurts when I think about it."

"Aw, jeez, I'm sorry," Rafe said. "Just forget I said anything, okay?"

"That's not necessary." Hannah gave him a misty smile. "Why do you want to know about pregnant women?"

"A good friend of mine's going to have a baby and she's acting pretty weird. I wondered if that was normal."

"I'll tell you whatever I can if you'll tell me the truth."

''The truth about what?''

''This pregnant woman. She's more than a friend to you, isn't she?''

''What makes you think that?''

''Well, I've never known a grown man to get this interested in babies without a dang good reason for it.''

Hannah removed the bottle from the warmer, tested the temperature of the formula on the inside of her wrist and brought the bottle to Rafe. He tried to hand Becky to her, but Hannah nagged him into sitting in the rocking chair and proceeded to give him a lesson in feeding a baby. Becky sucked hungrily on the bottle's nipple.

When she was about a third done, Hannah showed him how to burp little Becky. Rafe resumed feeding and Hannah perched on a child-size chair and watched.

''So, tell me about your pregnant friend,'' she said.

''What pregnant friend?'' Cord asked from the doorway.

If he hadn't been afraid of disturbing Becky, Rafe would have groaned out loud. He really wasn't in the mood for any of Cord's teasing, but on the other hand, Cord was going to find out about Caroline's pregnancy one of these days. There wasn't much point in waiting any longer.

''It's Caroline,'' Rafe said.

Cord's jaw dropped open as he stared at Rafe. Then he blinked and shook his head. ''Caroline Carlyle?''

''Yep,'' Rafe said. ''You know any other Carolines?''

''Is the kid yours?'' Cord asked.

''I think so. She's not admitting it, but I'll be mighty surprised if I'm not that baby's father.''

Grinning, Cord crossed the room and slapped Rafe on the shoulder. ''That's great, little brother. Now

Becky'll have a cousin and a playmate. Won't you, sweetheart?''

Becky looked up, her eyes a little glazed from all of the formula she'd ingested. She smiled around the bottle's nipple and dribbled formula down her chin. Chuckling, Cord grabbed a tissue and leaned forward to clean her up.

Rafe burped her again, feeling like quite the pro when she obliged him with a gusty little belch.

"Are you going to marry Caroline?" Hannah asked.

"Soon as I can talk her into it," he replied.

Cord frowned. "She doesn't *want* to marry you? What's wrong with her?"

"Nothing's wrong with her," Rafe said. "She's just a little confused is all. Don't you think so, Hannah?"

"I've never met her," Hannah said with a shrug. "What did you mean when you said she was acting weird?"

Rafe considered his response for a long moment. "She's real moody. One minute she's happy and laughing and the next minute she's madder than a rattler with a sore fang or she's weepy."

"That sounds about right," Hannah said. "A pregnant woman's hormones can put her emotions into an uproar pretty easily. But are you sure that's why she doesn't want to marry you?"

"I don't know anything for sure," Rafe said. "She's always been a complicated woman."

"That's the best kind," Cord told him, winking at Hannah.

"You got any advice for me, Hannah?" Rafe asked.

"Well, first off, you need to learn everything you can about pregnancy," she said. "A woman goes through tremendous changes you can hardly imagine if you haven't experienced it personally. Is she close to her mama?''

''Her mother died years ago.''

''Oh, that poor thing.'' Hannah swiped at her eyes again. ''A woman who's pregnant for the first time really needs her mama to give her advice.''

''You didn't have your mama around,'' Cord said.

''I sure didn't, and I missed her so much, I thought I'd die.''

''Couldn't you take classes to teach you what you needed to know?'' Rafe asked.

''Oh, you can learn a lot of things from classes, all right. But it's just not the same as having the woman who gave birth to you there to tell you what's what. I'll bet your Caroline is scared silly and doing her best not to show it.''

Rafe stood, handed Becky and the bottle over to Cord and walked over to Hannah. ''Scared of what?''

''Of everything.'' Hannah stood up, giving Rafe the impression that she didn't like having someone tower over her. ''There's so many questions you can't answer. Stuff like, can I get through labor and all that pain? Will I be a good mother? Is the baby really all right?''

''I can't bring Caroline's mama back,'' Rafe said. ''What else can I do to help her through this?''

''Like I said, you need to learn as much as you possibly can about pregnancy and labor. There are lots of books on the subject and videotapes, too. And you've got to be real patient and understanding with her when she gets upset. Reassure her that she can handle the birth and the baby afterward.''

Rafe leaned down and kissed Hannah's cheek. ''Thanks. I'll remember everything you said.''

''Well, while you're at it,'' Cord drawled, ''remember to keep looking for Dad's files. I'd really like to know what became of our own mama.''

''I'm working on it, Cord.'' Rafe left the nursery and went back to his own room to grab his wallet and car keys. He had to get to the bookstore before it closed.

Chapter Six

Caroline stood in front of the living room window, waiting for Rafe to pick her up for the first Lamaze class. She felt absurdly nervous, but she couldn't have said why. She hoped that would ease once the class began. While she wouldn't admit that she might actually need him for anything, she was awfully glad Rafe was coming with her.

He'd become amazingly attentive, helping her to get into and out of cars and chairs, steadying her when she walked upstairs or over an uneven surface and carrying everything that was heavier than a box of tissues for her. Though she really didn't need quite that much assistance, each brush of his fingers against the small of her back, her elbow or her hand made her feel sexy. Every warm touch of his skin on hers and lusty flash of heat in his eyes reminded her that even though she was big and ungainly at the moment, she still was a woman, with a woman's needs and desires.

Of course, he had to make his visits to her around his heavy work schedule, but he somehow saw her at least once and sometimes twice a day. He always brought her a flower, a new flavor of herbal tea or some other thoughtful little gift that made her smile. She didn't know how he managed it, but again, she was awfully glad that he did.

Oh, she knew that spending so much time with her was a deliberate tactic on his part. He'd made no secret of his intention to carve out a new place for himself in her life, or more likely, in her baby's life. From the moment she'd seen him again at the office, she'd feared that very thing. But somehow, she simply couldn't bring herself to send him away and mean it.

When he was around she felt less burdened, less lonely, less vulnerable. The man who had once kept her out dancing until the wee hours of the morning gave every impression of enjoying her company, no matter how quiet or mundane the activity they shared. He even played with Truman and tolerated his continued hostility with equanimity.

They'd finished only half of the file boxes in her garage with no trace of the information the Stockwells needed. Though she knew Cord would be demanding results daily, Rafe never uttered a single impatient remark about their lack of success. Knowing that he must be every bit as frustrated with the situation as she was, Caroline sincerely appreciated his restraint.

Now that she was working at home, she felt better both physically and emotionally, and she promised herself that she would get more file sorting done during the next few days. Rafe's green sedan pulled into her driveway. Her heart beating faster, she watched him climb out, shrug on his sports coat to hide his pistol and head toward her front door.

Lord have mercy, but he was a handsome man. Much too handsome for her peace of mind. How on earth he could stand to wear a jacket in this sweltering heat, she didn't know. She didn't know why he felt the need to wear his gun to a Lamaze class, either. Most of all, she didn't know why this man, who had, for as long as she had known him, been completely negative about the idea of having a family of his own, was still hanging around her on the off chance that he had fathered her baby.

He'd never once said that he loved her, and she'd never told him the baby was his. She'd also given him every opportunity to go on with the single, carefree life he'd planned for himself. So why was he still here? Why was he putting himself through the long, uncomfortable process of helping her get through this birth? Well, perhaps it really didn't matter. Whatever his reasons for staying, she was awfully glad that he was. She opened the door for him.

"Hi," he said with a charming smile. "Ready to go?"

"Yes, of course."

She turned away, picked up her purse, a spiral notebook and the pillows she'd been instructed to bring. While she said goodbye to Truman, Rafe took everything but her purse from her, tucked it under his left arm and offered his right arm. Slipping her hand into the crook of his elbow, she accompanied him down the steps and across the yard to his car. Anyone looking at them now would probably think they were married.

The air carried the lush scents of rosebushes in full

bloom and steaks grilling, and the sounds of children laughing and splashing in the swimming pool behind the house next door. Across the street a young couple ambled side by side, the woman pushing a stroller and the man walking a Great Dane on a leash. They looked happy and relaxed, and Caroline tried to imagine herself and Rafe doing something like that after the baby was born.

She couldn't do it, couldn't allow herself to visualize her most secret wish, which might lead her into hoping for something that couldn't happen. When the baby was born and Rafe left her, she already knew it was going to hurt. She would have the baby for consolation, of course, at least until the child started asking about her daddy....

The realization upset Caroline so much she wanted to turn around, go back into her house and stay there. But how on earth could she explain it to Rafe? Arriving at his car, he helped her into the passenger seat, then hurried around the hood and slid behind the steering wheel.

"Are you as excited about this as I am?" he asked, starting the ignition.

"That depends. How excited are you?"

Chuckling, he backed into the street and turned east toward the hospital. "I'm pretty excited. I've had a little training in delivering a baby, but I think we'll learn a lot more in these classes."

"I suppose we will."

Frowning, Rafe glanced at her. "Something wrong, sugar?"

"Not really. I'm just feeling a bit...ambivalent."

"Why?"

"Why do you think?" she replied. "I'm the one who has to go through labor in a couple of months."

"Are you afraid?" he asked. "Of the pain, I mean?"

"A little," she reluctantly admitted, "but no more than most women. Wouldn't you be?"

"I probably would." He reached across the seat and squeezed her hand. "But that's why we're going to this class, isn't it? To find ways to help you get through labor with a minimum of pain?"

She nodded, then shrugged. "I just hope it'll work."

"Lamaze classes have been around for a long time. If they didn't work, nobody would take them."

Caroline nodded, then fell silent until they arrived at the hospital. Again, Rafe carried everything but her purse and held her hand as they crossed the parking lot. A volunteer directed them to a conference room, where a friendly, middle-aged woman with short gray hair and brown eyes introduced herself as Nancy Kelly, the instructor.

When the rest of the class had arrived, Nancy directed them all to sit cross-legged on the floor in a circle. Faced with a combination of surprised laughter, dismay and even a touch of mutiny, she explained that it was a good exercise for the mothers-to-be, to strengthen their pelvic floor muscles and stretch their thigh muscles in preparation for giving birth.

Once everyone was finally settled into the proper position, Nancy said, "Let's go around the circle, and one at a time, tell us your name, why you're here tonight and what you expect from this class."

Caroline noted how young the other couples looked, most in their early twenties and one couple obviously still in their teens. They all appeared to be blissfully in love with each other, however, the women seeming more confident and relaxed than Caroline had felt since discovering she was pregnant.

Though she realized her maturity and financial stability would make it easier in some ways for her to raise a child than some of these couples would find it, Caroline envied them. While these young women had been bursting with excitement to tell their husbands the wonderful news about their pregnancies, she'd been sweating bullets figuring out ways to avoid any possibility that Rafe would find out about hers.

She envied the quiet pride in the young men's faces and the fierce, but gentle aura of protectiveness they cast around the young mothers-to-be. Whatever the future might hold for their relationships, they adored their young wives and unborn babies now. Caroline had no doubt whatsoever that they would do anything within their power to make their women happy and see their children safely born.

Most of all, she envied the closeness evident in the other couples' body language and the happy light of anticipation glowing in their eyes. Watching them, she felt like a penniless child with her nose pressed against the window of a candy store. What wouldn't she give to have someone who loved her that much?

And wasn't that the story of her life? For as long as she could remember, she'd always been on the outside, looking in at others who were happier, more secure, loved in ways she could only imagine. But that would change when her child was born. She knew it would. She would love her baby so much, surely they could become a family of sorts, even if it only consisted of the two of them.

With a start, Caroline realized it was her turn. Her face felt hot as she stammered out her name and clumsily added, "This is my, um…, my friend. Rafe."

"Why are you here tonight, Caroline?" Nancy asked.

Caroline's mouth went painfully dry. She licked her lips and cleared her throat, then held her hands out on either side of her abdomen and blurted, ''Well, just look at me. Isn't it obvious why I'm here?''

Everyone laughed, and though she didn't detect any ridicule in the laughter, Caroline's face felt even hotter than before. Rafe put his hand on her shoulder and gave it a squeeze she supposed was meant to reassure her.

''I think what Caroline meant to say is that we're here tonight because we want to make sure we have the safest, most positive birthing experience possible. We hope this class will teach us how to do that.''

His answer had been so close to what she would have said had her brain been cooperating, Caroline gave him a grateful smile. He smiled back and squeezed her shoulder again. She wanted to lean against him and have him put his arm around her. Dammit, for once in her life, she just wanted to be like everybody else.

To hide her frustration, she picked up her pen and notebook, taking neat, careful notes as Nancy explained the basic principles of the Lamaze method and outlined what would be covered in the rest of the class. Next she showed a movie about pregnancy and delivery, which included graphic scenes of a real birth.

Caroline watched in fascinated horror as the woman in the film sweated and groaned, shouted and wept as she complied with instructions from the doctor, the nurses and her husband. The entire procedure seemed fraught with pain and numerous indignities, and not even the joyful tears pouring down the mother's face when the doctor handed her the squirming, red-faced, crying baby eased Caroline's doubts about her own ability to handle such an ordeal. Not that she had any choice in the matter now, of course. The thought nauseated her.

While the film projector was rewinding, Nancy called for questions. Wanting only to go home, crawl into bed and hide her head under the covers, Caroline stretched her legs out in front of her and shifted around, searching in vain for a more comfortable position. To her surprise and dismay, Rafe raised his hand.

"Can you explain more about toxemia?" he asked. "What, specifically, should we be looking for?"

Nancy gave him a list of symptoms including hypertension, fluid retention, headache, nausea, vomiting and distorted vision, all of which sounded awful to Caroline. She breathed a sigh of relief when Nancy finished. Until Rafe raised his hand again. Caroline nudged him, hoping to shut him up, but he simply patted her back and asked his question.

"What should we do if her water breaks in a public place?"

The instant Nancy finished answering that one, Rafe raised his hand again. Caroline repeatedly tried to shush him, but he went on to ask about the percentage of strokes during delivery, the incidence of breech birth, suggestions for emergency home delivery and, best of all, hemorrhaging.

The other men and women in the class stared at him in open-mouthed shock, as if none of these potential problems had ever occurred to them. Some of them had occurred to Caroline, but she wasn't ready to think about any of them just yet. She cheerfully could have killed Rafe for raising these awful topics for discussion.

Nancy simply smiled and shook her head at him. "Tell me, Mr. Stockwell, are you always this optimistic?"

Caroline thought it was easy for Nancy to be pleasant to him. After all, *she* wasn't pregnant. The other men laughed, no doubt because *they* weren't pregnant, either. And damn glad of it, judging by the relief she could hear in their voices. The other women remained absolutely silent.

Rafe glanced around the room. "Sorry," he said with a grin that belied his apology. "I didn't mean to upset anyone. I just like to be prepared for emergencies."

"You're a real boy scout, all right," Caroline grumbled.

He shot her an odd look, then addressed the instructor again. "I work in law enforcement. When we're planning to do something, we always try to figure out the worst-case scenarios. If you plan for every possible eventuality, you do a better job of minimizing trauma and damage."

"All right," Nancy said, nodding at him. "Now I know where you're coming from, and it makes sense, but we'll cover that sort of information in due time. For now, I think we should learn what constitutes a normal labor and delivery and do what we can to prepare for that."

The class quickly broke up, the other couples gathering their things and rushing out the door before Caroline managed to struggle to her feet. Fearing what she might say if she spoke, she accompanied Rafe out to the car in a tight-lipped silence.

"What's wrong?" he asked, frowning at her.

"Nothing." She exhaled a deep sigh and fastened her seat belt without looking at him, then said, "Please, just take me home."

Baffled and more than a little irritated by her attitude, Rafe drove back to her house and carried her things inside. Before he could get the back door properly shut, she turned on him, cheeks flushed, her eyes glinting with anger, her voice sharp with demand.

"How could you?" she said, raising her hands beside her head, fingers spread wide in an uncharacteristically dramatic gesture.

Keeping a wary eye out for Truman, Rafe asked, "How could I what?"

Caroline lowered her hands to her sides and curled her fingers into fists. "I have never been so embarrassed in my life," she ranted. "How could you be such an insensitive dolt?"

Clearly affronted, Rafe propped his hands on his hips and stuck his elbows straight out at his sides. "What the hell are you talking about?"

"Those questions you asked."

"Hey, she asked if we had any questions, and I did. What's wrong with that?"

"Good Lord, Rafe, you scared everyone in that room to death," she scolded. "I'm surprised you didn't ask about infant and mother mortality rates while you were at it."

"Hey, if my questions were so bad, why didn't you ask some?"

"Because I didn't go there to ask questions."

"You already know all of this?" he demanded.

"A lot of it. I've read everything about pregnancy and childbirth I could find."

"Then what did you want to get out of the class tonight?"

She let out an exasperated snort. If she'd been a teenager, she probably would have rolled her eyes at him, too. "Number one, I wanted to listen and take notes and get a feel for Nancy's basic approach. Number two, I wanted to hear what other people asked and compare the information I've gathered with what Nancy offered."

"Which is exactly what I helped you do," Rafe said. "I asked good questions. Admit it."

She opened her mouth as if to speak, then paused, studying him with a puzzled frown wrinkling her eyebrows. "How did you know about toxemia?"

"You're not the only one here who knows how to read."

"What?" Her eyes bugged out and her mouth dropped open. "You've been reading about pregnancy? And childbirth?"

"Hell, yes," Rafe said, silently thanking Hannah for steering him in that direction. "Did you think I wouldn't take my job as your Lamaze partner seriously enough to learn about what you're going through?"

"I wouldn't put it quite that way," she said, her tone softening. "It simply didn't occur to me that you'd do anything on your own. Or even that you should."

"Well, I did. As soon as you agreed to let me help, I went down to the bookstore and bought three books about pregnancy and childbirth and one about what to expect during the kid's first year."

"But you've been so busy at work and with sorting all these files, I can't believe you found the time."

"You and the baby are important to me. Don't you know that by now?"

Her smile wobbled and she asked faintly, "What books did you buy?"

He named the titles and had the pleasure of watching her get surprised all over again. "Not bad, huh?"

"You chose very well," she agreed.

"Well, I asked a pregnant clerk for help, and—"

"You actually asked for help?"

She'd turned so pale with that last question, Rafe started to feel concerned. He'd enjoyed surprising her, all right, but he figured enough was enough. He didn't want her to pass out on him. "Yeah. I didn't know what to buy, and I figured she'd probably know which books were the best."

Caroline shook her head in amazement. This ranked right up there with seeing a man willingly ask for directions. Rafe was a nice guy, but he was still a *guy*, which made it difficult to imagine him being quite that thoughtful.

"So, do I get to ask about mother and infant mortality rates next week?" He expected her to smile, maybe even laugh, but she pulled her arms in tight to her sides and sort of withdrew inside herself. He didn't know why or how, exactly, but in a matter of seconds, she'd built an unbreachable wall between them. Rafe found himself standing there, staring at her and feeling as if she'd just slapped him. Her next words added another layer of bricks to the wall.

"Please, no," she said without looking at him. "In fact, I think it would be better if we forgot about this whole thing. I don't believe the Lamaze method is quite right for me."

"Why not?"

"After watching that film, I'd really rather sleep through the birth and wake up with a new baby in a bassinet beside my bed."

Appalled, Rafe demanded, "You'd rather be drugged unconscious than help bring your own child into the world?"

"It didn't look like much fun, did it?"

"Not all the way through, but that lady coped pretty well. And you will, too, sugar. You're braver than this."

"No, I'm not."

"Of course you are. You're the strongest woman I've ever met, and I know you're going to be a great mother. All of my books say it's better for the baby if you don't take all of those drugs. Don't forget he gets whatever you get."

"She," Caroline corrected him. "My baby's a girl."

"How do you know that? Did you have amniocentesis or one of those other tests?"

Caroline shook her head. "I just know, all right? Call it a mother's intuition."

"What does your mother's intuition tell you about doing what's best for the baby?"

"That's not fair, Rafe."

"Of course it is. And we're going to do the Lamaze thing. I'm right about this, and you know it."

"No, you're not. This is *my* baby. I'm going to do this *my* way, and I will *not* tolerate any interference from you."

He stared at her for a long moment, then took her by the arms. She gave him a fierce scowl and tried to shrug off his hands, but he held her fast. "Oh yeah? Maybe it's time to admit it's my baby too."

She went completely still, but a pulse beat visibly at the base of her throat. Her gaze darted back and forth as if frantically looking for someplace to land that wouldn't allow her to meet his gaze. Suddenly he knew just as surely as if she'd finally said the words. He *was* the father of Caroline's baby.

A warm sense of something—satisfaction maybe, pleasure certainly, he wasn't exactly sure what else it was—started in the pit of his stomach and spread through the rest of his body. He stretched out his now trembling left hand and lay it across Caroline's belly.

The baby thrashed away inside her, as if acknowledging, even welcoming, his presence.

Rafe's eyes stung a little, a lump grew in his throat and he had the craziest urge to lean down and plant a kiss where he'd felt the baby's movement. But Caroline was watching him with a wary—no, it was a frightened—expression that cut him to the quick. What did she think he was going to do? Yell at her? Beat her? Even the idea of either option made him sick.

Holding back a curse he pulled his hands off her and stepped to the side. "Caroline, please, talk to me."

She turned away from him and stooped to pick up Truman, who for the first time, hadn't even tried to bite Rafe. Of course, the fast food hamburger he'd slipped the mutt might have had something to do with that, but Rafe wasn't planning to mention it.

Brushing her cheek across the dog's smooth head, she murmured, "I don't know what you want me to say."

"Just tell me what's going on with you. You don't really want me to leave, now. Do you?"

She looked over her shoulder at him, then, biting her bottom lip, she lowered her gaze and slowly shook her head.

"Why was that so hard?" he asked.

"Because I want to be able to handle things for myself." Her voice softened to a near whisper, but he distinctly heard her say, "I've been alone forever."

"Aw come on, honey. Not forever."

"You don't know anything about it." She turned around to face him, her eyes so sad, it was almost as bad as if she were crying. "No one does."

"But you had your folks—"

"Did I?" She tipped her head to one side as if giving her own question serious consideration, then firmly shook her head. "Not really. I had people who hired other people to look after me, but it wasn't the same as having real parents."

"Be glad your dad wasn't as mean as my old man," Rafe advised. "Every time I turned around, there he was, ready to tear another strip off my hide for some piddly little thing nobody else would've noticed."

"I might've preferred that to being ignored," she said. "My father spent most of his time at work. He was pleasant enough when he finally came home, but I rarely saw him. I certainly never knew him. I still don't."

Rafe raised his eyebrows in surprise. "But Clyde was always real proud of you. I know he was."

"Well, he never bothered to tell me," she said with a nonchalant little shrug Rafe seriously was beginning to dislike.

"What about your mom? You saw her, didn't you?"

Laughing softly, Caroline shook her head. "Didn't you ever know why they sent me off to boarding school?"

"It wasn't for the education?"

"I was six years old when they sent me away. I couldn't stay at home because my mother was a drunk."

"No way," he said. "I remember her as a real classy lady."

"She hid it well when she was out in public. But at home, she was just...a drunk."

Dumbfounded by what she'd revealed, Rafe could only ask, "But why?"

"Why does anyone have an addiction? She was lonely. My dad loved the law more than he did her or me, and she didn't know what to do about it. She drank to forget the pain, and it worked. The only problem was, she forgot me, too.'' Caroline looked straight at him, then added, ''I used to envy you Stockwells.''

That surprised a laugh out of Rafe. ''Good lord, why? Caine beat us and berated us, and now it looks like our mother probably abandoned us to be with her lover. Some great family we were.''

''But you weren't alone, Rafe. You always had Cord and Jack and Kate.''

''You're serious about this,'' he said, amazed to find himself certain that she'd told him no less than the truth.

''Of course.'' She studied him for a moment, her eyes narrowing with suspicion. ''But save your sympathy for someone who needs it. I've become quite good at taking care of myself, and I'll do the same for my baby.''

Rafe's perception of her changed in the time it took to blink. Why hadn't he seen this part of her before? She'd always seemed so self-contained, so independent, it had never occurred to him that she might actually be lonely or that she might want a man in her life on a long-term basis. Her I-don't-need-anybody attitude had attracted him to her at first, mainly because he hadn't wanted any intense relationships, either.

Eventually, however, her fierce independence had driven him away when he hadn't yet wanted to go. Without her prodding him, he wasn't at all certain he ever would have left her. They'd been that good together.

But she'd asked him to go, hinting that she had another man in her life. From Rafe's viewpoint, there hadn't appeared to be any room in her life for him, and he wasn't the kind to push himself in where he wasn't wanted. He'd had more than enough rejection during his own childhood. He hadn't been willing to risk getting another dose of it from Caroline.

But now…well, now he could see the truth. She wasn't self-contained by nature; she'd been forced to become that way by necessity. Hell, she was so used to being abandoned, she probably expected that to happen with every relationship in her life. And now he knew why she kept trying to push him away. It was safer for her to reject the other person first than to risk being the one rejected.

Well, he wasn't going to buy into that anymore. Whether or not she would admit it, Caroline needed him. That baby would need him, too, and come hell or high water, he was going to be there for both of them. Caroline would damn well have to get used to the idea.

Chapter Seven

After breakfast the next morning, Rafe stepped into Cord's office and caught his brother in the middle of a play session with Becky. Supported by Cord's hands, she sat upright in the middle of his massive desk, squealing with delight when he made faces at her and then, making motorboat noises, jiggled her tummy with the top of his head. She grabbed fistfuls of his hair and drooled on his blotter, his shirtsleeves and the back of his neck, but he didn't seem to mind.

On the contrary, Cord appeared to be having the time of his life. Rafe was glad to see his brother acting so silly with Becky. That way he wouldn't have any room to talk when Rafe acted the same way after his own baby was born.

"Hey, what're you doing to my best girl?" Rafe scooped the baby out of Cord's grasp. Shifting her to the crook of his arm, he moved away from the desk.

"Dang it, Rafe. Give her back," Cord said.

A bewildered expression flitted across Becky's face and she turned her head toward her daddy's outraged voice. Carrying her to the window, Rafe tickled her under the chin and drew her attention to himself.

"Hi there, peanut," he said, smiling into her sweet little face. "Remember Uncle Rafe? The handsome one?"

Becky gave him a big grin and gurgled at him. He smoothed her wispy hair down with one finger, marveling at the softness of her skin, the delicacy of her features, the complete trust in her blue eyes. Rafe's throat tightened, his heart contracted, and suddenly he wanted to cuddle her against his chest and shelter her from any pain or sorrow for the rest of her life.

Oh, man, what was happening to him? How could this tiny scrap of humanity get such a complete hammerlock on his heart in only a few weeks? And if he felt this strongly about his niece, how much stronger would his feelings about his own kid be? He didn't know how he'd survive it.

Feeling weak in the knees, he turned away from the window, glanced around the room for an empty chair and discovered Hannah sitting about five feet away, studying him. Her eyes had a misty sheen. A soft, trembling smile played around her lips, and he instantly felt more exposed than if he'd stripped himself naked in the middle of downtown Dallas.

"Hi, Rafe." She stood up and crossed the space between them. Laying her hand on his shoulder, Hannah gazed at the baby, her expression reflecting a depth of love and devotion that mirrored his feelings with astonishing precision. As if she couldn't bear not to touch the baby, she cupped her palm around the side of

Becky's face before looking back up at Rafe. "How did the Lamaze class go last night?"

"It was okay," he said, after taking a moment to collect his thoughts. "Pregnant women sure are sensitive, though."

"Well, don't judge them until you've been there," Hannah said.

"There's not much chance of that happening." Chuckling, Cord joined them and lifted Becky out of Rafe's arms.

Hannah rolled her eyes at him, then turned back to Rafe. "How's Caroline doing?"

Rafe started to say, "Oh, she's fine," but changed his mind in favor of the truth. "I don't know, Hannah. She seems okay physically, but I think you were right when you said she was probably scared. In fact, I think she's scared about labor."

"Most women are a little," Hannah said. "Especially the first time. There's no way anyone can really explain how it feels and there's always some old biddy who has to tell you every labor horror story she's ever heard."

"Damn," Rafe muttered.

"Exactly," Hannah agreed. "Just keep reassuring her that she can do this. She needs to go into it with a positive attitude."

"I'm trying to help her with that," Rafe said. "But I don't think I'm doing it right. I keep wondering if a girlfriend couldn't help her more. Any chance you would like to meet her?"

"Golly, doesn't she have any women friends of her own?"

"She has lots of acquaintances, but I don't think she has any close girlfriends. She spent most of her life in boarding schools up north until she graduated from college.''

"Oh, my." Hannah shot a worried glance at Cord. "Well, sure I'd be glad to meet her, but—"

"Aw come on, Hannah, say yes," Rafe coaxed. "You're exactly what Caroline needs, I'm sure of it."

"Hannah's busy," Cord said.

"I'm not talking about a big time commitment," Rafe said, frowning at his brother. "You could take care of Becky for one evening, couldn't you?"

"Of course I could. And I will, once we get back."

"Cord, maybe we should put it off," Hannah suggested.

"No way," he said. "We're not waiting one more day."

"For what?" Rafe demanded, looking from one to the other. "Are you going somewhere?"

"Yes. We're going to Las Vegas," Cord said with a broad grin. "To get married."

Rafe couldn't help but smile back at his twin. "That's great. When are we leaving?"

"You're not invited," Cord said.

"The hell I'm not," Rafe shot back. "You're not going to ask anyone else to be your best man."

Cord shook his head, then handed Becky off to Hannah and slung his arm around Rafe's shoulders. "I'm not going to have a best man. Besides, we've got a more important job than that for you to do."

Rafe shot him a questioning look. "What's more important than being in your wedding?"

"Hannah wants to get married the same way her folks did, and they eloped to Vegas. Nobody in the family is coming with us. In fact, you're the only one who's even going to know where we are."

''But, Cord—''

''It's not up for negotiation, Rafe. I want to get my ring on Hannah's finger before she changes her mind, all right?''

''All right,'' Rafe grumbled, but the thought of his twin brother getting married with no family there to support him still didn't sit right. He stepped away, dislodging Cord's arm. ''What's the job you want me to do?''

Hannah took Rafe's place beside Cord. ''We want you to take care of Becky for us,'' she said.

''Are you serious?'' Stunned by the trust Hannah was giving him, Rafe stared at her. ''I mean, maybe you should get a real nanny. Somebody who knows more about babies than I do.''

''You're better qualified than any nanny,'' Hannah said. ''You've got the one qualification we can't buy, Rafe.''

''What's that?'' Rafe asked.

''You love her.'' Smiling, Hannah caressed Becky's head. ''That's more important than anything else. You'll do a fine job and she'll feel real safe with you.''

''It's just for the weekend,'' Cord added. ''Friday afternoon until Sunday night. Can you get that much time off?''

''For you two?'' Laughing, Rafe shook his head to make sure he wasn't hearing things. ''Of course. I'll do anything I can to help. Want a ride to the airport?''

''We'll see,'' Cord said.

''Maybe you could take this little punkin here over to see your Caroline.'' Hannah wrinkled her nose at the baby. ''Might help her to stop worrying so much about labor and start thinking about what she's gonna get out of it on the other side.''

''Yeah,'' Rafe said, nodding slowly at first, and then

more enthusiastically. "Yeah. Hannah, that's a brilliant idea. Would you mind if we take care of Becky together? Over at Caroline's place?"

Hannah looked to Cord for his opinion.

Cord shrugged. "I don't see why not. Caroline's a nice lady, and she's as responsible as they come. You'll like her when you meet her, Hannah."

"She'll go nuts over Becky," Rafe added. God knew anyone who could lavish so much affection on an ugly little mutt like Truman would have to find a beautiful baby like Becky irresistible.

"Well, all right," Hannah decided. "If I'm gonna trust you to take care of Becky, I'm gonna trust you all the way, Rafe."

He leaned down and kissed his soon-to-be sister-in-law smack on the lips, drawing out the kiss until he heard Cord suck in a harsh breath. Rafe raised his head, winking at Hannah. Her eyes looked huge and her face was nearly crimson.

Straightening up the rest of the way, Rafe took one look at Cord and started laughing. As expected, his twin was puffed up like a big toad, ready to rip out Rafe's lungs for taking liberties with his woman. Rafe cheerfully punched his shoulder.

"Hey, it's bad enough I don't get to go to my twin brother's wedding. You wouldn't cheat me out of kissing the bride, would you?"

Cord scowled at him until Hannah shook her head and carried Becky out of the office muttering something about grown men who oughtta know better, for pity's sake.

"I can see why you're in such a hurry to marry her," Rafe said when she was safely out of earshot. "She's great."

"Tell me something I don't know." Cord gave him a rueful smile. "What are you doing here so early? Did you find Dad's files?"

The hopeful light in Cord's eyes saddened and frustrated Rafe. He hated adding to Cord's stress, but there was no way to avoid it. "Not yet."

"Dammit, Rafe. It's time for the rest of us to help you and Caroline with this."

Rafe shook his head. "Not yet. I think we might be getting closer."

"What makes you say that?"

"We're finding more Stockwell files now. Just not the right ones yet."

"All the more reason to push harder," Cord said. "Mom's not that much younger than Dad. If she's still alive, who knows what kind of shape her health's in? And I'll bet she'd love to see Becky."

"What if she doesn't give a damn?"

"Come on, Rafe—"

"No, *you* come on," Rafe said. "If she *is* still alive, she left us without a backward glance. She didn't bother with phone calls, birthday cards or Christmas presents. Not one damn thing. If she didn't care any more than that about her own children, what makes you think she'd care about a grandchild?"

Cord lowered his gaze to the floor as if Rafe's question had probed too close to a tender spot. Finally Cord walked to his desk and sat in the big leather chair behind it. Rafe took the visitor's chair and leaned forward, bracing his elbows on his knees while he rubbed his palms together and waited for his brother to respond.

"You're probably right," Cord said after an agonizing moment of silence. "It might be easier on all of us if we found out she was dead all along. Lord, that's a terrible thing to say. Dammit, I want this settled.''

"No more than I do," Rafe said.

"Then let's bring Jack and Kate in on the search, and I'll join the rest of you when I get back from Vegas.''

"Caroline's not up to a Stockwell invasion," Rafe said. "Just hold off on that until you get home. If we haven't found what we need by then, we'll figure out something. All right?''

Cord hesitated, then gave Rafe a grudging nod. "All right. But only until I get back. Then we start a massive search.''

Rafe left for work five minutes later, wishing for the first time in his career that he didn't have to go. The thought shocked him. His career had been his life since he'd graduated from college. He and Vic were so close to Percy Jones now Rafe could almost smell him. They wouldn't fail again.

Under normal circumstances, Rafe would have been breathing, eating and sleeping this case, focusing every ounce of his attention and energy on putting Percy behind bars for the rest of his miserable life. Rafe still wanted to do that, of course, but at the moment, he was more concerned about Caroline and his family than he was about Jones. Realizing that made him feel odd, as if he'd become a different person during the past twenty-four hours.

Mentally brushing aside that ridiculous notion, Rafe pressed harder on the gas pedal. This distraction from duty was nothing more than a temporary glitch in his wiring brought on by his conversation with Cord and his unsettled relationship with Caroline. He was the same dedicated Deputy U.S. Marshal he'd always been. He had to be.

He'd always held himself apart from intense relationships with family and friends, often using his work as an excuse to justify keeping his distance. He longed to go back to that life, where the lines between the good guys and the bad buys were easy to see. The chain of command within the Marshals Service kept work relationships simple, and as long as there were violent criminals, he could always count on having meaningful work.

In comparison, personal relationships—especially family relationships—were too emotional, too messy and too damn unpredictable. No wonder he preferred to spend most of his time at work. Today, his work called to him, telling him it was time to come back and forget all this other stuff that made him feel so blasted confused.

The temptation to go back to business as usual was huge, but he couldn't do it. He'd already gone too far in the opposite direction. He had to consider Caroline and the baby. He'd made a commitment to take care of Becky for Cord and Hannah. Jack and Kate must be every bit as anxious as he and Cord were to learn about their mother's fate. The weight of those responsibilities rested squarely on his shoulders.

He had no intention of letting anyone down, but the timing for all of this couldn't be worse. After tracking Percival for ten months they finally were so close to catching him, Vic couldn't understand why Rafe suddenly wanted to cut his workday from sixteen or eighteen hours to twelve. Though he liked Vic well enough, Rafe didn't discuss personal matters with him or anyone else at work.

Shaking his head in disgust, Rafe drove up the entrance ramp to the interstate to Fort Worth. Dammit, the more he thought about all of this, the more ambivalent and confused he felt. This was why he'd always insisted that law enforcement careers and marriages just plain didn't work.

But now, the only thing he knew for sure was that whenever he saw Caroline, he felt connected to her and to the baby she carried in ways he'd never suspected were possible. The stress of his day at work faded from his mind, and he no longer had to be a hotshot Deputy U.S. Marshal or even a Stockwell heir. With Caroline, he was just an ordinary man who'd found a place he was needed, a place where he really belonged.

He wasn't head over heels in love with Caroline the way Cord was in love with Hannah. Rafe doubted he even knew what real love felt like, but that really didn't matter. No other man could ever care about Caroline and the baby as much as he did. Now that he'd had a taste of that kind of connection, he couldn't imagine giving it up. No matter what happened.

"Hey, Caroline! Dinner's here."

The sound of Rafe's voice booming from the back door brought Caroline's head up with jerk. Oh, dear Lord, what was he doing here already? She wasn't ready to tell him yet. Why hadn't he waited just one more hour to show up?

"Where are you, sugar?"

She heard a rustling noise in the kitchen, then the sound of his boots walking across the tile floor, moving in her direction. Frantically closing the two files she'd spread out on the dining room table, she stacked them together and shoved them into the middle of the box she'd been working on, then rubbed her palms down the sides of her khaki maternity shorts as if she could wipe the dirty history contained in those papers from her hands.

"Ah, there you are." Smiling, Rafe entered the room and crossed the space between them, his smile faltering a little more with every step. Stopping in front of her, he leaned down and pressed a quick kiss on her forehead. "Are you feeling all right, Caro?"

"Of course." She wiped her hands on her shorts again and moved a step sideways. Dammit, she needed more time with those files, so she could absorb all of the information and find a way to deliver it that wouldn't hurt him so much. "I feel...great."

He tipped his head to one side and studied her so closely, she began to feel intense sympathy for zoo animals.

"You look a little pale," he said. "When did you eat last?"

She glanced at her watch, though she knew perfectly well what time it was. Anything to buy a few seconds to compose herself. "Oh. Gosh it's been quite a while. Are you hungry enough to eat?"

"Caroline, what's going on here? You're acting strange. If I didn't know better, I'd say you'd just committed a crime of some kind."

And that was exactly how she felt. Lord, she had to tell him. And she would. Just...not yet. She forced herself to laugh, then shook her head. "Don't be silly. I'm a little tired and hungry."

"You're sure that's all it is?"

"Yes, dear," she said in a teasing, singsong voice. "Did you have a slow day catching bad guys, so you came here hoping for an emergency?"

"Are you accusing me of being an adrenaline junkie?"

"Yes. And don't try to deny it. You deputies are simply a bunch of overgrown boys playing cowboy."

"You could be right about that." Chuckling, he put his arm around her shoulders, pulled her against his side and started them both off in the direction of the kitchen. She slid her arm around his waist and couldn't stop herself from giving him a little hug. He came to a halt and turned to face her, putting both of his arms around her.

"You hugged me."

"Didn't you like it?"

"Yeah." His voice dropped an octave and took on a raspy edge. "I did."

He pulled her as close as her belly would allow, leaned down and kissed her on the mouth. It started out as a slow, sweet kiss, but then he broke away and made a nibbling foray down the side of her neck that raised gooseflesh while it heated her blood. Instinctively she blocked his path with her shoulder. He switched to the other side and nibbled his way up to her ear.

"Ah, Caro, you taste good and you smell good and you feel good in my arms," he murmured, biting her earlobe with just enough pressure to thrill her. "I've been thinking about you all day."

"You have?" Ever since he'd come back into her life, he'd treated her so gently, so cautiously, it was almost as if they'd never had the sexual relationship that had made her pregnant in the first place. After that one time he'd hugged her at the office and she'd noticed his arousal, he'd treated her with the casual affection of a brother. But there was nothing casual or brotherly about what he was doing to her now. The man definitely was feeling amorous.

"Uh-huh." Inhaling harsh-sounding breaths, he

rested his cheek against the side of her forehead. "I'm sorry. I've been trying hard not to do this, but I want you so much—"

She looked up at him, seeing the truth in his eyes, but having a difficult time believing it. "But I'm huge."

"And it's so damn sexy I can hardly keep my hands off you."

Eyeing him skeptically, she pulled back and rested her right hand on top of her belly. "Is it really that, or have you simply gone too long without...?"

"Without what?" His grin was positively wicked, making it impossible for her not to return it.

"You know what." He raised his eyebrows and stared at her until she laughed. "All right. Without sex?"

He rubbed his jaw and scrunched his mouth up to one side, narrowing his eyes as if he were thinking hard. "Well, it's been an awful long time, all right." Then he reached out, cupped the side of her face with his palm and stroked her cheek with his thumb. "I haven't wanted anyone since you."

His answer floored her, but she couldn't deny the sincerity in his voice or the intense, utterly serious expression in his eyes. "I...I don't know what to say."

"You don't have to say anything." He gave her a crooked smile. "You don't have to do anything about it either. I just wanted you to know. And baby or no baby, I think you're sexy as hell."

"Thank you." She stood there, feeling her response had been woefully inadequate, but completely unable to come up with anything else to say. Rafe was a very physical man. The thought of him going without sex for over seven months was hard to believe. But she did believe him. It deeply touched her to know that he hadn't simply gone out and replaced her in his bed with the first available woman who crossed his path. It would have been so easy for him to do. Had she meant more to him than she'd realized? With a man as reluctant to talk about his feelings as Rafe, who could tell?

"Look, why don't you go and freshen up?" he suggested, still with that crooked smile. "I'll have dinner on the table in five minutes."

"All right." She turned and fled to the bathroom off the family room, doing her level best to avoid looking at herself in the mirror. Rafe was so impossible sometimes, so impossibly dear at others. Right now was one of those dear times, and she felt like a rat for not telling him what she'd found. But, jeez, how could she tell him, knowing that it most likely would break his heart? There was no good way to soften the blow with news like this.

When she entered the kitchen, she found the table set with her favorite place mats, a fat bouquet of daisies and a basket of dinner rolls. Rafe stood at the work island, spooning a crisp, colorful salad of greens, chicken, mandarin oranges, pineapple and sliced almonds onto two plates. He carried them to the breakfast nook, then helped her to slide onto the bench.

The salad was delicious, but Caroline's appetite vanished the instant Rafe sat down across from her. She forced herself to take a few bites for the baby's sake, but every time she glanced up, she caught him looking at her mouth, her neck, her breasts with a wicked gleam in his eyes and a sexy smile playing at the corners of his mouth. Her own mouth went dry and her throat constricted. Her heart thumped hard against her rib cage. Knowing she'd never be able swallow another morsel, she played at rearranging the food on her plate, hoping to make it look as if she was eating.

"Don't like the salad?" he asked.

"Oh, it's lovely," she assured him. "I'm just not as hungry as I thought." Not for food, anyway.

She was, however, hungry for Rafe. If she didn't have this wretched news to tell him, she suspected that she might have told him she wanted him regardless of the consequences. But while he started an easygoing conversation and continued to flirt with her, she felt too guilty about withholding information from him to give him much of a response.

He reached across the table with his fork, scooped up an orange section and raised it to her lips. "Come on, sugar, just one more little bite. It'll be good for you."

When she started to refuse, he popped it into her mouth. The flavor spread across her tongue, prompting her to close her mouth and chew. By the time she swallowed it he had a bite of pineapple waiting for her. This was too intimate, too...sexy to continue. Leaning away from it, she shook her head.

"No, thanks. I really don't want any more."

"All right." He set the fork on his plate, then smiled and hit the side of his head with the heel of his hand. "Hey, I forgot to tell you about Cord and Hannah."

"What about them?"

"They're getting married next weekend."

"I suppose you're going to be the best man," she said, imagining him in the black tux he'd worn twice while they were dating. That was a big mistake. Along with the memories of seeing him in that tux came even stronger memories of peeling him out of it.

"Nope."

"Oh, that's a shame." Wondering what on earth could have possessed Cord not to give his twin the honor, she felt indignant on Rafe's behalf. Then she noticed his smile had widened and his eyes gleamed with what looked like anticipation. ''You're not unhappy about that?''

''Nope,'' he repeated, shaking his head this time. ''They're eloping to Las Vegas, and I'm going to stay here and take care of my niece, Becky. Want to help me?''

''I didn't know you had a niece. Is Cord her father?''

''Uh-huh.'' Rafe told her about Cord's relationship with Marnie Lott, a young woman who had borne Cord a daughter and then later died. He went on to relate how Hannah had been the social worker assigned to Becky's case and had nearly driven Cord crazy making sure that everything was in order before allowing Becky to stay at the Stockwell mansion. ''They're going to be quite a pair. And just wait'll you meet Becky.''

''How old is she?''

''Almost four months now.''

''Heavens, I don't know that much about babies yet,'' Caroline fretted. ''Do you really think we could handle her for a whole weekend?''

''No problem. Becky's a real sweetheart and Hannah's been teaching me how to take care of her. I can make bottles, change diapers, give a great bath. It'll be a good chance for us to practice being parents before little whoozit arrives,'' he said, pointing at her belly.

It sounded like fun. She would be spending the whole weekend with Rafe, and she might learn a lot of things about babies that would come in very handy. But she still hadn't told him about the files and she couldn't go on making plans with him as if nothing had happened. Her anxiety must have shown in her face, because he reached across the table and covered her hand with both of his.

"It'll be all right, Caro. I promise it will. If we run into anything we can't handle, I won't hesitate to call for help."

"Oh, stop." Groaning, she yanked her hand away and buried it in her lap. "Will you please just stop being so damn wonderful?"

"Huh? What are you talking about?"

Rafe looked so perplexed she wanted to laugh. Only the fear that her laughter would change to hysterical tears stopped her. "Never mind."

"I can't never mind when you say something like that. Caro, I know you're worried about the baby and the labor and everything, but I promise we'll all get through it somehow. And when you finally get to hold that little one—"

"You don't need to do this," she said, interrupting him.

"Do what? I'm just saying that you don't have to worry so much about this. People have babies all the time, and whatever it is that's troubling you—"

She pounded her fist on the table in frustration, then found herself shouting at him like some madwoman. "Dammit, Rafe, will you listen to me? It's not about the baby!"

Chapter Eight

Eyeing her warily, Rafe settled back against the bench seat and folded his hands together on top of the table. "I'm listening," he said. "If it's not about the baby, what's bothering you?"

Caroline took a deep breath, then blurted it out. "I found them."

"Found what?"

"The files you wanted. Caine's files."

Rafe's eyes widened. Shoving his plate to one side, he leaned forward, resting one forearm on the table. "Why the hell didn't you say so?"

"There's a lot of information. I haven't had a chance to read it all carefully yet."

"You know the basics of what's in there, don't you?"

She nodded. While she hadn't read the documents with her own professional standard of carefulness, she'd already memorized most of the salient points. Lord, but she didn't want to do this. Didn't want to tell him. Didn't want to hurt him.

"Well then," he said, "just hit the highlights."

She could see that his body was practically vibrating with tension and impatience. "What do you want to know?"

He rubbed the back of his neck for a moment, then thumped the table with his index finger. "I want to know which time Caine lied about her. When he said she died in that boating accident or when he claimed there was no accident and she still might be alive."

"She could still be alive, Rafe."

Without so much as a grimace in reaction, he asked, "What's the evidence?"

"A divorce decree," she said. "It's dated six months after she was supposed to have died."

"I see." He fell silent for a long, thoughtful moment before quietly adding, "Dead people don't need divorces."

"No, they don't," she said, aching for him. For his brothers and sister. For his mother and even for Caine, though she suspected he was the actual villain in this case. She had no actual proof of that, however, and chose not to mention it.

Rafe slid out of the booth and straightened to his full height. Shutting his eyes, he turned away from her and inhaled a deep breath. His attempt to project a calm bearing failed miserably. His face and neck flushed an alarming shade of red, his nostrils flared and his hands became fists. The muscle along the side of his jaw stood out in rigid relief. She wouldn't have been surprised if the salad greens had wilted from the anger rolling off him at such close range.

He'd always been such a model of self-control she couldn't imagine him seriously losing his cool. Unless she was badly mistaken, however, his temper was about to blow sky-high. The thought was as alarming as it was fascinating, but she didn't know whether she should sit here and watch the explosion or run for cover. What would happen if she tried to get close, perhaps even hug him?

No, on second thought, that obviously was a bad idea. A very bad idea. How else could she offer him comfort without offending his dignity?

Maybe she should tell him it was too late to get into all of this now. He could take some time to absorb this much information and get the rest of it in smaller doses. But that might be like pulling off a bandage millimeter by millimeter, drawing out the pain rather than ripping it off with one hard yank and ending the pain immediately.

It probably wouldn't be any easier for him to hear the details tomorrow or any other day. In fact waiting would only give him too much time to imagine worse things than what actually was in the documents. The best thing to do was to get it over with.

"All right," she said, struggling to her feet. For the first time since he'd come back into her life, he didn't help her, didn't seem even to notice that she could use some help. Sighing inwardly, she led the way out of the kitchen.

By the time they reached the dining room, his face had lost all expression; looking at him, no one ever would suspect that he'd just received a terrible blow. In fact, he seemed eerily calm. And there was a brittle quality to his movements that made her think of a big tree that would break rather than bend in a strong wind.

Caroline thought an explosion of temper would have been healthier for Rafe.

He sat in the chair she normally used. She located the files and pulled them out of the box, opening the one with the divorce decree and setting it in front of him. He reached for it, but she laid a hand on his arm. He looked up at her, eyebrows raised in question.

"I'll give you some privacy, but I'll just be in the kitchen," she said. "Call me if you have any questions."

He gave her one quick nod and turned back to the file. She returned to the kitchen and spent fifteen minutes putting away leftovers and loading the dishwasher. Then she put a can of dog food out for Truman. He didn't come running at the sound of the can opener. Had she even seen him since lunch?

Concerned, she stepped out the back door. Oh, there he was, chewing on something near the fence surrounding the pool. She walked over to see what he'd found this time. Truman wagged his tail as she approached, but he didn't stop gnawing on a big soup bone with lots of meat scraps still attached.

"Where did you get that?" she asked. "As if I didn't know."

Truman wagged his tail again, still gnawing with enthusiasm.

"Will you be nice to Rafe now? Hmmm? You certainly ought to. What exactly will it take for him to buy your affection, anyway? A whole steak? A roast? A ham?"

As if tired of her chatter, Truman stood, picked up the bone in his mouth and carried it ten feet away before flopping down on his tummy and resuming his feast.

Caroline smiled. "If you keep eating like that, before

long your tummy's going to drag on the ground whenever you walk.''

Truman ignored her completely, and she turned back toward the house feeling absurdly rejected. It was nothing compared to what Rafe must be feeling. Perhaps she was only feeling this way out of sympathy for him. After all, Truman wasn't really rejecting her. He was only acting like a dog.

But it was easy to know that sort of thing with your intellect. It was something else to know it with your heart. A child's broken heart was the most difficult thing to mend. Rafe was a grown man, of course, but the heart being broken in her dining room right now belonged to the little boy Rafe had been when he lost his mother. Accepting the death of a parent was hard enough. Accepting abandonment was impossible.

Wanting, for once in his life, to give his temper free rein and sling these damn papers against the far wall, Rafe forced himself to close them carefully and stack them up before pushing them away. He'd thought he was ready for this. He'd thought he'd imagined every possible scenario for what might be in those files and come to terms with all of them. He'd thought this whole mess had happened so many years ago, whatever he found wouldn't matter a bit. He'd been wrong on all counts.

It was easy enough to blow off the ravings of a sick and dying man who was drugged to the eyeballs with pain medication. There was no way to blow off legal documents that told the same story. It was time to face the truth, ugly as it was.

And it was damned ugly.

He couldn't remember much about his mother, but

he'd always carried an impression of a warm, affectionate woman who laughed a lot and had unending patience for little boys. It was impossible to reconcile that image with the documents he'd just read. How could any mother do what she had done?

Propping his elbows on the table, he held his head in his hands and closed his eyes, trying to shut out the mental pictures that kept popping up in his mind. The nights he'd lain in his bed, desperately wanting his mother and biting his lower lip until it bled to stop himself from crying loud enough for Caine to hear him. The beatings all four of them had endured, but especially himself and Jack. The day Caine had banned him from Stockwell Mansion and stripped him of all financial support because he'd changed his college major from pre-law to criminology.

He'd learned enough about frugality and found enough menial, part-time jobs to finish school on his own. After graduation, he'd joined the U.S. Marshals Service and enjoyed showing his old man that he could get along fine without his backing. But the wound of essentially being ousted from his family had never fully healed.

Looking back, Rafe didn't blame his mother for leaving his old man; he'd never understood why she'd married such an abusive, humorless control freak in the first place. But he did blame her for leaving him, Cord, Jack and Kate behind without putting up any sort of a fight. She must have known, or at the very least suspected, what kind of a father Caine would be. How could she have saved herself but not her children?

Had she really left them to be with his Uncle Brandon? Everything Caine had said was proving to be true. And where the hell was she now?

A hand gently touched his shoulder. He started violently, then raised his head to find Caroline standing beside him, studying him with a worried frown. She squeezed his shoulder in a gesture he supposed was meant to be comforting. Dammit, he didn't need or want her feeling sorry for him, which she obviously was. He shrugged off her hand and stood up.

"Are you all right, Rafe?" she asked.

"I'm fine."

"Do you have any questions about the papers?"

He considered that for a moment. "Was that kind of custody arrangement fairly common back then?"

Caroline shook her head. "Just the opposite. Women almost always retained custody of their children."

"What happened in this case?"

"I don't know. The court documents only tell what actually happened. They don't have to say why."

"What were the usual reasons a woman might lose custody?"

Caroline's lips tightened and she looked away, clearly reluctant to answer his question.

"Don't worry about hurting my feelings now," he said, not caring how harsh his voice sounded. "I have a pretty good idea what probably happened. I just want confirmation."

"All right." She took a deep breath before continuing. "Usually, for a woman to lose custody of her children, especially children as young as you all were at the time, someone would have to prove she was an unfit mother. That would include abuse, neglect, mental illness, adultery. That sort of thing."

"Or maybe she didn't want custody in the first place," Rafe suggested.

"That's another possibility." Moving closer to him,

Caroline reached out and offered him her hand. "Let's sit down in the family room and talk about this."

Rafe would rather be tortured by a crazed drug lord, and was just about to say so when his beeper went off. Gratefully yanking it off his belt, he checked the number and stepped around Caroline, intending to use the phone in her kitchen. It was his partner, Vic, calling to say he'd just watched Percival Jones check into a fleabag motel in Fort Worth. Did Rafe want to be there for the arrest?

"Does Texas get hot in the summer?" Rafe asked. With Vic still chuckling on the other end of the line, Rafe hung up, then turned back toward the dining room. Caroline stood in the doorway, watching him with troubled eyes.

"That was Vic," he said. "I've got to go to work."

She crossed the space between them and would have reached for him if he hadn't sidestepped her to grab his sports coat. "Rafe, you're understandably upset, and you need to talk about this. I don't think you should go to work."

"I'm fine. Don't worry about it." Rafe gave her a brief salute and escaped out the back door. When they had Percy behind bars, he might have to shake the man's hand for rescuing him from a terrible fate. The very last thing he wanted to do tonight was talk about his mother. Wherever she was, he hoped she was miserable.

Caroline stood at the back door, shaking her head as she watched Rafe back out of her driveway. Darn it, if she'd had another ten minutes with him, she might have broken through that, I'm-just-fine-don't-worry-your-pretty-little-head-about-me line of baloney Rafe had been giving her. Now he'd get his macho defenses back in place and bury his feelings so deep it would take dynamite to bring them back to the surface.

On the other hand, men processed emotional issues differently than women did. Having something else to think about for a while might be good for Rafe. But when he was called out in the evening, he usually had to make an arrest, which many times involved gunfire. She only hoped he wouldn't be distracted enough by what he'd learned tonight to get himself killed.

Her breath caught in her lungs and her stomach clenched. Lord, what a thought. But if he did get killed tonight, she would have serious regrets. She'd never told him the baby was his. She'd never told him how much she appreciated his help. She'd never told him she loved him.

"No, I don't," she whispered, raising one hand to her throat. Her impossibly tight throat. "I can't love him. I just…can't."

But she did love Rafe. Second by second, minute by minute, her certainty of that fact grew. If she didn't love him, she wouldn't be standing here, fearing for his safety. She wouldn't have worried so much about finding a way to soften the news about the contents of the files. Her heart wouldn't ache just a little every time he left her.

Had she ever really stopped loving him? She doubted it, but decided it didn't matter. She couldn't burden him with her feelings now. He had more than enough to deal with at the moment. Perhaps when things settled down for him and his family she could bring up the subject. For now, she needed to concentrate on helping him find out everything there was to know about his mother's long absence.

Determined to do something useful, she returned to

the dining room and carefully went through the files again. She brought a small, portable television into the room and turned it to a local station in case there was any news regarding Rafe's activities. Then she searched for more files pertaining to Caine and Madelyn Stockwell's divorce, but didn't find any.

The evening passed with excruciating slowness. Midnight came and went. She was too tired to do anything useful, too worried about him to sleep. By one-thirty she'd had enough. After checking on Truman, she grabbed her car keys and left.

Rafe would want to be alone tonight, she was sure of it. He wouldn't go out to the mansion, but he still had a town house in Grandview. She wouldn't intrude; she just wanted to know he was all right. She'd drive by and if his car was there, she'd turn around and drive right back home.

Swearing under his breath at the hot stale air in his town house, Rafe walked from the hallway to his bedroom, turning on lights and opening windows. Stripping off his clothes and his gear, he left it all in a heap, stepped into the shower and let the hot water pound on his head and neck. Damn, but he was beat.

His partner and the rest of the crew were out celebrating Percival's arrest, and he felt like some surly old badger who only wanted to hole up in his burrow and stay there. When the water finally ran cold, he dried off, pulled on an old pair of jeans and went to the kitchen for one of the beers he'd bought on his way here. Carrying it into the den, he sat in his recliner and picked up the remote control.

His being here wasn't any big deal. This was his real home, after all, not the mansion and not Caroline's house. He hadn't wasted much time decorating the town house, but it suited him fine. He hadn't had much privacy lately, and it felt good to be alone. He'd drink his beer, do a little mindless channel surfing and go to bed.

He'd just gotten settled and found an all-night sports channel when the doorbell rang. He froze. He hadn't told anyone he was coming here. Jeez, he hoped it wasn't Cord, but it probably was. Maybe if he stayed quiet, whoever it was would give up and go away.

The bell rang again, more insistently this time, and he realized that with the lights on and windows open, he could hardly pretend he wasn't home. Swearing under his breath, he got up and stomped through the house. He yanked open the door, and there was Caroline, still wearing the same clothes she'd had on at dinner.

"Hello, Rafe," she said, her voice soft and hesitant.

"It's the middle of the night," he said. "You should be at home in bed. What are you doing here?"

"I couldn't sleep." She looked down at her hands as if she felt embarrassed. "I just planned to drive by and see if your car was here, but when I noticed all the lights on, I…I just wanted to make sure you were all right."

Jeez, he should've known she'd still want to talk about his family. Well, too bad. He wasn't going to do it. Not now. Not ever. How he felt was nobody's business but his. "I'm fine, Caroline."

"Of course you are." Hurt flashing briefly in her eyes and red spots staining her cheeks, she stepped back from his doorway, clutching her purse against her side with her bare arm. "I understand, Rafe. I'm sorry to have bothered you. Good night."

She turned away and, using the wrought iron handrail, went down the five steps to the sidewalk. Every step she took screamed of fatigue far greater than his own.

He realized he should have called her, but it hadn't occurred to him that she cared enough to worry about him, much less drive all the way across town at this time of night to check up on him.

No one else had ever done anything like that for him. She was almost to her car now and she was rubbing her back as if it hurt. What if she was too tired to drive? Dammit, he felt like a jerk. The least he could do was offer to drive her home.

"Caroline," he called. "Wait a minute."

She looked back, gave him a stiff smile and a little wave, then walked on to her car and awkwardly lowered herself into the driver's seat. She really was going to leave. Suddenly, he felt a cold, aching crater of loneliness open up inside of him, and he wanted her to stay more than he wanted his next breath.

He rushed outside, stubbing his big toe on the sidewalk and hopping three steps on one foot like a big, clumsy kid trying to play hopscotch. "Please, Caroline," he called, loudly enough to wake his neighbors. "Don't go."

By the time he ran the rest of the way to her car, she'd climbed out and stood waiting for him with one arm resting on the car's roof and the other across the top of the open door. "What is it?" she asked in a husky voice.

"I want you to stay. If you want to, I mean." He shoved a hand through his hair, feeling damn uncomfortable. He still wasn't sure he wanted to talk, but he didn't want her to leave, either.

Her gaze roamed down his bare torso, then she looked up at his face again with a hint of a smile teasing the corners of her mouth. "Were you getting ready for bed?"

He glanced down at himself and grinned. "No. Just unwinding after work."

"Let me guess. You've got a beer, a remote control and a recliner."

"How'd you know?"

"I've been here before," she said. "Besides, it's a guy thing. You're a guy. Elementary deduction."

Chuckling, Rafe reached out and offered her his hand. "Come on, sugar. I'm sorry I was so rude. Stay awhile."

She hesitated long enough to make him feel anxious, but finally slipped her hand into his and stepped out from behind the car door. Still holding hands, they slowly walked back to the town house. Once inside, he led her into the den and seated her on the black leather sofa he'd bought to celebrate his last birthday.

She glanced around the room, and he suddenly wondered what she thought of it. Whenever she'd been here before, they'd usually been in too much of a rush to get to his bedroom for her to pay much attention to anything else. His philosophy of home decor emphasized comfort and ease of maintenance rather than style. Compared to her place, his looked downright Spartan.

"Would you like something to drink?" he asked, turning off the TV and all but one lamp, leaving the room in semidarkness.

"No, thanks. What happened at work tonight?"

He sat beside her, stretched his arm behind her head across the sofa's back and told her about Percival's arrest, which had turned out to be surprisingly easy once Percy realized he was severely outgunned. Caroline smiled and nodded in all of the right places, and gradually, Rafe began to relax. When she leaned against his side, it seemed perfectly natural to wrap his arm around her shoulders.

The next thing he knew, the conversation had drifted to the files she'd found that afternoon. He had no idea what kind of magic she used on him, but somehow, talking about his mother went from being impossible to being necessary. It was as if Caroline had opened a gate hidden inside him and released a torrent of pent-up words that had been clamoring for release for God knew how many years.

"I'm not sure what I wanted to find in those files," he said. "But I sure wanted to be able to call Caine a damned liar to his face. Now I can't, and I don't know what to think of either one of them anymore."

Caroline squeezed his hand. "Give yourself some time."

"I had my mom all built up in my head as this warm, loving, delightful woman." He sighed, then sadly shook his head. "And now, to find out she just left us...I can't quite get my brain to accept that. I read those papers. Saw the words with my own two eyes. But I still don't want to believe any of it."

"That's normal," Caroline assured him. "Denial is the first part of the grief cycle."

"I went through all of that when I thought she was dead." He turned his hand over and caught hers between his palms. "This really doesn't change anything, so what's left to grieve?"

"In a way, you're losing your mother all over again, Rafe. The wonderful woman you believed in gave you comfort even though you thought she'd died. Now you're discovering a different sort of mother and you miss your old one, so your loss is new and just as real as the original one. Your brothers and sister have probably been feeling it, too, ever since Caine raised doubts about her.''

"I guess that makes sense in a weird sort of way," Rafe said thoughtfully. "If denial's the first stage of grief, what comes next?''

"Anger," she answered without hesitation. "You've been feeling it yourself. When you tell the others, you should be prepared to see a lot of anger in them, too.''

"How do you know so much about all of this?''

She shifted around on the sofa until she faced him almost directly. "I've been there, remember? I learned all about betrayal firsthand from both of my parents.''

"Your mother didn't betray you the way ours did," Rafe said. "If Caine's telling the truth about the rest of it, our mom gave us up to be with her lover. But your mom was sick. She couldn't help herself.''

Caroline reached up and clasped his hand where it hung past her shoulder. "I'd like to believe that, but I don't. It's just that my mother's lover was a bottle of vodka instead of a man. And have you noticed that your mother's betrayal hurts twice as much as your father's?''

After a moment's consideration, Rafe slowly nodded. "You're right. I guess we all want at least one parent to love us. Dads tend to handle discipline and make us earn their respect. But it's different with mothers.''

"That's right." Caroline rested her hand on her abdomen, spreading her fingers protectively. "Mothers usually provide most of the nurturing we get as children. We feel closer to them and simply expect them to love us more than anyone or anything else. It's a nasty shock when they don't. I'm not going to make that mistake.''

Rafe stared at her. "Do you really think people can avoid making the same mistakes their parents did?''

"Yes, I do. The fact that you recognize it's even a possibility is your best defense against it." She pressed her palm to the side of his face. "For example, you couldn't be more different from your father."

They fell silent then. Rafe cuddled Caroline closer, using his free hand to press her head into the hollow of his shoulder. She caressed the palm of his other hand with her thumb. He felt a strong sense of contentment settling over him, filling him, sinking into his bones.

It had nothing to do with sex, but it reminded him of those amazingly peaceful moments following a bout of lovemaking where you felt as if you'd connected with your partner on every level and understood each other completely. He kissed the top of her head, then rubbed his cheek over her soft hair. He knew she must be exhausted, but he wanted to stay right here with her for the rest of the night.

"Don't give up on your mother just yet, Rafe," she said softly. "Madelyn may have loved all of you more than you think, no matter what the divorce settlement implies."

"What makes you say that?"

"Caine obviously got exactly what he wanted out of the divorce, but the papers only tell us what happened in the end."

Rafe raised a doubtful eyebrow at her. "I didn't see any evidence that she put up a fight to keep us with her."

"That's the point I'm trying to make," she said. "The papers say that Caine won, but they don't tell us anything about the process they all went through to get to that final decision. She might well have fought for custody of her children and lost for whatever reason. That settlement is really quite unusual for that time."

Rafe looked into her eyes. "You think there's something fishy about it? Like, maybe Caine bought off a judge or a witness? Or made threats? Something like that?"

"Given his reputation for questionable ethics, don't you think it's possible?" Caroline asked.

"Hell, yes." Shaking his head, Rafe snorted. "With my old man, anything's possible."

"That's why I'm saying, don't give up on your mother until all of the facts are in."

"I don't know if we'll ever be able to find all of the facts. Even if Caine was willing to be honest, he's probably too far gone to tell us much. And we don't know where my moth...I mean, Madelyn is."

"I went back through the file with all of the financial information and picked up one lead that might be worth following. It's a return address on the envelope of one of the checks she refused to keep. It was in Paris."

"All right. We'll look into it."

"When are you going to tell the others?" she asked.

"Not until after Cord and Hannah's wedding. Might as well let them enjoy their weekend away without bringing this up. A few more days won't make any difference in the long run."

Caroline tipped back her head and with a sweet, sleepy smile, slid her fingers into the sides of his hair. Gently raking his scalp with the tips of her fingernails, she slowly licked her lips. "You're a nice man, Rafe Stockwell. If you leaned down where I could reach you, I'd probably have to kiss you."

"If you did that," he said cautiously, "I probably wouldn't stop with a kiss."

She laughed softly. "What makes you think I'd want you to?"

Chapter Nine

Rafe wanted her so much, he hardly dared to breathe, but he finally found the courage to ask, "Are you serious?"

Neither her eyes nor her smile wavered. "I am if you are."

"What about the baby? Making love won't hurt her?"

A naughty glint entered Caroline's eyes and she slowly shook her head from side to side. "My doctor said that as long as I don't do anything too athletic, it's fine until the ninth month."

She gave him her special wink, the one that had been a signal back when they'd been dating. He'd always loved seeing it, because it had been her private way of telling him, "I've had enough of this party. Take me home and ravish me, you fool."

Seeing that wink here and now nearly stopped his

heart. He'd been completely focused on convincing her to let him back into her life at least until the baby was born. Fearing he might offend her if he tried to reintroduce a sexual element into their relationship, he'd kept his libido on a tight leash.

With no more warning than that wink, she'd severed the leash. Months of celibacy, weeks of wanting her threatened to overwhelm him. If he wasn't very careful, he'd wind up taking her right here on the floor of his den.

That wouldn't do, of course. He'd read enough books about pregnancy, all of which had contained chapters on making love to a pregnant woman, to know that a little finesse was in order here. He'd read the how-to-have-sex chapters several times, in fact, but he really hadn't expected to have the opportunity to apply what he'd learned. Not during this pregnancy, anyway.

Instead of making a fool out of himself, he needed to get her upstairs where he could make her comfortable and show her that he could be a great lover under any circumstances. *Please. Let me do this right.*

"No athletics, sugar. You won't even have to stand up." Hoping like hell he could manage this, he scooped her into his arms. He discovered that she wasn't much heavier than when he'd done this before and carried her to his bedroom. "Don't you worry one little bit. I'll gladly do all the work. No athletic moves at all."

Laughing, she raised one hand to the back of his head and pulled him down for a kiss. It was a soft, warm kiss at first, and the simple affection it offered stopped him halfway to the king-size bed. Then she raised her other hand to clasp the side of his face and deepened the kiss, slipping her tongue into his mouth and exploring it until his self-control wavered alarmingly.

"I won't break," she murmured, kissing him again. "And neither will the baby."

He laid her on the bed and gathered an armful of pillows, propping up her back and neck, automatically watching for tension in her arms and legs the way he'd learned at their most recent Lamaze class. Sitting on the edge of the bed, he rested his hands on either side of her hips and took a moment just to gaze at her. She looked lush and ripe, like some gorgeous fertility goddess with magical powers designed to lure men into her arms.

He sure wouldn't put up much of a fight, and he could hardly wait to see those delicious curves hidden by her maternity clothes. Smiling at the thought, he was startled to see his goddess blush and turn her head away.

"Hey, what is it, sweetheart?" He hooked a finger around the side of her chin, coaxing her to look at him. "You can tell me anything."

"Would you turn off the light?" she asked, her voice barely audible. "I don't want you to see me like this."

Disappointment was a fierce ache in the middle of his chest. He tried to keep his voice even, but suspected there'd be a whining edge to it. "Why not?"

"I don't—" She paused and cleared her throat. "I don't think the beached whale look is in this summer."

"There aren't any beached whales in this room." He brushed the backs of his fingers over her cheek. "All I see is one very beautiful and sexy lady who's going to become a mother soon."

"You're just saying that to make me feel better."

"Not true. I've read all about the changes your body's been making." He stroked her breasts through her clothes, giving special attention to her nipples. She inhaled a sharp breath and arched her back, pushing herself more firmly against his hands. "I know your breasts are bigger and more sensitive now, and I really want to see them. Don't deny me that pleasure, Caro.''

She watched him through half-closed eyelids. Holding her gaze, he slid one hand under the hem of her top and stroked her through her bra, grazing bare skin with his fingertips wherever he could reach it. A darker flush rose from the neckline of her top and swept over her face. He continued his verbal seduction, hoping it worked half as well on her as it was working on him. It had been one heck of a long time since he'd touched her like this.

"Doesn't that feel good?" He leaned down and kissed her sweet mouth, gently nibbling on her lips. She wrapped one arm around his neck and kissed him back. He stroked her breasts again until her breathing came harsh and shallow.

He moved his hands around her rib cage and under her back, and she obligingly arched her back again while he unfastened her bra. She sat up just enough to allow him to pull the top and bra off over her head, then lay back.

"Happy now?" she asked, giving him a wry smile.

"Oh yeah, sugar." Now his breath sounded harsh and shallow, in his own ears, anyway. The breasts he'd only been able to imagine so far were even more beautiful than he'd expected. He cupped them in his palms, loving their weight and the satiny texture of her skin as well as the larger, darker nipples. "You're gorgeous. Just tell me what you like."

He kissed one, then the other, carefully watching her reaction to make sure she was enjoying his attentions. He needn't have worried. The next instant she was guiding him with her hands and her sighs. Her pleasure was an incredible turn-on.

Still loving her breasts with his mouth, he caressed her sides and then gently rubbed his hands all over her belly, nudging her shorts and panties out of the way a little at a time. He felt a little thump and experienced a renewed sense of awe at the knowledge that his child was nestled inside this round, firm mound, all safe and snug while Caroline's amazing body fed and nurtured it. It seemed the most natural thing in the world to lavish her belly with kisses.

The baby thumped his nose. "Hey, you in there," he said to her belly. "What do you want?"

He put his ear to her navel, earning a giggle from Caroline. "You want what? An inner tube? No, I don't think there's enough room in there, kid. You want a chocolate sundae instead of all those vegetables your mama eats? That's not up to me but I'll pass along your request."

Caroline's laughter made her abdomen jiggle. He gave her a stern look that only made her laugh harder. He put his ear to her navel again.

"Uh-huh. Uh-huh. Well, what's it gonna take for you to settle down so I can have a little fun with your mama? A complete video game library? A custom bike? Your own horse? A hot car? A full ride at Harvard? Jeez, kid, have a heart. I'm just a civil servant."

"You nut," Caroline murmured, ruffling his hair.

He raised his head and laid one hand flat on her abdomen. "This is the coolest, most wonderful thing I've ever seen. Your body is doing what it was created to do. How could it be anything but beautiful?"

Her eyes took on a misty sheen, but he didn't want her to cry now, for heaven's sake. Kissing her soundly, he stripped off her shorts and panties without giving her a chance to protest. He couldn't stop caressing her, exploring her, loving her all over. She urged him to move up onto the bed with her.

He shucked off his jeans and underwear, then stretched out beside her and pulled her into his arms. Until that moment, he'd been proud of his control, but feeling so much of her warm, naked skin flush against his made him ache with the need to be inside her again. She snuggled into his embrace, exhaled a soft sigh that ruffled his chest hair and relaxed so completely against him, he feared she would fall asleep.

His body cried out in silent protest, but a wave of tenderness for her tugged on his heartstrings. If this was all she wanted right now, it was all he would give her. He couldn't help thinking back to the way they'd made love before—hot, urgent, even greedy at times, there'd always been too much fire and excitement to leave a whole lot of room for softer emotions like this. He had to admit there was something to be said for it. He just wished—

Her hands suddenly came alive, stroking, petting and exploring his body, finding his most sensitive spots. Her tempo was slower than usual, but her touch felt so good, so right after all this time, he couldn't hold back a moan of sheer delight. Was she reading his mind or what? He slid his hands into her hair and kissed her for all he was worth.

She responded with a passion that rocked him to his soul. Turning onto her back, she draped her legs across his hips and guided him into her body from the side. He moved as slowly and gently as he could, but she was so ready to welcome him, he encountered little resistance.

When he was deep inside her, he put both arms around her and held her close for a moment, feeling as if he'd finally found his way home after a long, dangerous mission. Was this what love felt like? Or was it simply contentment? Before he could come up with an answer, she moved her hips in a circular motion, and the friction wiped out any inclination on his part to think.

Unable to hold still anymore, he matched himself to her rhythm as he'd often done before. This new position gave him easy access to her mouth and her breasts. He indulged himself in playing out his recent fantasies. He indulged her, as well, lavishing her with attentions he knew she enjoyed.

Making love like this seemed more restrained than usual. Then time stretched out and nature took over, banishing any sense of awkwardness or hesitation, giving each stroke, each sigh, each kiss a sweet, fluid quality he'd never guessed was possible. Everything felt new and different, as if they were making love for the first time all over again. But every bit of their lovemaking was as powerfully satisfying as any wilder, more athletic sexual encounter he'd ever had.

When they both tumbled over the edge into completion, he lay on his side, still inside her and panting for breath, watching her panting in perfect time with him. Secure in the knowledge that he'd pleased her, he propped himself up on one elbow, leaned forward and kissed the tip of her nose.

Caroline opened her eyes and smiled at him with a smug, satisfied gleam in her eyes that matched his own feelings so exactly, he chuckled.

"Wow," she said, stroking his cheek with her fingertips, scratching lightly at his night whiskers.

"Yeah." He turned his head and nibbled on her fingertips. "Wow."

Luxuriating in the sweet aftermath, they cuddled and caressed each other with long, languid strokes that might have incited another round of lovemaking had they continued. Caroline pulled away from him, however, struggled into a sitting position and covered herself with the sheet. He wanted to reach for her, pull her back down beside him and kiss her senseless, but his instincts told him to let her go.

Looking away from him, she sank her teeth into her lower lip. Her eyes took on a serious, thoughtful expression, giving him the impression that she was carrying on some kind of internal debate. Her modesty with the sheet tickled him, but her sudden change of mood worried him. Only a moment ago, she'd seemed happy and relaxed. What on earth was going on in her head?

"What is it?" he asked when he couldn't tolerate the suspense any longer. She started, then met his gaze again and smiled at him, easing the worst of his anxiety.

"There's something I have to tell you," she said, lacing her fingers together on top of her abdomen.

"What's that?" he asked.

"The baby *is* yours, Rafe."

"I know." He grinned at the thought that he soon would have his own little Becky. Then his mood took a somber turn. "If there really wasn't anyone else in your life, why did you break up with me?"

"There *was* someone else I wanted to spend more time with," she said. "The baby."

He frowned. "That wasn't logical, Caroline. You led me to think there was another man in your life. Why didn't you tell me when you first found out about the baby?"

"I was afraid you wouldn't believe me." Her voice sounded soft, hesitant.

"Aw, Caroline—"

"Don't pooh-pooh me," she said, scowling at him. "You were always such a gentleman about taking care of protection, I didn't see how I could expect you to believe me when *I* didn't even know how I got pregnant."

"You could've tried. Even I know that all methods of birth control have occasional failures."

"I considered that," she admitted.

"So why didn't you tell me?"

"What would have been the point?"

"I deserved to know. Isn't that point enough?"

"Not when you were always so...adamant about wanting to stay single. You didn't want any permanent commitments. You were already married to your work, and law enforcement marriages rarely succeed anyway. Does any of that ring a bell?"

"Unfortunately," Rafe agreed, feeling like an idiot for having said all of those things. "And I doubt I ever would have intentionally done anything to change that. But I'm not such a louse that I wouldn't accept responsibility for my own behavior. You knew that, didn't you?"

"Of course I did." She reached over and squeezed his hand. He supposed she meant to reassure him, but it didn't help much. "I knew you were a good man, and I knew if you believed the baby was yours, you would feel obligated to help support her. But I didn't want you to do that, because obligation is a poor substitute for love. Anyway, I was so pleased to be having her, I didn't see any reason to disrupt your whole life."

"That was my choice to make. Not yours."

"I understand that. Now. At the time, though, I really didn't think you'd want to know. I'm sorry I misjudged you."

He gently squeezed her bare shoulder. Obviously they had both made some mistakes. "I gave you every reason to think that way, so forget about it. And forget those dumb things I said back then. It's taken a while, but I've gotten used to the idea of being a dad. Now I'm excited about the baby."

Caroline gazed deeply into his dark blue eyes and felt as if her heart was swelling inside her chest, filling up the empty, lonely places with warmth and happiness. She imagined she could hear her defenses against loving him crumble one at a time, and for once, that thought failed to frighten her. Maybe, just maybe, this could all work out.

Of course, Rafe's excitement about the baby didn't necessarily mean that he loved the baby's mother. But the way he'd just made love to her and the way he was looking at her now gave Caroline hope that someday he might love her. Someday, they might be able to form a family and—

The cordless telephone on the bedside table rang, shattering her rosy dreams of a happily-ever-after future for all of them. Rafe leaned across her, grabbed the handset and rolled away from her before putting the receiver to his ear.

"Yeah?" He listened intently for several minutes, then muttered a pungent curse Caroline had never heard him say. "All right, I'll meet you there."

He got off the bed, walked around it and hung up the phone, then bent down and kissed Caroline's forehead. "Sorry, sugar, duty calls."

She stared at him, feeling as if she'd been swept to

the top of a roller-coaster and then sent straight to the bottom without the benefit of the car or the tracks. How could he blithely get up and go to work when they hadn't really finished what she thought had been an extremely important discussion?

"But you've hardly been home," she said. "You haven't even had any sleep yet."

"Doesn't matter." He scooped his jeans off the floor, carried them into his walk-in closet and continued his side of the conversation through the open doorway. "There's a bad guy out there and it's my job to bring him in."

"You already brought in Percy or whatever his name was."

"This is a different bad guy." Rafe came back to the bedroom dressed in a navy blue suit, a crisp white shirt and a shiny black pair of boots. He needed a shave, but she'd bet her law degree he had a rechargeable electric razor in his car. "God knows, we never run out of them, but that's what gives me job security."

He grinned at her, obviously enjoying his own little joke. The jerk. How could he be so pumped about going out and risking his life, when she suddenly felt like bursting into tears? "What about Becky's visit? We still don't have the crib or the changing table put together. And I'll need to do some cleaning. When are you bringing her?"

"That's not until the day after tomorrow," he said.

She pointed at his radio alarm clock. "It's already tomorrow."

"It'll be all right, Caroline. I don't expect you to do anything out of the ordinary. You don't need to worry about any of this."

She bristled at the hint of impatience, or maybe it

was dismissal she detected in his voice. "Right. And when should I expect you to come back from work today?"

"I don't know yet, but I'll be there in plenty of time to take care of everything. I promise."

If she had a dollar for every time she'd heard that phrase from her parents, she could build a mansion and pay cash for it. "Don't make promises you can't keep. I don't have any patience for men who promise to be around and then put their family relationships at the bottom of their list."

"I'm not your dad, Caroline."

"It's not just him, Rafe. I see this problem all the time in my law practice. It's a major cause of divorce."

"I'll be there." He bent down again, gave her a sexy grin and dropped a quick, but thorough kiss on her mouth. "Trust me."

"That's hard for me to do," she said.

"I understand." He went down on one knee beside the bed and framed her face with his hands. "I'm doing the best I can. I've already got Friday through Monday off, so be patient with me for just a little while longer and I'll get the rest of it figured out. Okay?"

He looked so earnest and so dear, how could she refuse? He'd repeatedly surprised her with his thoughtfulness since he'd discovered her pregnancy. Maybe he'd surprise her this time and prove he wasn't a workaholic like her father. At the very least, Rafe deserved a chance to try.

Dredging up a smile for him, she nodded. "All right. I'll do my best."

"Thanks, babe. Why don't you sleep here tonight? I'll call you tomorrow." He kissed her again, ruffled her hair and hurried out of the room.

She lay back, listening to the sounds of his leaving, debating whether she should stay in Rafe's bed or go home to her own. Without him in it, however, his bed felt huge and far too empty for her to sleep in it. Five minutes later she got up, dressed, tidied the room, then let herself out the front door.

All the way home she lectured herself about thinking positively for a change. Given enough time, Rafe would find an appropriate balance between his personal life and his job. Just because her father had broken every promise he'd ever made to her, it didn't mean that Rafe would do the same thing. Everyone had to tolerate certain compromises to make relationships work.

By the time she arrived at her house, she'd almost convinced herself that everything would work out fine. She entered the back door and Truman trotted out to greet her. Doing his usual dance of joy, he sniffed and licked at her hands as she petted him and talked to him. She finally pushed herself upright and watched him sniff a path to the door. He reared up on his hind feet, put his front paws just below the screen and gazed out into the darkness as if he expected someone else to come inside.

"Oh, Lord," she murmured, "he's looking for Rafe."

Truman barked once, waited a couple of seconds, then dropped back onto all fours and walked through the kitchen with his tail at half-mast. He looked so much like a disappointed child, Caroline felt tears stinging the backs of her eyes.

Instead of giving in to them, she locked up and wearily climbed the stairs to her bedroom. Truman came with her, and she didn't have the heart to send him back downstairs to his basket.

She climbed into bed and curled up on her side with only a sheet for a covering. Though her bed was only queen-size, without Rafe, it felt big and lonely, too.

A cold, wet nose prodded her hand. Grateful for the company, she stroked Truman's head and scratched around his ears. After three futile attempts at jumping onto the bed, he sat on his haunches and let out the most pitiful howl she'd ever heard.

She called him back to the bed and on his next attempt, she boosted his rump. He happily stomped around her entire bed, sniffing and poking his head under the pillows. Finally he settled into the hollow behind her knees with a soft sigh and promptly went to sleep.

Caroline wasn't so lucky. No matter which way she turned or which pillows she used, she couldn't get comfortable. She couldn't stop thinking about Rafe, either. Where was he? What was he doing? Was he in any danger? She hated worrying like this.

Still, the questions chased each other around and around in her mind until she dragged herself out of bed and crossed the room to stand by the window. Opening the curtains she looked out at the moon and the stars and finally allowed the tears to fall. She wanted Rafe Stockwell for a bed partner, a husband, a father for her baby and perhaps other babies.

She wanted it all with him—the kids, the messy house, the minivan and soccer games, the braces, skinned knees, broken bones and homework. Her heart already loved him and desperately wanted to trust him, but she'd been disappointed too many times in the past. She glanced back at the rumpled bed and grimaced. At the rate they were going, she was afraid that her long-term bed partner was far more likely to be Truman than Rafe.

Rejoining Truman on the bed, she petted him, then murmured, "Sorry, buddy. I love you dearly, but you're a damn poor substitute for Rafe."

Chapter Ten

On Friday afternoon Truman started barking and ran to the front door. The doorbell rang. Silently vowing to kill Rafe if he was the one ringing the bell, Caroline went to answer it. He'd lulled her into a false sense of security yesterday by handling the preparations for Becky's visit just as he'd promised.

He'd been called out again early this morning, but he should have been back almost an hour ago. The rat. He hadn't even called, though she'd dialed his pager twice.

She pulled open the door and found not Rafe, but Cord Stockwell standing on her stoop. She hadn't seen Rafe's twin brother since she'd discovered her pregnancy, and God only knew what Rafe had told him about their situation. She'd never met Cord's fiancée, Hannah, from Oklahoma. And for all Caroline knew, little Becky might take one look at her and start screaming.

This was Rafe's family. *He* should be here to welcome them and make this transition easier for everyone. So where was he? Plastering a lawyer smile on her face, Caroline nudged Truman out of the way. "Hello, Cord. I understand congratulations are in order."

"Thanks, Caroline." Cord gave her a charming smile she'd seen on Rafe's face too many times to count. His gaze swept from her face to her abdomen and back to her face again. "It's been a long time."

"Yes. It has." Feeling her cheeks getting warm, Caroline stepped back. "Please, come in out of the heat. Would you like something cold to drink?"

"No, thanks. We can't stay that long." He ushered a pretty young woman with shoulder-length brown hair and a beautiful, wide-eyed baby in her arms into the entryway. "Caroline, I'd like you to meet my bride, Hannah, and my daughter, Becky. Why don't you ladies get acquainted and I'll bring in Becky's things?"

"That'll be real nice, honey," Hannah said with a strong Oklahoma accent.

She turned to Caroline with an expectant expression, but Caroline had no clue what it was that Hannah expected her to do. "Well, um, why don't you come in and sit down?" Caroline led the way to the sofa. "Are you sure you don't want something to drink?"

"No, thank you very much." Hannah followed her to the sofa, slid a bulging, flowered diaper bag off her shoulder and sat down, holding Becky on her lap. "Have you had much experience with babies, Caroline?"

"Not too much," Caroline answered truthfully, sitting on the cushion beside Hannah's. Truman sat beside Caroline's feet, tipped his head to one side, perked up his ears and watched the baby as if he couldn't figure out what it was. Caroline looped one finger through his collar to make sure he didn't make any sudden moves that would frighten Becky. "Of course, I've been reading a lot, and Rafe told me you've been giving him lessons."

Laughing, Hannah nodded. "I sure have, and he does real well with little Becky."

Hannah seemed like a nice person, but she looked a good five years younger than Caroline, and with her twangy, small-town Oklahoma accent, Caroline wondered what, if anything, they could have in common. Other than being attracted to tall, dark-haired, sinfully handsome men with incredible blue eyes, of course.

Spotting the dog, Becky leaned forward over Hannah's supporting arm, waved her little arms and started making excited, gurgly sounds that made no sense whatsoever to Caroline.

"That's a doggie, sweetheart," Hannah said, holding out a hand for Truman to sniff. "Nice doggie."

Wagging his tail enthusiastically, Truman stood up and would have put his front paws on Hannah's knees if Caroline hadn't had a firm hold on him. Hannah patted his head, then turned her attention back to Caroline. "When are you expectin' your little one to arrive?"

"In about five weeks," Caroline said. "Do you have any special instructions for Becky's care?"

"Oh, just a few."

Hannah handed Becky to Caroline, then rummaged through the diaper bag. Caroline held the baby at eye level for a moment, loving the feel of her solid little body. Becky gave her a big, toothless grin, and Caroline realized with a jolt that she would be holding her own baby in just five weeks. And in five short months, her baby would be about the same size as Becky was now.

Coming up with a thick sheaf of papers, Hannah set them beside Caroline and held out her hands to take Becky back. Becky lurched toward her. Startled by the child's strength, Caroline quickly released her, feeling incredibly awkward and foolish when Hannah gave her an odd look and scooped Becky up against her shoulder.

"My goodness," Caroline said. "She's quick."

"Why don't you look through those notes so you can ask any questions you have before we leave?" Hannah suggested.

Cord walked in loaded down with an amazing array of baby equipment. "Where do you want all of this stuff, Caroline?"

"Oh, well, why don't you take it in the family room?" She gestured toward the doorway. "Rafe can sort it out when he gets here."

"Cord, honey," Hannah said quickly. "Why don't you leave the baby seat out here? She'll probably need it."

Caroline flipped through page after page of instructions and immediately felt incredibly overwhelmed. Good heavens, there were three pages of instructions for preparing Becky's formula alone, not to mention photocopies of emergency procedures for administering infant CPR, charts of common childhood illnesses, home remedies, phone numbers for every imaginable emergency and a list of approved specialists "just in case."

Just in case *what?*

The question danced on the tip of her tongue, but one glance at Hannah's anxious eyes made Caroline swallow it. Oh, dear. She couldn't spoil Cord and Hannah's wedding plans by acting like an idiot. Unfortunately it was already too late.

Clutching Becky tightly, Hannah got up and went to

meet Cord in the doorway to the family room. "Honey, could I talk to you for just a minute?" she said with a brittle smile.

He shot Caroline a puzzled glance, then retreated into the family room with Hannah right beside him. At first all Caroline could hear was the buzz and hiss of whispering, but gradually, Cord and Hannah's voices grew loud enough for her to make out what they were saying.

"Hannah, please," Cord said, "we've got to go now or we'll miss our flight."

"But, Cord, I really don't feel good about leavin' Becky here without Rafe. Caroline doesn't seem to be that comfortable with the baby. It's just not right to do this."

"Caroline's an intelligent woman. She'll figure out what Becky needs. Besides, Rafe will be here any minute."

"Oh, I don't know."

"Well, I do," Cord said. "I want to marry you now, Hannah. Dad could pass on just about any time, and if he does, I'll have to handle his funeral and settle the estate. It could be months before I can get away again."

Unable to tolerate any more, Caroline heaved herself to her feet and walked into the family room. "I didn't mean to upset you, Hannah. I promise you Becky will be fine. If I have any problems before Rafe arrives, I have several friends I can call who are doctors."

"Really?" Hannah asked, her pretty green eyes lighting with hope.

"Cross my heart," Caroline said, making the appropriate motions. "I wasn't expecting quite such detailed instructions for a weekend visit. She's not very likely to get the measles, chicken pox and otitis media at the same time, is she?''

''No,'' Cord said with a laugh. ''That's just Hannah's streak of superstition showing up.''

Hannah elbowed him in the ribs, but she smiled at Caroline. ''He's right. I have this silly feeling that if I cover all of the possible problems, you won't have any. But if I forget to tell you something, you're bound to need it. I just love this baby girl so much...''

''I understand.'' Smiling back at her, Caroline reached out for Becky.

Hannah kissed the baby's wispy hair, then handed her over with obvious reluctance. Standing behind Hannah, Cord blew Caroline a kiss and gave her a thumbs-up before taking Hannah's hand and hustling her out of the house. Caroline carried Becky out to wave bye-bye.

''Have a wonderful wedding,'' she called, helping the baby with her wave.

''We'll see you Sunday night,'' Cord called back, then drove away.

The instant his car rounded the corner, Caroline turned back toward the house, and Becky's gorgeous blue eyes, the exact same color as her daddy's and her Uncle Rafe's, puddled up with big, fat tears. Her lower lip poked out and her chin trembled, and by the time Caroline got inside and shut the front door, Miss Becky Stockwell was crying at the top of her healthy little lungs.

If dark, angry thoughts could have killed, the Stockwells would be planning a funeral, all right. But it would be for Rafe, not Caine.

Pulling into Caroline's driveway, Rafe checked the dashboard clock and swore under his breath. He was a full forty-five minutes late and Caroline was going to be madder than hell at him. He climbed out of the car and hurried toward the house. Hearing Becky's screams when he was only halfway across the yard, he sprinted the rest of the way.

He used the key Caroline had given him and barged inside, where he found her frantically walking the baby back and forth in the living room. Becky's whole face was redder than a third-degree sunburn, and Truman was howling, no doubt at her ear-splitting shrieks. Eyes round with fear and lips trembling, Caroline looked equally distressed.

She took one look at him and burst into tears. "Oh, Rafe, thank God you're here." She rushed across the room and shoved Becky into his arms. "We have to take her to the hospital."

"Why? What happened?" He looked for signs of an injury, but didn't see any.

"Nothing happened," Caroline wailed. "Cord and Hannah left and Becky started crying. She's been crying like this ever since. I've tried to comfort her, but she just keeps getting louder, and she's really hot, so I think she's got a fever. There must be something terribly wrong with her."

"Let's try a few things first and we'll see what happens."

He carried Becky to the sofa and laid her on her back. Talking softly to her, he stroked her little head, but she kept screaming. "Hey, there, little bit, what's all this noise about? Uncle Rafe's here. There's no need to carry on like that, baby."

Caroline paced like a lioness kept in too small a cage. He didn't blame her for being upset, but her tension was only aggravating Becky's. Calling Caroline over, he dug around in the diaper bag, brought out a washcloth, a bottle of formula and the bottle warmer.

Handing them to her one at a time, he said, "Put the bottle in the warmer and plug it in somewhere. Then take the washcloth to the kitchen and wet it down with cold water."

While she was gone, he continued talking to Becky, checked her diaper and peeled off her tiny T-shirt. Jeez, her neck, back and tummy were nearly as red as her face and she was sweaty, too. Must be all that aerobic crying she was doing. He fanned her tummy with her T-shirt and her cries abated a little.

"That's right, sweetheart, calm down. We're going to have a great weekend, now. If you stop that cater-wauling, maybe Uncle Rafe will take you in the swimming pool. He might even sneak you a bite of ice cream."

Becky's cries subsided to a few hiccuping sobs, and a moment later, Caroline quietly walked back into the room.

"Does bribery work as well on babies as it does on dogs?" she asked, handing him the wet washcloth he'd requested.

"I sure hope so." Rafe shot her a wry grin. "The kid could wake up a whole cemetery, couldn't she?"

"The thought crossed my mind a time or two," Caroline admitted. "Do you think she's all right?"

Nodding, he gently wiped down Becky's face, neck and torso. She shivered, but didn't seem to mind it. When he added a light touch of baby lotion and smoothed it over her skin, she actually smiled at him, then stuck her fist into her mouth. "I think she was just having a little tantrum."

Caroline rolled her head from side to side and covered

her eyes with her hands. "Lord, I hope you're right. I kept thinking she was going to die and it would be all my fault."

"You did fine, Caroline."

She lowered her hands and stared at him with obvious disbelief. "Fine? That poor child was headed for a seizure at the very least, and I was so completely flipped out, I couldn't even remember that I had a telephone, much less where it was or how to use it."

Becky's eyebrows climbed halfway up her forehead and she looked up at Rafe with an anxious little frown.

"Babies are real sensitive to moods. If you're uptight, so are they," Rafe told Caroline. "Try to keep your voice down."

Caroline let out a gusty sigh, then rolled her eyes at the ceiling. "I'm sorry."

"No need for an apology." Rafe tilted his head toward the television, where the bottle warmer sat. "I'll bet that bottle's ready now."

"Coming right up."

Becky's color was back to its normal color now, Rafe noted with relief. He put a dry T-shirt on her, fished a burp towel out of the diaper bag and slung it over his shoulder. When Caroline brought him the bottle, he tested the formula's temperature on the inside of his wrist, then settled Becky into the crook of his arm and poked the nipple into her mouth.

She eagerly suckled it, but a few moments later, her eyelids fluttered shut and her mouth opened, leaving a gap around the nipple. Rafe lifted her to his shoulder and gently patted her back until she burped. Caroline hovered uncertainly near the other end of the sofa. Smiling at her, he relaxed back against the cushions and nodded at the empty space beside him.

"Have a seat," he murmured. When she did so, he carefully removed the bottle. Transferring Becky to Caroline, he held his breath and prayed the baby wouldn't awaken and start crying all over again. Becky's mouth made funny kissing motions for a moment. Then she let out a squeaky little sigh, snuggled into Caroline's arms and fell asleep. Caroline shot him one tremulous smile before turning back to study Becky's face as if she'd never seen anything quite so fascinating in her entire life.

At first, Caroline sat absolutely still, and Rafe suspected she would allow her muscles to seize up before she would do anything to risk disturbing the infant. Fifteen minutes later, she'd relaxed enough to settle into the cushions and stretch out her legs. Finally she traced Becky's delicate features with feather-light strokes of her fingertips, avidly watching a variety of expressions flitting across the baby's face.

It was one of the most sensuous things Rafe had ever witnessed, almost as if she was drinking in the baby's essence with her touch and her sight. Caroline looked warm and sweet and motherly, and at the same time, she looked so sexy, he wished her fingertips were stroking him. If that wasn't kinky, he didn't know what was, but as long as he could keep watching her, he didn't particularly care.

"You're good at this baby thing, Uncle Rafe," she said, her voice low and soft.

"Thanks. I've had a good teacher," he murmured.

"Are you willing to pass on the lessons?"

"For you? Anything," he said. "Most of it's just common sense."

She gave him a rueful smile. "It's easy to lose track of common sense with a screaming baby in your arms."

"That's true enough. But all it takes is a little practice," he said. "Once you figure out their screams are just a way of communicating that won't be ignored, it's not nearly as terrifying."

"Speaking of terrifying, why didn't you call back when I paged you?"

"I didn't get any pages." Rafe pulled the pager off his belt and studied the readout. It looked fine.

She hitched Becky up a little higher, then turned her attention back to him. "I dialed it twice, Rafe."

"Let's dial it again now and see what happens." He picked up the phone on the end table and punched in the number. His pager vibrated right on time. He held it up to show Caroline the readout. "It's working now."

"It didn't this morning," she insisted.

Reading the fear in her eyes, he managed to contain his impatience. "I'll keep an eye on it, but this is the best pager on the market. The chances of it malfunctioning are slim to none."

Clearly unconvinced, she muttered, "If you say so."

He moved close to her side and slid his arm across the top of the sofa behind her neck. "Caroline, I'll be here when you need me."

"You promise?"

"I promise."

"All right," she said with a slight smile. "My next question is why were you so late?"

"I wasn't that late." He got up and carried the bottle of formula to the refrigerator, hoping that when he came back, she would've forgotten the issue. No such luck.

"If someone kept you waiting for forty-five minutes, would you think it was that late?"

"I did the best I could," he grumbled. "I only stayed long enough to make sure we'd nailed him before I took off. Vic got stuck with all of the follow-up and paper-work.''

''That's too bad for Vic, but Hannah almost refused to leave without you here to take care of Becky.'' Caroline laughed, but there was little, if any humor in it. ''She knew right away that I didn't know anything about babies. Cord had a tough time convincing her to go.''

''What changed her mind?''

''I lied and told her I have friends who are doctors.''

Rafe tipped back his head and laughed softly. ''Oh, I'll bet you know a few doctors.''

''Not any pediatricians.''

''Did you tell her they were pediatricians?''

''No, but that's what she thought. And I don't mind saying, I felt terrible about misleading Hannah that way.''

''It was for a good cause, Caro.''

Caroline let out an indignant huff. ''It didn't do little Becky much good. I wish I knew what I did wrong that made her cry like that.''

''It's not your fault,'' Rafe said.

''How can you say that? She was fine until their car turned the corner, and then she just started...shrieking. It's a wonder the neighbors didn't call the police and report me for child abuse.''

Rafe shifted around until he faced her more directly. ''Didn't you hear what you just said? She was fine until their car turned the corner. Becky wasn't crying because of anything you did. She was crying because her folks drove off without her. She would've cried just as hard if I'd been the one standing there holding her.''

''Do you really think so?''

''No, I know so. It would've been a miracle if she hadn't cried in that situation. The only thing you did wrong was not be Hannah, and you couldn't do a blessed thing about that.''

Caroline's shoulders rose, then fell in what looked to Rafe like a silent sigh of relief. She definitely needed to have her confidence boosted. Luckily, he liked doing that sort of thing, and this weekend was the perfect time to do it.

''Anyway, sugar, I'm sorry I made you so angry by being late,'' he said after a moment of silence. ''I really appreciate your talking about this in such a calm, rational way.''

She wrinkled her nose at him. ''The only reason you're getting a calm, rational discussion is that I don't want to wake this little angel. And I wasn't angry. I was scared. If you'd been here when you promised, I wouldn't have had anything to be scared about.''

''Jeez, you don't give an inch, do you?'' She just stared at him as if she was still waiting for him to say something intelligent. When he couldn't take it anymore, he pushed himself to his feet, and said, ''All right, I'll do better next time. Will you be scared now if I go out to my car and bring in my gear?''

Caroline bit her lower lip to keep from grinning openly at his grumpy voice. ''I doubt it.''

He walked out without so much as a glance in her direction, quietly closing the door behind him. Caroline looked back down at Becky and wondered if her own baby would be even half as dear and perfect and precious as this one. If she hadn't seen it with her own two eyes, she never would have believed that Rafe Stockwell could handle a screaming infant with such ease. And such confidence.

Maybe she'd let him off too easy for being so blasted late, but he couldn't have been more gentle or tender with Becky if she'd been his own child. It was nearly impossible to stay angry at a man who did such things. Her own baby was going to be lucky to have Rafe for a father.

That was, *if* he wanted to be a real father for the next eighteen or twenty years. The kind who played with his child, read her storybooks and taught her how to dance. The kind who fed her bottles and kissed her boo-boos and told her she was beautiful.

She could see Rafe doing all of those things, and there it was again. That stubborn kernel of hope lodged somewhere in her foolish heart that simply refused to give up on the notion that she could build a regular, full-fledged family with Rafe, the baby and Truman, and they all would live happily ever after. Holding Becky only fertilized that stubborn kernel, but Caroline couldn't make herself let go of the baby. Or of the hope.

Not now. Not yet. She might only have this one weekend to pretend she could have everything she wanted. Why not go ahead and allow herself to enjoy it? If it all fell apart when Cord and Hannah returned for Becky, at least she finally would know what it felt like to be part of a real family.

Having made her decision, Caroline allowed herself to put aside her worries about the future. For the first time in her life, she lived for the moment, and each moment became a magic, wonderful experience. Rafe entered into the spirit of her fantasy without even knowing about it.

After Becky's nap he found a tiny red swimsuit with a green frog on the front and took Becky into the swimming pool. Sitting on the side of the pool with her feet dangling in the water, Caroline took pictures of him making motorboat noises while he propelled the giggling baby back and forth.

When Becky tired of the pool, he took her into the shower, rinsed away the pool water and taught Caroline the fine art of diaper changing. As an added bonus, he found a pink T-shirt with Daddy's Girl written across the front and allowed Caroline to put it on the baby.

After struggling and struggling some more to get Becky's busy hands and arms to go through the little sleeves, Caroline laughed and tossed up her own hands in surrender. "Good grief, this is like trying to poke a worm into a pinhole."

Rafe came to the rescue. Making it look easy, he put the shirt on Becky, picked her up and gave Caroline a triumphant grin that made her laugh again.

"You think you're so smart, Stockwell."

"That's because I am." Becky smacked his chest with her right hand. "Yeah, kid? What do you want to do now?"

From the soft, random syllables Becky babbled, Caroline never would have guessed that she wanted to lay on her tummy on a blanket spread out on the family room floor and bat around a whole herd of plush animals, rattles and squeaky toys. Rafe solemnly swore on his badge, however, that his niece had demanded this very activity.

"It seems awfully convenient that she wants to do this while the Texas Rangers are playing the Seattle Mariners," Caroline said dryly.

"Hey, can I help it if the kid's got great taste in baseball?"

Lowering herself to the floor, Caroline sat tailor fashion as she'd learned to do at Lamaze classes. She ruffled Rafe's hair just for the fun of it, then dangled colorful squeaky toys over Becky's head and enjoyed watching her go into excited gyrations. Truman snuggled up beside Caroline, observing the action from the edge of the blanket.

They had supper, changed diapers and took a walk around the neighborhood with Rafe pushing the stroller and Caroline holding Truman's leash. Caroline watched Rafe bathe Becky in the little plastic tub Cord had brought. Caroline had one exactly like it upstairs in the nursery, and she was grateful to have a better idea of how one put it to use. While she wrapped the wet baby in a hooded towel and dried her off, Becky chortled, reached out a tiny hand and patted Caroline's face. Rafe came back from emptying the tub, put his arm around Caroline's shoulders and watched the baby's antics with her.

Caroline read Becky a story. Rafe fed her a bottle of formula. Together they climbed the stairs and lay Becky on her back in the brand-new crib. They stood there holding hands and watching her sleep, and Caroline realized she had never felt so close to another human being as she was to Rafe at this moment.

Tired from a busy, emotional day, she carried the baby monitor downstairs and curled up beside Rafe on the family room sofa, half dozing through a documentary he wanted to watch about the famous Western artist, Charles M. Russell. Rafe put his arm around her, pulled her close to his side and rested his hand on her abdomen.

She felt comfortable, happy and protected. She probably would have fallen fast asleep if Rafe hadn't started tracing light, random patterns across her abdomen with his fingertips. A glance at his face told her he was so involved in the program, he probably didn't even realize what he was doing. However, her body's response to his touch more than made up for his lack of awareness.

A pleasant, low-key tingle skated across her skin, following the path of his fingertips. She found it incredibly relaxing and settled more fully against him, laying her head in the hollow of his shoulder. His fingertips began to move in wider arcs, sweeping from one side of her belly to the other, and she arched her back slightly, giving him easier access.

When his touch strayed to the lower curve of her abdomen, however, the tingle blossomed into a deeper, warmer, sexier sensation that nearly made her gasp at the strength of it. She wanted him touching her skin, not her clothes. She wanted him to forget about his documentary, to kiss and caress her. She wanted to spend an hour making love with Rafe.

Since she was living for the moment, she didn't have to worry about future emotional consequences for anything she did now. And the moment meant Rafe Stockwell. Acting as substitute parents for little Becky today, she and Rafe had bonded in a new way. Now she wanted to go back and share a different kind of bond with him, and the first order of business was getting his attention.

Smiling to herself, she rested her hand on his thigh, waited a few minutes, and then started tracing random patterns on his jeans with her fingertips. When he didn't appear to notice, she shifted her theater of operations to his hard, flat belly. Now using her fingernails, she drew fat, lazy circles, quick, sharp-edged squares and triangles with rounded corners.

''What are you doing, sugar?''

At the sound of his amused drawl, she looked up at

him with an ingenuous smile. "What do you think I'm doing?"

"Taking a wild guess, I'd say you're trying to turn me on. That's what you're doing, anyway."

"Really?"

"Move your hand about five inches lower and you'll find out for yourself."

Keeping a straight face, she followed his directions, encountered an impressive ridge under his fly and let her mouth drop open in feigned surprise.

"Well, now, isn't that a lovely stroke of luck?"

He made a choking sound that might've been a cross between a snort and a laugh. "Sure feels like one to me. Is there anything in particular you want to do tonight?"

Feeling sexy and playful, she batted her eyelashes at him. "Move your hand about six inches higher and you'll find out for yourself."

He followed her directions with unconcealed delight, and when his hand gently closed over her breast, she shut her eyes and gave herself up to the sensations he created for her. She covered his hand with her own and guided him to her other breast, using pressure to tell him she would welcome a firmer touch. He kissed her hair, the side of her forehead, her earlobe.

"Anything you want, darling." His voice was low and husky. "Show me what you want and I'll make it good for you. So good."

"Kiss me," she whispered, craning her neck to reach his mouth. "Please, kiss me."

Shifting around, he slid his hands under her arms and lifted her onto his lap, with her left hip flush against his middle. He framed her face with his palms and swept the pad of his thumbs across her cheekbones while he gazed into her eyes, as if he were looking for some secret that might be hidden in their depths. Then he lowered his head and made love to her mouth with his lips and his teeth and his tongue.

She melted into him, returning the pleasure with all of the passion she felt for him. His arms wrapped tightly around her, as if he would hold her and kiss her forever. She had no intention of objecting if he did exactly that.

One by one, articles of clothing drifted to the carpet. Murmurs and sighs of pleasure became moans and ecstatic cries loud enough to drown out the sound of the television. Their need for each other grew rapidly, along with the ache of their mutual desire for fulfillment.

He tasted her, explored her, drove her crazy with teasing nips across her collarbones and a stubborn refusal to be coaxed into moving along just a little faster. By the time he helped her to straddle his lap, she had to clutch at his shoulders to keep herself from dissolving into a quivering mass of need. Again, with his help, she slowly lowered herself to take him inside her. Having him inside her felt fantastic. With her knees braced on the cushion, she held herself still and rested her forehead against his, savoring the sensations.

Cupping her breasts with his hands, he kissed her eyelids, her temples, the bridge of her nose, her mouth. She stroked his hair, fondled his ears and gently raked her nails across the back of his neck. Everywhere they touched she felt exquisitely alive.

She tentatively rocked her hips forward and back, gasping at the jolts of pleasure radiating from the place their bodies were joined. A low, ragged sound came from somewhere deep in his chest, and his body was rigid with what she supposed was restraint.

"It's your show, sugar," he murmured, confirming her guess. "You set the pace."

As if she couldn't wait any longer, she began to move, slowly at first, and then picking up speed. Occasionally she alternated the forward and backward motion with an up-and-down one, smiling to herself when he clamped his hands onto her bottom and clenched his teeth as if he was teetering on the edge of losing control.

She slowed down, wanting to prolong his pleasure as well as her own. Hooking one hand behind her head, he pulled her close enough to kiss. Her head spun as he released her mouth. When he put his hands under her arms and lifted her just enough to suckle at her breasts again, the added sensations sent her reeling out of control.

He uttered a hoarse shout and they were frantically moving against each other, straining, racing toward that state of ultimate completion. She reached it first, he followed a second later and they wound up slumped against each other, panting like a pair of Olympic sprinters.

Before either of them could breathe normally, the baby monitor crackled and a piercing wail filled the room. They stared at each other in shock for a moment, and when the next wail came, Caroline felt as if she'd been drenched with a bucket of ice water. She scrambled off Rafe's lap with what little grace she could muster and was reaching for clothes by the time her feet made contact with the floor.

Rafe ran for the stairs stark naked. The sight of him streaking through the house with God only knew how many windows exposed to the street or the neighbors tickled Caroline's funny bone. Not even Becky's crying could stop her laughter. By the time she managed to pull her own clothes back on and gather up Rafe's, he returned the family room with a teary-eyed Becky cuddled against his chest. He leaned over and kissed Caroline before trading her the baby for his clothes.

"Sorry I had to leave you like that, but I didn't want her to get all wound up again." He pulled on his jeans and his shirt.

"I understand," Caroline said, patting the baby's back. "I hope she wasn't crying too long before we heard her."

"She's pretty tough." He gently smoothed Becky's wispy hair to the side. "I guess we'd better get used to interruptions, though. It's a cinch our baby's going to do the same thing."

Caroline's breath caught in her lungs and she wondered if he realized that was the first time either of them had said, *our* baby.

Chapter Eleven

Caroline dragged herself out of bed at nine o'clock the next morning and went downstairs to check on Rafe and Becky. The baby had been restless all night, and though Caroline had tried to take turns walking her, Becky clearly preferred her uncle. After a final, unsuccessful attempt to soothe Becky sometime around four, Caroline had given up and gone to bed. She had no idea how long Rafe had stayed up, but knew he must be exhausted.

Halfway down the stairs she caught the scent of freshly-brewed coffee; it smelled so wonderful she could almost taste it. Of all the things she'd given up for the baby's sake, she missed coffee the most. Three steps from the kitchen doorway, she heard Becky chortling and a rattling sound. Then Rafe said, ''That's it, kid. Do it again.''

Not wanting to interrupt whatever was going on, Caroline tiptoed the rest of the way and peeked around the door casing. Becky reclined in her portable baby chair in the middle of the kitchen table, gazing up at a set of measuring spoons dangling from the carrying handle positioned over her head. Rafe batted the spoons with a pencil, making them rattle and dance, which, in turn, made Becky laugh and thrash her arms and legs. While she was performing, Rafe hunched over something on the table directly in front of him, occasionally glancing up at the baby.

Caroline crept into the room, stood close to Rafe and looked over his shoulder. His hand guided the pencil over the pad of paper she kept by the phone, making quick, fluid strokes. The end product was a sketch of Becky that managed to capture her mood and personality in a few simple lines.

"That's adorable," Caroline said, startling him. "I didn't know you were an artist."

"I'm not." Abruptly pushing the paper to one side, he slid out of the bench seat and stepped around her on his way to the coffeemaker for a refill.

She slid into his seat, jangled the spoons for Becky and picked up the pad. Flipping through the five other drawings he'd made, Caroline shook her head in disagreement.

"For someone who's not an artist, you've got an awful lot of talent," she said. "One of my college roommates was an art major, and she would've raved over your work."

"Give me a break." Looking disgruntled, Rafe turned away from the coffeemaker and crossed his arms over his chest. "It's just doodling."

"How can you call that doodling?" Waving a hand toward the sketches, Caroline climbed to her feet, then propped her hands on her hips. "Does your family know how good you are?"

"Not hardly." He let out a choked laugh. "And I'd appreciate it if you wouldn't talk about it." His voice took on a teasing tone she didn't believe for a second. "It's not the kind of thing us macho-cop types want to get around."

Wondering why he'd deny such a talent, she decided to play along with him for the moment. She rolled her eyes in mock exasperation, went to the refrigerator and took out a carton of yogurt. "Of course not. We wouldn't want anyone to think you were even slightly civilized."

She took a teaspoon from the drawer and returned to the table, jangling the measuring spoons for Becky again. The baby's laugh made her smile. She couldn't wait to hear her own baby laugh that way. Rafe silently drank his coffee, finally asking, "Mind if I use your phone?"

"Be my guest," Caroline said with a shrug, though she felt intensely curious about who he might be calling on a Saturday morning. She sincerely hoped he wasn't going to call anyone from work, but saw no profit in bringing it up. They'd had such a good time so far, she didn't want to do anything that might jeopardize the rest of the weekend.

"Hello, Mrs. Hightower," he said into the receiver. "How are you this morning? Good. Jack or Kate there? No, it doesn't matter which one. Thanks, you're a peach."

Caroline opened her yogurt, spooned a bite into her mouth and made no attempt to act as if she were doing anything other than listening to his side of the conversation. If he didn't like it, he could always take the phone outside or use one in another room. Becky made a raspberry sound. Caroline laughed and tickled the bottom of her tiny foot.

"Kate, it's me," Rafe said. "Yes, I know where they are. They're fine, sis. Calm down. Becky's with me. I was supposed to call you last night and let you know, but I got distracted." He gave Caroline a sexy wink. "Never mind what distracted me. I'm sorry."

He crossed his eyes at Caroline and rapidly pinched his thumb and fingers together in a yakety-yak-yak motion. "I'm not supposed to tell you that, but if you'll be quiet for two seconds, I'll tell you what they're doing. Cord and Hannah are getting married this weekend."

Rafe held the handset a foot away from his ear, letting Caroline hear an angry, female voice talking loud and extremely fast on the other end of the line. When he spoke again, he said, "Katie, it was their decision. Cord deserves our support and we're going to give it to him. We weren't invited to the wedding. Get over it."

There was another long pause before Rafe jumped back into the conversation. "I've got my hands full with Becky. Why don't you and Jack do something? I don't know what. A family party or a dinner or whatever, but keep it small and simple. I'm free Monday night. Great. See you then."

Heaving a sigh, Rafe hung up the phone, then sat across from Caroline and rubbed one hand down over his face. "My sister doesn't like being left out of the loop."

"Most of us don't." Caroline searched his face, noting the signs of exhaustion she'd expected to see earlier—deeper lines around his eyes, dark circles beneath them, tousled hair and a healthy crop of whiskers. Poor man. But even in his rumpled condition, she found him extremely appealing. "Did you get any sleep at all?"

"Nope." He tapped the spoons and shot Becky a rueful smile. "I couldn't believe how stubborn the little squirt was. Probably got that from the Stockwell side of the gene pool."

"No doubt." Caroline reached across the table and squeezed his hand. "I can take over now. Why don't you get some sleep?"

"There's something I want to ask you first."

"What's that?"

"Kate said she'd arrange a dinner on Monday night for Cord and Hannah. Will you come with me?"

Caroline's heart fluttered. She'd gone to Stockwell Mansion before, accompanying her father to various social functions, but she'd never gone there with Rafe. He'd told Kate to plan a *family* dinner. Besides celebrating Cord's marriage, could Rafe be planning to make this an official, "meet the family" evening?

"I'd love to," she said with a smile, telling herself that made perfect sense as part of her weekend fantasy. And she knew exactly where to find the perfect wedding gift for Cord and Hannah.

When the newlyweds picked up Becky on Sunday night, Caroline felt like a seasoned baby-sitter. She assured them that the weekend had been a delight, and offered to take care of Becky any time. She felt sad to see Becky leave, but was grateful for the time she'd been able to spend with the baby. Now she could only hope and pray that her weekend fantasy with Rafe would extend to her own child's birth. And beyond that to the rest of their lives.

By the time Rafe escorted her into the Stockwell mansion on Monday night, Caroline felt as if she'd gone from a normal sense of anticipation to wobbling on the edge of having an anxiety attack. It was silly to be so nervous, of course. She was hardly a novice at handling social gatherings, and after a day of primping and pampering, she knew she looked good for a woman in her condition. Even her hair had cooperated, which was saying something with one hundred-degree-plus heat outdoors.

Not that it was doing her much good. She still felt twitchy as a fox hearing the call of a bugle and the baying of hounds. She'd tried to start a conversation with Rafe to distract herself, but he'd been too preoccupied to be of any help. Was he feeling the tension, too? But why would he be nervous with his own family? She stepped into the foyer with him, grateful for the coolness.

A tall handsome man waved to them from a doorway farther down the hallway. ''We're in here, Rafe,'' he called.

''Thanks.'' Rafe slapped the man on the back. ''Caroline, this is my oldest brother, Jack Stockwell. Jack, you remember Clyde Carlyle, don't you? This is his daughter, Caroline. She's running the firm now.''

Clyde Carlyle's daughter? Was that all she was to Rafe? She'd have to see about that later, Caroline told herself. Hiding her hurt behind her polite smile, she extended her hand to Jack. ''Hello, Jack.''

''It's a pleasure, Caroline.'' Jack Stockwell's features were more rugged than Rafe's and Cord's, his hair was a medium brown and his eyes a lighter shade of blue, but he had their same build and there was no missing the family resemblance. ''We're glad you could share our little celebration tonight.''

''Thank you.'' Aware that he was studying her with

more than a casual interest, she met Jack's gaze without flinching. She couldn't tell whether or not he liked what he saw, but there was a fierce light in his eyes, and she had the distinct impression he was not a man she wanted to have for an enemy. It was as if he carried some invisible aura of danger with him. She usually attributed such wild thoughts to her busy hormones, but with Jack Stockwell, the impression was impossible to deny.

"It's about time you got here, Rafe," a feminine voice called from the far side of the room. "Well, don't just stand there in the doorway. Come in and let us meet your guest."

Rafe and Jack walked into the room with Caroline between them, and a tall, slender woman about her own age came forward.

"Hello, I'm Kate Stockwell." She gave Caroline a quick once-over, her blue eyes widening when she noticed what even a cleverly-designed maternity dress no longer could hide. Then she shot Rafe a speculative glance while he gave her Caroline's name and nothing more.

Hurt that he hadn't at least called her his friend, Caroline offered her hand to Kate. Then Hannah caught sight of her and came to the rescue.

"Hi, Caroline. How're you feeling tonight? All rested up from your wild weekend with li'l Becky?"

Grateful to hear a genuinely friendly voice, Oklahoma twang and all, Caroline hugged Hannah. "I'm fine. And I meant it when I said how much I enjoyed having Becky there."

"Rafe and Becky were at your house?" Raising an eyebrow, Kate glanced again at Caroline's abdomen. "So, how long have you and Rafe been seeing each other?"

Caroline felt heat sweep up her neck and into her face. She looked at Rafe, hoping he would jump into this conversation and give her a little help. She suspected Cord and Hannah knew something about their relationship, but it was fairly obvious that Jack and Kate didn't. She didn't know what that meant, or what, if anything, he wanted them to know.

Unfortunately the big dope excused himself and went over to talk to Cord. Caroline watched him walk away from her with a queasy feeling in the pit of her stomach. She knew he had better manners than to walk off and leave her on her own like this. What was going on with him tonight?

"Let's all go get a cold drink." Linking her arm with Caroline's, Hannah filled the awkward silence with happy chatter about her trip to Las Vegas.

Kate gave Caroline one last speculative glance, then, with obvious reluctance, let the matter drop. During dinner Caroline sat beside Rafe, pushing the food around on her plate. She was too confused by his behavior to have an appetite. While his brothers, his sister and Hannah entered into the spirit of a party, talking and teasing each other, Rafe remained quiet.

He didn't look angry or upset about anything, but she sensed he was putting an emotional distance between himself and his siblings. No one else appeared to notice anything amiss, and that bothered her, as well. Something was wrong here, and she wanted to understand it.

Her eyes sparkling, Kate stood up when everyone had finished. "We're going to have our dessert in the parlor, so let's all move right along."

Rafe helped Caroline to her feet, tucked her hand into the crook of his elbow and led her into an elegant parlor next door. She smiled in delight at the silver-and-white streamers, enormous bouquets of flowers, glowing candles and a five-tiered wedding cake complete with a miniature bride and groom on top. Dainty silver baskets holding little net bags filled with birdseed and tied with satin ribbons flanked the cake.

This might have been a quickly arranged wedding celebration, but it was a lovely one. Caroline felt a tug of regret that she would never have the kind of wedding she used to dream of. But she refused to feel envious.

Popular wedding songs played in the background and a servant stood at one end of the table holding a tray of champagne flutes. Elaborately-wrapped gifts covered a smaller table beside the French doors on the south side of the room. Caroline set her own small gift beside the others.

"Jeez," Rafe muttered, "Kate went overboard again."

Caroline nudged him in the ribs with her elbow. "You told her to plan a party. What's bothering you tonight?"

"Nothing," he said with a careless shrug that failed to convince her. "This kind of stuff just isn't for me."

"Then why did you suggest it to Kate?"

"I thought we should welcome Hannah into the family."

Cord and Hannah stood behind the cake, laughing and holding a ceremonial knife while a photographer snapped pictures. Rafe's grim expression softened as he watched Hannah feed Cord a small piece of wedding cake.

"They look happy, don't they?" Rafe asked.

"Yes." Finally seeing a side of Rafe she recognized, Caroline squeezed his arm in reassurance. "They really do."

Everyone gathered around the cake table then, congratulating the bride and groom. The servants passed around cake and champagne, which Caroline declined. What little dinner she'd eaten wasn't sitting well with her. Smiling, Kate and Jack brought the gifts over for Hannah and Cord to open. It seemed like any other wedding reception until Hannah opened Caroline's gift and promptly burst into tears.

"Oh, Caroline," she said, clutching the box to her chest, "this is the sweetest thing I've ever seen."

"What is it?" Kate said.

"Oh, I'm sorry," Hannah said with a flustered laugh, turning the box around to let everyone see the collage of the sketches Rafe had done of Becky. "Did you do the drawings yourself, Caroline?"

"No, Rafe did," Caroline said, pleased with Hannah's reaction. "I just had them framed. Aren't they wonderful?"

Hannah's smile wavered as she glanced around the room, and Caroline suddenly realized that the Stockwells were staring at her gift as if it might explode and splatter a vile substance all over them. The one exception was Rafe, who was looking at her as if she'd somehow betrayed him. She had no idea what had caused this shocked silence, but the longer it continued, the more embarrassed and humiliated she was.

She looked to Hannah for support or leadership or simply an explanation, but Hannah looked every bit as perplexed as Caroline felt. She knew those sketches were adorable, and having them framed made a perfectly appropriate gift. What on earth was going on with these people?

Cord finally cleared his throat and said, "Well, um, thank you all for the party and the wonderful gifts. If you don't mind, I think Hannah and I will go check on the baby now."

Rafe surged to his feet and looked around the room at each member of his family, his face devoid of any discernible emotion. "Go ahead and do that, Cord, but then you'll need to come back for a meeting."

"A meeting? Now?" Kate demanded, clearly perturbed to have the party she'd planned end so early and on such a questionable note. "What for?"

Rafe responded in a flat, businesslike tone he might've used to testify in court. "We located the old man's files. I want to tell you what we found out while we're all together and Caroline's here to answer any legal questions you have."

Another shocked silence followed Rafe's announcement. As dumbfounded as everyone else appeared to be, Caroline scrambled to get her lawyer's face in place. Goodness, when she misjudged a situation, she certainly did it in a big way. So much for indulging her stupid fantasies about "meeting the family" and living happily ever after with Rafe.

If she'd known he only wanted her here as a legal consultant, she wouldn't have spent so much time primping, and she wouldn't feel like such a complete idiot right now.

"I'll go see about Becky, hon," Hannah said, automatically touching Cord's arm in a loving, wifely gesture of support. "You go on ahead and have your meeting. I'll be waitin' for you."

She headed for the doorway, taking Caroline's gift with her. Caroline went after her, fearing she would burst into tears if she didn't get away from the suffocating tension already filling the room. She'd come back as soon as she could maintain her composure.

"Where are you going?" Rafe called after her in a sharp tone that set her teeth on edge.

Pausing, she looked over her shoulder and forced herself not to answer him in kind. "Just give me five minutes. Ten minutes, max."

Even with her promise to come back, Rafe wanted to drag her back into the room. How could she leave him now? She knew how important this information was to his brothers and his sister.

God knew he'd been dreading this moment since he'd read those damned files, and he didn't know if he could get through this without her. But maybe he wouldn't have to. She probably just needed to use the bathroom. She'd been doing that a lot, lately. It wasn't time to panic. Yet.

His tension grew as he got a cup of coffee he didn't want and Kate suggested that they move to more comfortable seating so the staff could clear away the party mess. The others agreed, and Rafe found himself continually watching the doorway, praying that Caroline would return. Dammit, he wanted her to be there for him the way Hannah was for Cord. Didn't she know that?

He busied himself arranging chairs around the coffee table, berating himself for letting her leave in the first place. Hands in his pants pockets, Jack ambled across the room while Cord and Kate were getting their own coffee.

Stopping beside Rafe, he said, "Thought you gave up that art stuff."

"It's just a hobby." Rafe dismissed it with a shrug, but he felt resentful for having to defend himself over something that was nobody else's business.

"Maybe it shouldn't be," Jack said.

Rafe snorted in disgust. "You think Caine's going to get out of that bed and beat me now?"

Smiling slightly, Jack shook his head. "That's not what I meant, little brother."

Jack had more right to call him that than Cord did, but Rafe scowled at him anyway. "What did you mean?"

"Those were excellent drawings of Becky. I always thought it was a damn shame the old man took that away from you."

"Water under the bridge," Rafe grumbled.

"Doesn't have to be. Maybe you should take some classes and see what happens."

Before Rafe could begin to digest what Jack had said, Cord and Kate joined them. In desperation, Rafe looked at the doorway, silently willing Caroline to come back. As if she had heard him, she walked into the room rubbing the small of her back with one hand. He wanted to ask if she was all right, but she took the chair beside his without even looking at him. Well, hell, he'd better get this done so he could take her home.

He cleared his throat to get everyone's attention. When they all turned and looked at him, he began. "It appears that Caine was telling the truth when he said our moth...Madelyn Stockwell could still be alive. Caroline and I found some evidence that backs up his story."

"What evidence?" Cord said, his voice tight.

Rafe told them about the divorce decree and the record of payments Caine had sent to Madelyn. The others listened in stony silence, but Rafe saw the flashes of hurt in their eyes as the implications of his words sank in. When he finished, Cord jumped up as if he'd been goosed and started pacing.

''I don't know about the rest of you,'' he said, smacking his right fist into his left palm, ''but I don't see much point in trying to find her now. Even if she *is* alive, I don't want to see her.''

''Me neither,'' Kate agreed. ''All these years I've told myself it didn't matter that much if Daddy was mean, because at least our mother had loved us. It wasn't her fault she died, and if she'd lived, she would've taken us away somewhere we could all be happy.'' Her voice broke and she swiped at the tears on her cheeks with the backs of her hands. ''Oh, silly, stupid me.''

''Aw, Katie,'' Cord said with a groan, then knelt down beside her chair. He tried to give her a hug, but she shook her head and pushed him away.

''This isn't some little boo-boo you can make all better with a kiss and a bandage.'' She scrambled out of the chair and turned to face him, her body trembling, her voice filled with bitterness. ''The truth is, our dear moth—I mean Madelyn—deserted us, to go screw around with her own brother-in-law. No wonder Dad was such a bastard. She must've been one cold, selfish—''

Jack's deep voice thundered through the room. ''That's enough, Kate. You don't know what you're talking about. She wasn't anything like that.''

''After what Rafe's told us, I'd say Kate's right on the money,'' Cord said. ''You know something about her we don't?''

''I remember her better than the rest of you,'' Jack said. ''That's all.''

Remembering his own pain when he'd learned the truth, Rafe felt his siblings' natural responses like a knife twisting in his gut. He wished he could think of something to say that would make them all feel better, but he couldn't imagine what it would be. He looked at Caroline and grimaced when he saw how pale and tense she looked.

Damn, he'd planned to ask her to marry him soon, but after hearing all of this, it was a wonder she hadn't already run screaming into the night. But that had never been her way. She was a strong woman who'd handled everything life had thrown at her. She could handle the Stockwells, too. With the great weekend they'd spent with Becky, he was determined to make her his wife, raise their baby together, and God willing, have some other children, too.

Jack turned to Caroline then. "Did you find any evidence that she actually had another child?"

"There's no evidence either way," Caroline said.

"How much money are we talking here?" Jack asked.

"The payments were quite substantial, even by today's standards," Caroline told him. "They were sent and returned every month, and my father deposited them into the escrow account right on schedule. After earning interest all of these years, it's become a small fortune."

"What'll happen to it when Dad dies?" Cord asked.

"Madelyn will inherit it. When she dies, or, if she's already dead, if there *was* another child, he or she will inherit it."

"What if there wasn't another child?" Kate chimed in.

"That will depend on your father's latest will, but most likely, whoever his principal heirs are will divide it equally." Caroline paused for a moment, then added, "It's up to all of you to decide what's best, but eventually, you'll need to find out what happened to Madelyn in order to settle Caine's estate."

"I'm going to find her now," Jack said, his tone indicating he didn't intend to argue the matter. "If you'll give me that return address in France, I'll start looking right away."

Caroline's voice was calm and composed in contrast to the strain in the room. "I've actually located return envelopes with several addresses in France. For the last few years the checks have all been returned stamped Address Unknown."

"It's a place to start. I'll stop by tomorrow on my way to the airport to get them."

"Any more questions for Caroline?" Rafe asked.

"I want copies of the files," Cord said.

When Caroline agreed, Cord, Kate and Jack abruptly left the room. Though he knew they hadn't meant to be rude, Rafe glared after them. Once they'd had a chance to lick their wounds in private, he'd have a talk with them about their manners and how to treat Caroline. Mightily relieved that the worst was over, however, he turned to her with a rueful smile.

"Ready to go, sugar?"

"Yes." She pressed one hand to her sternum for a moment, then nodded. "Please."

"What is it?" He went down on one knee beside her and pressed the backs of his fingers to her forehead. "You look a little pale. Are you all right?"

"Not really." She pushed his hand away and stood up. "I don't feel very well, and I want to go home."

"Is it that heartburn thing again?" he asked.

"I don't know." She gave her head an impatient shake. "Let's just go. All right?"

Hurt by her attitude, he walked her to the car. Once she was settled, he climbed in beside her and headed back to Grandview. He could feel her withdrawing from him more with each passing minute and found himself talking to fill the silence. "It's earlier than I thought, but wow, what an evening."

"That's one way to describe it," she said dryly.

"Yeah. It was tough giving everybody the news, but thank God that's over. I'm sure glad you were there."

She shot him a look he couldn't decipher, but she didn't say anything.

"Look, Caroline," he said, "I'm sorry you had to see us at our worst, but we usually get along fairly well with each other. We're not that dysfunctional all the time."

"I didn't think you were," she said, turning her face toward the passenger window.

What the hell was *that* supposed to mean? Her tone was casual, but she wouldn't look at him and her neck and shoulders looked about as rigid as the mile marker posts flying past on the side of the road. He wished he'd never started this stupid conversation, but it was too late to back out of it now. He didn't have to dwell on the negative parts of the evening, though.

"Kate's party for Cord and Hannah turned out to be pretty nice, after all," he said.

"It was lovely until Hannah opened my gift and the rest of you acted as if I'd given her a dead cat," Caroline said in that clipped Boston accent cold as any blue Norther. "Would you mind telling me what *that* was all about?"

Aw man, in his anxiety over telling his siblings about Madelyn, he'd forgotten about the sketches. He didn't want to explain to her, either. Her impression of his family was already bad enough. "It didn't have anything to do with you, sugar."

"Don't patronize me." She huffed at him and crossed

her arms over her breasts. "I obviously made a huge faux pas, though I don't have a clue why. And it's equally obvious that your family must despise me."

"No way. It's just some more bad history with Caine. Once they all think about it, they'll realize you just didn't know."

"Didn't know *what,* Rafe?" she demanded, her voice rising in pitch as well as in volume. "And why didn't I know it?"

He'd been trying to be patient and make allowances for her hormones the way the books all said he should, but dammit, he was getting just a little tired of her surliness. "Maybe it never occurred to me that you would take my sketches and frame them, much less wrap them up for a damned wedding gift. If you'd asked for permission, I would've told you not to do it."

"It never occurred to me that there was any reason you would object."

"Oh, come on. I told you I'd rather you didn't talk about it. Wasn't that a big enough hint?"

"Evidently not," she said with a disgruntled sounding sigh. "I just thought you were being overly modest about your talent. I certainly didn't realize there was some big problem or secret or whatever you want to call it involved in your...hobby. I didn't mean to embarrass you. That's the last thing I wanted to do tonight."

Her voice wobbled a little at the end, and he suddenly realized this was not the way he wanted to spend the rest of this evening.

"It wasn't that I was embarrassed," he fibbed, choosing his words with extreme care. "It really isn't an issue anymore as far as I'm concerned. We have a lot more important things to talk about."

"Such as?" she asked quietly.

"Such as the weekend we had with Becky," he said. "And with each other. I thought it was great. Didn't you?"

She hesitated for a moment, then slowly nodded. He waited for her to say something, but when she didn't, he took a deep breath and went on.

"I've been thinking that we could build a good life together, and we could learn to be good parents together."

He paused, hoping for some kind of response, but the only thing he noticed was Caroline edging closer to the door. Jamming one hand through his hair he debated whether to give it up for now or go on pressing his case. His timing probably reeked, but he just couldn't stop himself.

"You know where I'm going with this, Caroline. We should get married. And we should do it before the baby's born."

Chapter Twelve

Caroline stared at Rafe for a moment, then blurted out the first thought that occurred to her. "Are you completely out of your mind?"

"Don't say no." His hands tightened around the steering wheel until his knuckles shone white, and he turned his head long enough to frown at her. "At least think about it."

"I already have, and it won't work," she muttered. Lord, she felt awful. The heartburn was back. Her back ached, she needed to use the bathroom again and if all of that wasn't enough, she was having Braxton Hicks contractions again. They were perfectly normal and while they didn't hurt, the extra pressure in her lower abdomen wasn't comfortable, either. And they were awfully distracting.

Rafe appeared to be winding up for a major sales pitch on the virtues of marriage. She wished something, *anything* would distract him, but it would probably take a full-fledged disaster. Unfortunately she didn't expect any tornadoes, earthquakes or hurricanes tonight.

"You obviously need to think about it some more." He pulled out to pass a farm truck, and when he returned to the right lane, he said, "We both know what it's like to grow up missing a parent. Don't you think our baby deserves better than that?"

"Our baby deserves the best we can give her. That doesn't necessarily mean we should get married." Closing her eyes against a pain in her chest, Caroline lay her head against the seat back and willed the car to go faster. She really didn't have the energy to cope with him right now.

"Of course it does," he said. "All of the studies say that children who come from two-parent homes do better than children from single-parent homes."

"With many notable exceptions."

He went on as if she hadn't spoken. "And fathers are a lot more important than anyone realized."

Caroline opened her eyes, raised her head and looked straight at him. "We don't have to be married for you to be a father."

He sighed with obvious exasperation. "Come on, be realistic. We want to give our baby the most normal, stable home we can. That means marriage."

He went on and on, hammering at her with impeccable logic until she tuned him out in self-defense. She closed her eyes again, pinched the bridge of her nose between her thumb and forefinger and shook her head. If she hadn't been so miserable, she might have laughed at the irony of the situation.

She'd started out this evening nervous, but expecting Rafe to make his family aware that she was an important person in his life and they would welcome her. Hopefully, with time, Rafe would realize he loved her and ask her to marry him. Then they would make a home together with their precious child and yada, yada, yada. She would have been more than happy with that progression of events.

What had she gotten instead? Rafe had introduced her as Clyde Carlyle's daughter and treated her as little more than an employee of the Stockwell corporation. The only Stockwell who truly had welcomed her was Hannah, the brand-new in-law. Outside of asking Caroline for her legal opinions, Cord had barely spoken to her, and Kate and Jack obviously didn't know much, if anything, about Caroline's relationship with Rafe.

Speaking of dear Rafe, here he was, using every logical reason in the world to convince her to marry him, except for the single one she would have been able to accept in spite of everything else that had happened this evening. But clearly, it was too much to expect that he might actually love her.

She shifted around in her seat, searching for a position that would ease her backache without finding one. The contractions continued, a headache blossomed between her eyebrows and tears rose up in a threatening rush, but she pushed them back down by sheer force of will. She would not cry in front of him.

Against her better judgment, she had allowed herself to hope for all of those things she'd missed out on as a child. A loving husband and a happy home with family all around who loved and cared about each other. After watching the Stockwells in action tonight, she suspected that family thing either didn't exist or it was highly overrated.

She and her baby might very well be better off living

on their own and letting Rafe have generous visitation rights. He was a good man. A very good man who would love his child without reservation, and she would do whatever she could to nurture that relationship.

But she would not be included in it.

It wasn't Rafe's fault. While he might like her, respect her, even desire her physically, there was something about her that wouldn't allow him or anyone else to love her. She didn't know what it was that she lacked, only that she lacked some essential ingredient. If even the baby didn't love her—

She couldn't even finish the thought without making her chest ache. Or was that heartburn? At this rate, before long she wouldn't be able to tell physical pain from emotional pain and wouldn't that be a fine mess?

"Caroline, are you listening to me?" Rafe asked, his tone giving her the impression this was not the first time he'd asked that question.

"Not really." She nearly laughed at the surprise and then consternation in his expression. He was so used to issuing orders and having them obeyed, it must be almost as frustrating for him to deal with her as it was for her to deal with him.

"Thanks a lot," he grumbled.

"You're not listening to me, either," she pointed out. "You're giving me a hard sell on getting married, but it's all coming from your head. I need more than that."

"What's more than that?" he asked.

"If I have to explain it, you probably wouldn't understand it anyway."

He shot her several perturbed glances when he could spare the attention from the road, but he remained silent for the rest of the trip. Ten minutes later, he pulled into her driveway. Ever the gentleman, he helped her out of the car and walked her to the door. She unlocked it, then turned to face him.

His grim, tight-lipped expression would have intimidated her if she hadn't caught a glimpse of pain in his eyes before he'd shut down all outward signs of emotion. No one should be so good at doing that. It broke her heart to realize what he must have gone through in order to develop that much skill.

"I don't want to hurt you," she said, meaning it. "It's just that marriage is a huge step, and we've never even talked about it. You really can be a father to the baby without having to marry me."

"We'll talk about it later." She'd heard automated phone systems with more warmth, but still, he asked, "Will you be all right if I leave now?"

She felt so lousy, she didn't know if she would or not, but she desperately needed some time alone to think and regroup. Nodding, she said, "I just need some rest."

He started to turn away, but changed his mind and turned back. "I'll bring dinner tomorrow before Lamaze class."

Before Caroline could do more than utter a quick, "Thanks, Rafe," he was back in his car. She stepped inside and stood at the screen door, watching Rafe leave while Truman let out a series of disgruntled woofs in the vicinity of her ankles. "I know he's won your affections," she told the dog, "but you'd be smart to remember who saved your hide at the animal shelter."

The house felt too empty without Rafe talking and moving around and simply taking up space the way a man did. Caroline fixed a cup of herbal tea and sat down at the breakfast nook to drink it. She turned on the small kitchen TV for noise. Picking up the notepad from under the phone, she tried to rebuild a sense of normalcy by making out a To Do list.

She had laundry, groceries to buy, bills to pay and she needed to get copies of the Stockwell files made for Cord. Her receptionist, Gina, was finally back at work and handling the office, but Caroline hadn't seen her father in over a week. She'd better get out to Rosewood Manor in the morning to check on him.

She looked at the list and burst into tears. Oh, she'd really done it now. This was exactly what her life had consisted of before Rafe had come back into it. Mundane chores and responsibilities, a certain level of contentment, but no real personal joy or excitement.

Ugh. She didn't want to go back to that. The baby might open up some new avenues for her to explore, but it was Rafe who spiced up her days and nights. Rafe who made her feel alive. He drove her crazy sometimes, but without him, her life was boring and so was she. The weekend with him and Becky had been the happiest time of her life. Other people somehow managed to have that for a lifetime. Why couldn't she?

And why couldn't Rafe just love her?

Rafe spent most of the night trying to figure out where he'd gone wrong with Caroline. He knew that he'd hurt her, but couldn't lay his finger on any one thing he'd done that was out of line. If the truth were told, he was hurt, too, by her adamant refusal even to think about marrying him.

Are you completely out of your mind? Now, there was a phrase he wouldn't forget anytime soon. Then, after he'd racked his brain to come up with good, solid reasons she should want to marry him, to find out that she hadn't even been listening to him—that had cut him down to the quick and whatever lay beyond it. Rejection didn't come any plainer than that.

He ought to know.

God knew that when it came to being rejected, Rafe Stockwell was an expert. Thanks to Caine, Rafe had lived with it on a daily basis for as long as he could remember. But, because Caine was mean to almost everyone, Rafe had been able to write his father's treatment off as not being personal.

Caine had been even more cruel to Jack than he'd been to Rafe, a fact which, to his shame, Rafe had often used to comfort himself. He'd taken a similar approach to coping with the truth about his mother's absence. Since he wasn't the only one she'd abandoned, Rafe didn't have to see it as a personal rejection of himself. Hell, maybe she'd just been trying to get away from the old man, and who could blame her for that?

But this thing with Caroline *was* personal, and he didn't have a clue as to why she would do that to him. And without a moment's hesitation. He could've handled a *Maybe* or even a *Let's think about that,* but what was he supposed to do with *Are you completely out of your mind?* It didn't make any sense.

Against considerable opposition on her part, he'd knocked himself out to help her in every way he could for the past month. They'd worked together, learned about pregnancy and childbirth together, made incredibly intimate love together. The weekend they'd spent with Becky had been, without a doubt, the happiest time of his life.

He'd shared more of himself with Caroline than he'd shared with any other human being. He'd thought they were building something brand-new between them that involved more than the baby they'd created. He'd obviously been wrong. Dead wrong.

And now she wanted something else from him, but if she had to explain it, he wouldn't understand. That didn't make any sense, either. Hell, knowing so-called female logic, she probably wanted him to say the *L* word.

Why? So she could reject him again? Not damn likely.

But on the other hand, could he just give up on the one relationship that had ever made him feel as if he really belonged? That being Rafe was an asset? That he was needed?

What if she just wanted him to say he loved her? He honestly didn't know what love was, but he sure as hell cared about Caroline. He wanted her to be happy, and he wanted to be happy with her and the baby. He wanted to be with them all the time, not at certain times when it was allowed in some custody arrangement.

If saying he loved her would give him a family of his own, it wouldn't kill him to say it. Of course, he didn't want to lie to Caroline. But maybe it wouldn't be a lie. How the hell did anybody know if they were in love, anyway?

His thoughts bounced around in his head like a handball on speed. He went back to that first time he'd seen her and realized she was pregnant, and replayed every encounter he'd had with her since then. By the time he was dressed and on his way to a task force meeting at the regional office in Fort Worth, he'd cleared away enough confusion to make some decisions.

First, he wasn't going to give up on his relationship with Caroline. She was the strongest woman he'd ever known, stronger than even she herself realized. When he added in her intelligence, her soft heart, her passion and her sense of humor, she was an ideal mate for him. He'd be a fool to walk away from her without putting up a fight.

Second, she was right when she'd said that he hadn't been listening to her, and that they hadn't even talked about marriage. Much as he hated the thought of their baby being born before they were married, he had to think of Caroline's needs as well as his own. If she needed more time to feel comfortable about marrying him, he could be flexible on that issue. After all, he still had five weeks before the baby was due.

Third, too many things had been happening in his life to distract him from building a solid relationship with Caroline. The demands of his job, looking for the files, learning about childbirth and babies, taking care of Becky had eaten up too much time he should have spent with Caroline. Not that those activities hadn't been important, of course, but he'd focused too much attention on Caroline, the mother-to-be, and not enough on Caroline, the woman.

He could fix that, he thought, smiling for the first time in what felt like forever. He wasn't sure exactly how, but he'd figure out something. One way or another he would convince Caroline that she was important to him for more reasons than the baby she carried.

"Oh, God, it's blood."

Too surprised to move, Caroline stared at the small crimson stain on the chair in her home office, irrationally hoping against hope that if she just looked at it long enough, it would go away. It stayed right there, of course, but she continued to stare at it until a Braxton Hicks contraction broke through her shock and propelled her into action. Grabbing the phone, she called her doctor's office, impatiently drumming her fingernails on the desk while she waited for him to come on the line.

When he finally said, "Hello, Caroline. What's the problem?" she wanted to scream at him for taking so long. Instead, she told him about the bloodstain and answered his questions, then held her breath while he digested the information she'd given him.

"You'll need to be checked sometime today, but I don't want you to drive. Is there someone you can call?"

Her thoughts immediately flew to Rafe, and she wanted him to be with her at that moment more than she'd ever wanted anything else in her life. "Yes. It might take a little while for him to get here, but the baby's father will come."

"All right then, I want you to keep your phone with you. Put your feet up or lie down, then call Daddy right away and have him bring you to my office. Stay calm and try to rest, but monitor your bleeding. If you're using more than one sanitary pad in an hour, don't wait for Daddy. Call an ambulance and get to the hospital. Have you got that?"

"Yes, I think so." Scared half to death and struggling to keep her voice from wobbling out of control, Caroline took a deep breath before asking, "It's really that serious?"

"It's impossible to tell without an examination, but there's no need to panic yet," the doctor said with a confidence she appreciated. "Chances are good this will resolve itself without any problem, but I prefer not to take any unnecessary chances. Now get off your feet and make your call."

Caroline thanked him, cleaned herself up, then carried her purse into the living room and stretched out on the sofa. She dialed Rafe's cell phone, only to be told, "The customer you have dialed has either driven out of the service area or is not answering at this time."

"Oh, Lord," she muttered, cutting off the rest of the message. "Please don't let him be in the middle of a shoot-out or some other big mess."

She tried his pager number next. While she waited for Rafe to call her back, she felt another mild contraction. When he hadn't returned her call in five minutes, she called his pager again. She waited ten minutes this time, but she still didn't hear from Rafe.

"No need to panic," she said. Sensitive to her tension, Truman put his front paws up on the edge of the sofa cushion, cocked his head to one side and let out a soft whine. Caroline petted his head and scratched around his ears, but told him, "Not this time, pal. This sofa's not big enough for the two of us."

He curled up on the floor beside her, and Caroline went back to trying to raise Rafe. She could have called Gina at the office, or even Hannah Stockwell, but it wasn't that late yet and her bleeding hadn't increased much. Rafe was the person she most wanted to be with her and she felt comfortable waiting a while longer to reach him.

She knew he'd checked out the problem with his pager. Of course, even the best pagers wouldn't work under certain conditions, but she was willing to bet that if she just kept trying long enough, eventually he would get her page. He would be here by five or five-thirty at the latest, anyway.

"Definitely no need to panic," she told Truman, dialing again. Still no response.

She moved into the family room so she could watch TV. A trip to the bathroom assured her the bleeding was still well within the doctor's guidelines. She raided the kitchen for a bottle of water and a carton of yogurt, then settled in on the love seat with her feet propped up on the coffee table and the remote control in her lap. Between sips of water and bites of yogurt she dialed and dialed and dialed again. The light contractions came and went.

Her anxiety mounted as the afternoon wore on. "No need to panic," became "Where the hell *is* he?" which became "He *said* he'd be here if I had an emergency. Dammit, he *promised.*"

At four Caroline discovered the bleeding was noticeably worse. Still not bad enough to go to the hospital, but enough to convince her it was time for plan B. She called her office number, got the answering machine and remembered Gina had asked to leave early for a dental appointment. She called the Stockwell Mansion and asked for Hannah, but Hannah and Cord had taken Becky out somewhere. Caroline went back to dialing Rafe's pager.

At four-thirty, she found the number for the U.S. Marshals Regional Office in Fort Worth. A woman with a Texas drawl that made Hannah's Oklahoma twang sound tame in comparison answered the phone. "U.S. Marshals. This is Urlene speakin'. How may I direct your call?"

"I'm trying to reach Deputy Rafe Stockwell, but he's not answering his cell phone or his pager," Caroline said, forcing herself to sound calm when she was anything but. "Do you have any way of locating him?"

"Why yes, ma'am, I do. May I ask what this pertains to?"

"It's an emergency," Caroline said. "For a family member."

"All right." Urlene made some clicking noises that Caroline recognized from her own computer keyboard. "Deputy Stockwell has been in a task force meetin' in this building all day, ma'am. I believe it broke up about twenty minutes ago, but I can page him if you'd like me to."

"Please." Caroline felt one more contraction, and then a sudden wetness between her thighs. Her heart stuttered and fear grabbed her by the throat. "Forget it. I can't wait for him."

With Urlene still sputtering in Fort Worth, Caroline ended the call, saw blood staining her slacks and dialed 9-1-1.

After his meeting adjourned, Rafe sat in the cafeteria drinking iced tea at a small table with his warrant supervisor, Art Franklin.

"Two months of vacation and six weeks of parental leave?" Eyes bulging, Art clutched at his thinning hair with both hands and pretended to pull out tufts of it. "Are you completely out of your mind?"

Rafe found Art's dramatics and his all too familiar question less than funny. "It's not negotiable. I've got the time coming and I'm going to take it."

"Do you have to take all of it at once?"

"Yes." Rafe made a production out of looking at his watch. "And it starts right now."

"Well, you sure picked a hell of an inconvenient time." Art drank from his glass, then banged it on the table.

A garbled page came over the public address system, but since he couldn't make any sense of it, Rafe ignored it. "It's never going to be convenient. No matter how many cases we solve, there's always another one."

"But what am I supposed to do with your workload for three and a half damn months?"

"Not my problem, Franklin. Uncle Sam pays you the big bucks to figure out that stuff."

Rafe climbed to his feet while Art was still chuckling. The warrant officer followed suit and together they walked to a junction where two hallways branched off in different directions. One led to the parking garage next door, the other to the elevators that connected the basement to the building's upper stories.

"Will you sign me out upstairs?" Rafe asked. "I want to get back to Grandview so I can spend some time with Caroline before Lamaze class."

"You bet." Clapping Rafe on the back, Art shook his head. "Never thought I'd see the day you settled down. Caroline must be quite a woman."

"She is." Rafe stepped back and raised a hand in farewell.

Whistling, he hustled out to the parking garage and headed for the highway. He called Caroline on his cell phone, frowning when she didn't answer. He couldn't imagine where she would've gone now, but he left a message on her voice mail.

"Hey there, sugar, it's me. It's four-fifty-five and I'm about twenty minutes from Grandview right now. I need to make a couple of stops, but I should be at your house by five forty-five. If you have any special requests for dinner, call me on the cell phone."

He stopped at a flower shop, bought a dozen red roses and hurried on to a deli that carried a pasta salad Caroline enjoyed. Feeling pleased with his day's work and himself, he drove on to her house and pulled into the driveway. He climbed out of the car, the cellophane-wrapped roses in one hand, the deli bag in the other.

A long, mournful howl came from the front yard. Curious, Rafe walked around the house and saw Truman frantically scratching at the front door. Caroline never would have let her dog carry on like that if she were home. She never would have left her dog outside if she was going somewhere, either. No way. Rafe dropped the deli sack and ran.

Truman bolted past him when he unlocked the door. Rafe hurried in after him.

"Caroline?" he shouted. "Caroline, are you here?"

He ran through the house, still shouting and clutching the roses, but he didn't find her. Forcing himself to slow down, he backtracked as far as the living room, where he found Truman pacing back and forth with his nose to the carpet like a bloodhound tracking a fugitive.

Rafe squatted down, grabbed the dog's collar and pulled him out of the way while he studied the carpet. "Oh, God. Not blood." But it was. He knew it before he touched the stained carpet with his index finger. There wasn't that much; not enough to be life-threatening unless there was a lot more somewhere else. Nevertheless, his lungs refused to breathe, his stomach knotted and the hair at the back of his neck stood straight out.

He'd seen some gruesome things during his career, but nothing he'd ever seen had struck such bone-deep terror in him as knowing those drops of blood belonged to Caroline. He wanted to vomit, but there was no time for that. He had to find her.

A timid knock at the front door drew his attention. He hurried to answer it and found a young redhead he recognized as one of Caroline's neighbors standing on the porch.

''I've seen you here a lot lately,'' she said. ''Are you looking for Ms. Carlyle?''

''Yes,'' Rafe said. ''Do you know what happened here?''

She gave him a sympathetic smile. ''I'm afraid not. I just saw the ambulance drive up about a quarter to five. They loaded her up and left in five minutes. I thought you'd like to know that much.''

''Thank you.'' Blocking Truman with his left foot, Rafe stepped outside with his right, then quickly shut and locked the door, trapping the dog inside.

The woman noticed Truman and sighed. ''Oh, I'm so glad he's all right. Caroline was so upset when he got out and they wouldn't put him back in the house.''

Rafe started down the steps. ''I need to go. Thanks for the information.''

''You're welcome. Tell Ms. Carlyle we'll pray for her.''

Rafe waved an acknowledgment and sprinted back to his car. The closest hospital was the one Caroline had planned to use for the baby's delivery. It was only about twenty minutes away when he drove the speed limit. Rafe pulled into the Emergency Room's parking lot in ten.

He jammed the car into a parking spot and ran for the building, his hand still clutching the now battered bouquet of roses. Fear left a metallic taste in his mouth and coated the pit of his stomach like an oil slick. At least he now had the answer to one of the questions he'd wrestled with last night.

There was no longer the slightest doubt in his mind that he loved Caroline Carlyle with every particle of his heart and soul. He loved their baby, too. Even the possibility of losing either one of them filled him with an unspeakable dread that made his eyes burn, his chest ache and his knees go rubbery.

He would die for her. Kill for her. Sell his soul if it would save her or the baby. Unfortunately all he could do was hope and pray that he wasn't too late to tell Caroline what he should have said months ago.

Dammit, why hadn't he used the *L* word?

Chapter Thirteen

The ambulance careened around a corner, then sped up again. Fearing that the slightest movement on her part might cause her to lose the baby, Caroline did her best to lie absolutely still, clutching her abdomen with both hands as an added precaution. When the driver hit a pothole that must have been the size of a bomb crater, she whimpered.

Without taking his eyes off the fetal monitor, the paramedic spoke to her in a low, soothing voice. "You're doing fine, Caroline. We'll be there soon and you're going to be all right."

"What about my baby?" she asked. "Is my baby going to be all right?"

"We're doing everything we can for both of you."

That was the best answer she was likely to get from this guy. He was good. He worked with the ease and confidence of a professional, reassuring her while he started an IV and took her blood pressure. But she'd never been so scared in her entire life.

Please, please, oh, please, God, let my baby be all right.

She silently repeated the prayer like a mantra. Everything else receded to a place where she knew what was going on around her, but she didn't have to respond. She would not lose this baby. Period. She just wouldn't.

She wanted Rafe. *Please, God, let my baby be all right. I'll do whatever you want. Just let my baby live.*

The ambulance turned another corner, but this time it slowed to a stop. The siren hadn't bothered her while they were moving. Now it was loud and shrill enough to make her grit her teeth.

The noise cut off. The ambulance doors opened wide. The paramedic pushed the stretcher to the doorway. Other faces filled her vision. Strong hands lowered the stretcher to the ground. People in hospital scrubs rushed her inside. The paramedic jogged behind them, reporting what he'd done and the readings he'd taken.

Please, please, oh, please, God, let my baby be all right.

She was in a room now. The bright lights made her squint. They rolled the stretcher beside an examination table. More hospital personnel converged on her from both sides. One of the men said, "On my count. One, two, three."

Moving as one, they transferred her onto the examination table. The paramedic wished her good luck and left. The doctors and nurses—at least she thought they were doctors and nurses—went to work on her, adjusting her IV, attaching another blood pressure cuff and a fetal monitor. The equipment around the bed beeped and lines squiggled across a screen. Someone else brought in an ultrasound machine.

"My baby?" Caroline asked. "Is my baby okay?"

A woman patted her shoulder. "We're taking good care of you, honey. You're going to be fine."

"I asked about my baby," Caroline said. "Please. Is she all right?"

"We're doing our best for the baby. Do you know for sure it's a girl?"

Caroline shook her head. "I think it is, though."

A man leaned over her from the other side of the table. "Hi, Caroline. I'm Dr. Garcia. Who's your OB?"

Her mind went blank. She couldn't think. "I don't know," she said, barely able to get the words past the lump in her throat. "In my purse." Oh, God, she wanted Rafe. Where was he? He knew her doctor's name. She couldn't get through this without him. A tear trickled down her cheek.

Dr. Garcia gently brushed it away. "It's all right. We'll find it or it'll come to you. The best thing you can do to help your baby is to help us by staying calm. Can you tell me your due date?"

"Yes," she said, and when she told him, Dr. Garcia's smile eased the lump in her throat.

"That's good," he said. "We'd like to keep your baby inside you a few more weeks. But, if we can't, the baby has a good chance for survival."

"Dr. Garcia, she's bleeding more," a female voice called.

He moved to the far end of the table. The activity in the room accelerated. The voices sounded more urgent, and they were talking in so much jargon, she only understood about every fourth word. She picked out "transfusion," "placenta previa" and "hysterectomy," all of which scared her witless.

"What's wrong?" She tried to clutch her abdomen, but someone pushed her hands down to her sides and told her she couldn't disturb the fetal monitor. "Is my baby all right?"

No one answered her. It seemed they were all too busy poking or prodding her somewhere. Or rushing in and out of the room. Or hooking her up to a new machine.

She ached everywhere. She was still having contractions. Her legs were going numb from lying flat on her back. With all of these people working on her, she couldn't move to alleviate the discomfort. She suddenly felt light-headed, but she couldn't make anyone listen to her.

Please, please, oh, please, God, let my baby be all right.

Rafe. He should've been to her house a long time ago and realized something was wrong. He tracked down fugitives, for heaven's sake. Finding out what had happened to her should've been easy for him. Half the neighborhood had gathered around the ambulance when paramedics had brought her outside.

So where the hell was he?

No matter what had happened between them last night, how could he abandon her now, when she needed him more than she'd ever needed anyone? Didn't he care enough about her or his own baby to be here? His continued absence was the only answer she received.

Turning her head to one side, she inhaled the deepest breath she could manage and blinked back scorching tears. She could handle this. She had no other choice *but* to handle it—alone, as usual. She couldn't believe she'd been stupid enough to believe Rafe would be any different than the other people in her life who were supposed to be there for her.

Well, she'd finally learned her lesson. It was over. She couldn't waste any more energy on Rafe Stockwell. Let the doctors and nurses do whatever they had to do to her. She would channel all of her thoughts, prayers and the force of her own will into saving her child.

"I'm sorry, Mr. Stockwell, but I can't release any information about one of our patients without permission, unless you're a relative. It's hospital policy."

Rafe sucked in a deep breath and silently counted to fifteen. He still wanted to throttle this self-important, sadistic little twit, but he figured it could wait until after the baby was born. Her name tag read Trudi. Give her five or ten years and she'd grow up to be a full-fledged bureaucrat. He didn't intend to help her get there.

"I want to talk to your supervisor," he said, using the same blunt tone he used on cornered fugitives. "Now."

"I'm sorry, Mr. Stockwell." Trudi looked far from sorry, but that could be fixed. "My supervisor has left for the day."

"Call him at home."

She let out a prim sigh, then gave him a patently false smile. "I'm sorry, Mr. Stockwell, but—"

"If you say, 'I'm sorry, Mr. Stockwell,' one more time, I won't be responsible for my actions."

Trudi finished her sentence as if he hadn't interrupted her. "My supervisor is *Ms.* Donovon. She's not available after regular business hours."

Rafe rested one elbow on the reception desk and leaned down, getting right in Trudi's face. "Let's get one thing real clear. I'm prepared to take this all the way to the top. You may not know or care what the Stockwell name means in this town, but trust me, your hospital administrator will.''

Trudi drew herself up tall and crossed her arms over her breasts. "I'm only doing my job. This hospital respects the privacy of its patients. You can't see Ms. Carlyle, and I can't reveal any information about her condition unless you have her permission or you're a relative. I can't change that for you, no matter what your name is, *Mr.* Stockwell.''

"Don't tell me about Ms. Carlyle, then,'' Rafe said. "Tell me about her baby. I'm the father. I'd say that makes me a relative.''

Trudi didn't even blink. "Do you have any proof that you're the father?''

Rafe turned his back on her, pulled out his cell phone and called Cord. When his brother came on the line, Rafe explained what was happening and asked him to start pulling every damn string he could find at this hospital. When he finished the call, Rafe turned back to face Trudi.

"You'll be getting new instructions within the hour. When you do, I'll be right over there in that waiting area. Don't try to pretend you couldn't find me.''

He walked away before she could reply. He'd never thrown the Stockwell name around to get special treatment before and he didn't feel good about doing it now. He'd always thought people who did that sort of thing were idiots, but he'd do anything to get to Caroline and the baby. Anything.

The waiting area had the usual uncomfortable plastic chairs, a television playing endless medical information programs and a collection of ancient magazines. He ignored all of them in favor of pacing. Eight steps forward, turn, eight steps back. It did nothing to ease his anxiety, but it was better than sitting.

An ambulance screamed into the ER's bay, bringing in some poor soul on a stretcher. A little boy waiting to be seen by a doctor caused a commotion by fainting. A weeping woman sat in a corner, her gaze glued to the hallway that held the examination rooms. Rafe barely noticed any of them.

He was too busy worrying about Caroline and the baby and bargaining with God for their safety. He'd faced danger and violence with less fear than he felt now. His stomach hurt, his chest felt tight and a cold sweat broke out all over his body.

Only the possibility that he somehow might interfere with Caroline's care prevented him from barging back there and finding her, hospital policy and security be damned. He just couldn't shake the conviction that whatever was happening to Caroline, she shouldn't be going through it alone. He'd give it half an hour and then all bets would be off.

The second hand on the wall clock dragged itself around the clock's face; he doubted the minute hand would budge at all. The tension built inside him until he thought a stroke was imminent. Dammit, he couldn't wait any longer. Ready to tear the place apart, he turned around and came face to face with a middle-aged male doctor holding a medical chart.

They both came to an abrupt halt and took a step back. The doctor scanned the waiting area. "Stockwell?" he called. "Mr. Rafe Stockwell?"

"That's me," Rafe said.

"Oh, hello. I'm Dr. Yeager, Caroline's obstetrician."

"How is she?"

Dr. Yeager motioned for Rafe to come out into the hallway. Leaning one shoulder against the wall, Dr. Yeager consulted the chart for a moment before looking back at Rafe. "She's stabilized now."

Relief washed over Rafe in such a rush his knees nearly buckled. "What about the baby?"

"He's fine as far as we can tell."

"He?" Rafe demanded. "You're sure about that?"

"Absolutely," the doctor said with a smile. "That much was extremely clear on the ultrasound."

"A boy," Rafe murmured, shaking his head in amazement. Oh, man, he'd been picturing another sweet little Becky that he could spoil and cuddle. Could he handle raising a rough-and-tumble little boy? Could Caroline? Then, realizing he was getting sidetracked over something he couldn't change if he wanted to, he asked, "What happened to Caroline?"

"She's developed a condition called placenta previa. Basically, the placenta implants too low in the uterus and causes bleeding. Sometimes it corrects itself. Sometimes it's dangerous."

"But she's okay now?"

"For now," Yeager agreed. "The baby is close enough to term to survive on his own if we have to do a cesarean section, but of course, we'd rather keep him in the uterus as long as we can to make sure all of his organs are completely developed."

"How do you do that?" Rafe asked.

"We'll keep Caroline in the hospital with complete bed rest until the baby's born."

"For a whole month?"

Dr. Yeager raised his eyebrows at him. "I don't think you understand how serious her condition is. If she'd waited much longer to call the ambulance, she and the baby might have bled out.''

''Bled out?'' Rafe asked, not wanting to believe what he was hearing and seeing in the doctor's grim expression.

''Died. The very same thing could happen again at any time. Until the baby's born, she literally can't go anywhere.''

A low roaring sound filled Rafe's ears, his field of vision started to shrink and he felt oddly dizzy. Calling for a chair, Dr. Yeager put a hand behind Rafe's neck and pushed his head down toward his knees. Suddenly too weak to struggle, Rafe collapsed onto the chair and found himself looking directly at the toes of his cowboy boots.

Gradually the dizziness passed, his vision cleared and the roaring faded away. Humiliated beyond belief, he slowly sat up.

Dr. Yeager grinned at him. ''Better?''

''Yeah,'' Rafe said, wiping his forehead with the back of his hand. ''Sorry about that.''

''Don't be. We see it all the time. It's tough to have to wait out here for news.''

''Will Caroline be able to have other children?'' Rafe asked.

''Probably. But, if she starts to bleed heavily again and we can't stop it, we'll have to perform a hysterectomy.''

Rafe closed his eyes and sat back in the chair, struggling to digest everything the doctor had told him. Finally he opened his eyes and asked, ''Does Caroline know all of this?''

''Yes, of course,'' Yeager said.

"Is there anything else I need to know about her condition?"

The doctor pursed his lips for a moment, then nodded. "I'm concerned about her mental state. She seems depressed and withdrawn. That's not unusual for people who've had an intense emergency like this, but I hate to see her so alone."

"She doesn't have to be if you'll let me in to see her."

"I want her to rest for at least a couple of hours. If she's still stable then, I'll be happy to let you see her."

"Will you at least tell her that I'm here and that I've been here for over an hour?" Rafe asked.

"Certainly."

"All right," Rafe said. "I'll wait two hours, but if nobody comes to get me, I'll go looking for her on my own."

The doctor left him. Rafe spent the next two hours making himself presentable and composing himself for Caroline's sake. If she was as upset as she had every right to be, he needed to be calm and comforting. The first bouquet of roses he'd bought was so badly mangled, he bought another one in the hospital's gift shop. By the time a nurse arrived to escort him to Caroline's room, he thought he was ready for anything.

But when he saw her huddled up in a big hospital bed, looking pale and exhausted, with lines of pain evident around her eyes and nose, he wanted to scoop her up and rescue her from any more suffering. She looked at him as he crossed the room, but her eyes held no welcome and she didn't say anything.

He leaned down and kissed her forehead. "Hello, sugar. How do you feel?"

"Tired." Her voice sounded flat and distant.

"You've been through a lot today." Flowers still gripped tightly in his left hand, he went to retrieve a visitor's chair, but Caroline called to him.

"I want you to leave."

He stood there for a moment, staring at her and debating whether or not he should do as she asked. No, he couldn't leave. This was too important. He dragged the chair to her bedside and sat down. She closed her eyes as if she couldn't bear to look at him. It hurt. He couldn't believe how much that simple action hurt, but he wasn't going to give up on her.

"Why didn't you call me when you started having problems?" he asked.

She shot him a look so fierce it could've melted a bullet in midflight. He was glad to see she still had that much life in her. He reached for her hand, but she pulled it away from him. He closed his own eyes, absorbing the sting of more rejection.

"All right, I'll assume you tried to call me, but for some reason you couldn't get through. I don't know why that—" He broke off his sentence, remembering where he'd been. He smacked his forehead with the heel of his hand. "Aw, dammit, I was in the basement of the federal building all day. Of course my cell phone didn't work. With all that concrete and steel overhead, there's no way the signal could get through."

Feeling like an idiot, he forced himself to meet her gaze. "I'm sorry, Caroline. I should've thought of that, but I promise, it'll never happen again. From here on out, I'll be with you every step of the way."

A tear trickled down her cheek. He pulled a handkerchief out of his pocket and would have wiped her face, but she turned her head toward the wall. He crumpled the handkerchief in his right hand and squeezed the rose stems harder in his left, ignoring the pain of the thorns biting into his palm and fingers. "Last night I decided that if I wanted our relationship to grow, I needed to give it the time and attention it deserves. So, this afternoon I met with my boss and arranged to take two months of vacation and six weeks of parental leave. It starts today, so I'm not just blowing smoke up your skirt when I say I'll be here with you every step of the way."

"No," she murmured, letting out a deep, shuddering sigh. "Go away, Rafe."

He paused and took a deep breath. Obviously his reassurances weren't getting through to her. Must be time for a different approach.

"Are you sure that's what you want?" he asked.

"Yes."

"All right, I'll go," he said, carefully keeping his voice calm and unemotional. "But I want to get a few things straight. First, I'm only going as far as the waiting room, so don't tell yourself I've abandoned you. Anytime you need me, all you have to do is send a nurse out to get me. If you wind up sitting in here feeling alone and scared for the next month, remember it was your choice, not mine.

"Second, I don't understand your definition of 'being there for you.' It seems to be an all-or-nothing deal. If I'm not physically with you twenty-four hours a day, seven days a week, then I'm not being 'there for you' at all. I don't know anybody who could meet those standards, and you wouldn't respect any man who did. You've already got one dog tagging around after you all day. What do you want with another one?"

She turned her head long enough to shoot him another

fierce look, then faced the wall again. Well, good. She might be mad as hell, but at least she was listening.

"Third, I love you, Caroline Carlyle. I have for a long time. I would've told you sooner, but I didn't know what these feelings I'd been having about you were."

He heard a derisive snort come from the bed, and nodded in agreement. "Yeah, I know that's pathetic, but it's the damn truth. I never thought I was even capable of feeling love, but you sure blew that theory to pieces."

Her shoulders were hunching, as if she wanted to fold in on herself in order to get away from him. She might as well rip out his heart with a fork, but he wouldn't stop now. He couldn't.

"You know all that stuff I said about never wanting to get married or have a family? Pure bull. I was afraid I might be too much like Caine to be a good husband and father. I sure didn't want to pass on his legacy, but you told me I'm not like him. Your belief in me meant...well, it meant everything. I want a chance to prove you were right."

He saw her throat work down a swallow. She was still listening. "I know you think I'm a workaholic like your dad, but I'm not. It's not the work itself that turns me on. It's just that at work I feel competent and the people I work with respect me for what I can do.

"If my name was Joe Smith they'd treat me the same, and I like that. I feel good about myself when I'm there. Maybe it sounds corny, but I like doing my bit to make the world a better place. But you try giving me a loving wife and a family who wants me, and I'll find plenty of reasons I want to be at home."

He paused, giving her an opening to respond, but she didn't take it. So be it. He'd gone this far, he might as well finish the job.

"Okay, this is the last one, sugar. You've been pushing me away ever since you found out you were carrying my baby. I know you did it because you were afraid I'd let you down. I've tried real hard to be understanding about that, but it still feels like a big fat rejection to me. If you think finding out you wouldn't even tell me about my own kid didn't hurt me, think again.

"You know something, Caroline? I'm just as afraid of being rejected as you are of being abandoned. Every time you've pushed me away, I've fought my fear because I believed we could have something real special together. I still believe that, dammit, but I can't fight my own fear and yours too. If we're ever going to create a real family for ourselves and our baby, at some point, you're going to have to let go of that fear and trust me.

"I can't promise to be a perfect husband or father, but you'll never find anybody who'll love you and our baby any more than I will. And I swear before God, I'll do everything in my power to do the very best I can for you. I'll never intentionally or willingly let you down. If that's not good enough for you... well, I've got nothing more to say."

Chapter Fourteen

Barely allowing herself to breathe, Caroline waited until the door closed behind Rafe. She'd been holding back tears for hours. She would have preferred to continue holding them back forever, but she was too exhausted to fight them any longer.

They streamed down her cheeks, dripping into her ears and off her jaw in hot rivulets. Tears of fear for the baby. Tears of anger at Rafe for not being reachable. Tears of relief when the bleeding stopped and the baby appeared to be fine. Tears of joy at hearing Rafe say he loved her, followed by tears of regret at knowing she'd hurt him. And tears of frustration that he made it sound so easy for her simply to let go of her fear and trust him. Oh, right.

Once started, it was as if someone had tipped over a huge vat of tears and there was no way to stop or divert the flood. Her body shaking with the force of each new sob, she could only wait for the contents to drain away. By the time they did, she felt as if she'd been hollowed out like a Halloween pumpkin. Her head ached, her nose was red and stuffy and her eyes were nearly swollen shut.

At the same time, she felt better, lighter actually, and she recognized a sense of clarity she hadn't had since discovering she was pregnant with Rafe's child. Maybe there was something to be said for crying, after all. Unable to reach the box of tissues, she wiped her eyes on the sheet, and when she lowered her hands to her sides, she brushed against something cool and smooth.

Glancing down, she saw the red roses Rafe had brought with him, and her heart contracted. She picked them up and studied them, carefully avoiding the thorny stems. The stems were oddly mangled in a wide band, and when she cast her mind back to picture the way Rafe had been carrying them, she realized that he must have been hanging on to them like a lifeline.

Oddly comforted by the thought, she cradled them in her arms and ran her fingertips over the silky petals. She had no idea what she was going to do about Rafe, or even what she thought of the things he'd just said to her. But right now, her body was demanding sleep and she didn't have the strength to deny it. Tomorrow she would deal with Rafe.

Wondering if he'd just done more harm than good with Caroline, Rafe found the waiting room and collapsed onto one of the upholstered chairs that were a step up from the plastic ones in the ER, but still managed to be uncomfortable as hell if you had to sit in them for long. Propping his elbows on his knees, he cradled his head in his hands and released a sigh that came all the way up from the depths of his soul.

"Rafe, what's wrong? Is it Caroline? Or the baby?"

Jerking his head up at the sound of Cord's alarmed voice, Rafe saw his brother rush into the room with Hannah hot on his heels. Touched by their obvious concern, he sat up and hurried to reassure them.

"They're both okay," he said. "I'm just a little... tired."

"I reckon you are," Hannah said, sitting on his left.

Cord took the chair on Rafe's right and stretched his legs out in front of him. "What did the doctor say?"

Rafe briefed them as best he could.

"Considering the possibilities, that sounds like pretty good news," Hannah ventured when he'd finished. "I mean, if there aren't any more complications."

Rafe nodded, then raised one shoulder in a half-hearted shrug. "Right now that feels like a pretty big if."

"You've got to think positively." Hannah tilted her head to one side and studied his face. "You look really sad to me, Rafe. Is there something else you haven't told us?"

He hesitated, but decide he needed feedback from somebody who wasn't so intimately involved in the situation. He gave them an abbreviated version of the problems he and Caroline were having and what he'd said to her only minutes ago.

"I don't know what's going to happen," he confessed. "I figure she'll either hate me forever for talking to her like that, or she'll give me another chance. I'm not sure even God knows which way she'll go."

"Oh, that was smooth, little brother," Cord said. "Real smooth."

Hannah leaned around Rafe and spoke directly to her husband. "Honey, I need some coffee from the first floor. Will you please get me some?"

"What's wrong with the machine right out there in the hall?" Cord asked.

"It's fresher on the first floor." She gave him a sweet smile, but her voice held a firm tone Rafe wouldn't have wanted to argue with. "There's no hurry at all, darlin'. Just take your sweet time."

"Oh, I get it," Cord grumbled, pushing himself to his feet. "You want to get rid of me."

"Thank you, sweetheart. I just knew you'd understand."

Rafe watched his brother slink off to the elevator, but couldn't dredge up the energy to laugh at how neatly Hannah had managed him.

When Cord was out of sight, Hannah put her hand on Rafe's forearm. "You did exactly the right thing. Even if Caroline's madder than a wet hen, I'm sure she needed to hear that you love her."

"I wouldn't mind hearing that from her, either," Rafe admitted.

"Don't fret about that," she told him. "I've seen you two together twice now, and I can tell she loves you. Why, that day we picked Becky up when we came back from Las Vegas, you two looked like a happily married couple."

"It felt that way." Rafe smiled at the memory, then grimaced as a wave of discouragement hit him in the face. "Aw, who am I kidding, Hannah? I've done so many things wrong, made so many mistakes with her, she's never going to forgive me."

"You stop that right now," she scolded him. "In case you didn't notice, Cord and I hit our share of speed bumps on the road to true love. Why should you and Caroline have it easy?''

Rafe found it impossible not to grin at Hannah. ''All right, all right, you've got a point. So what do I do now?''

''The same thing you've been doing, hon. Just keep loving her. Sooner or later she'll figure out that when it's really love, you stick it out during the bad times as well as the good times.'' Hannah fell silent a moment, worrying her bottom lip with her front teeth. Then she added, ''You know, it might not hurt for the rest of the family to make some sort of gesture to help Caroline feel welcome. We weren't exactly at our best last night.''

Rafe nodded thoughtfully. ''And since she's carrying my baby, that automatically makes her a part of the family. Maybe we should show her that the Stockwell resources are available to her the same way they are to the rest of us.''

''Now you're gettin' it,'' Hannah said.

Cord stuck his head around the doorway. ''They're out of coffee on the first floor. May I come back yet?''

Chuckling, Hannah her hand out to him. ''Of course you may.''

He sat beside Hannah this time and listened carefully as she and Rafe filled him in on their ideas.

''All right, Rafe,'' Cord said. ''You sit tight here and I'll put some things in motion that ought to get her attention. We'll take care of her dog and keep you supplied with clean clothes.''

Cord stood again and extended a hand to help Hannah up. She took it, then leaned over and kissed Rafe's cheek.

''Whatever you do, don't give up,'' she advised. ''It

may take Caroline a while to come around, but my money's on you. You tell her we'll be prayin' for her and that sweet baby.''

Watching Cord and Hannah walk away, Rafe remembered Caroline telling him that she once had envied the Stockwells because they had each other. At this moment, he understood why. One short visit from his twin and sister-in-law, and he felt reassured that he wasn't alone to deal with whatever lay ahead. Caroline had never had that luxury. He'd better remember that.

Caroline woke with a start early the next morning when a pretty young nurse swept into the room, checked her vital signs and her connections to the IV and the fetal monitor.

"Everything looks good here," the nurse said. "But as soon as we can get you organized, we'll be moving you to another room."

Caroline raised the head of her bed and rubbed the sleep from her eyes, which still felt swollen. The nurse studied her face for a moment, then brought her a cool, wet washcloth. "Rough night?"

"A little bit." Caroline took the cloth and wiped her face with it. It felt so wonderful, she immediately craved a whole bath. "Why am I moving?"

"You've got me," the nurse said. "All I know is, the orders came down from the top with the shift change."

An orderly arrived with a gurney. He helped the nurse transfer Caroline, her roses and her purse onto it, covered her with a sheet and whisked her into the nearest elevator. They rode up to the tenth floor in silence, and he rolled the gurney into a hallway. Three rooms to the left of the elevator, he pushed her into a room that looked like a luxury hotel room, with plush carpeting, impressionist paintings, an entertainment center and a wall made of windows.

Another nurse, this one in her late thirties and with a calm, motherly personality, helped the orderly transfer Caroline to the bed. It operated the same way a regular hospital bed did, but it was wider and more comfortable, and most of the equipment was cleverly concealed behind wooden cabinets. In an amazingly short time, Caroline had been reconnected to the necessary machines, fed a delicious breakfast, bathed and dressed in a so-called designer hospital gown that certainly fit her better than the standard one had.

The hospital administrator dropped in to welcome her to the hospital's VIP floor and jokingly scolded her for not mentioning her connection with the Stockwell family. Didn't she know that they were extremely generous contributors to this institution?

He'd no sooner left, than the huge baby-themed floral arrangements began to arrive. The card on the first one read,

> Caroline, we're thinking of you and the baby and sending good thoughts your way. Becky will be so delighted to have a cousin to play with. Please let us know when you're up to having visitors. A Stockwell takes care of his own. You're one of our own now. Yell if you need anything.
>
> Love, Cord and Hannah

Caroline grabbed the box of tissues, wiped her eyes and blew her nose before going on to the next one.

The card on the second arrangement said,

Dear Caroline, my fingers are crossed for you and
the baby. Can't wait to meet my new nephew. Take
care and don't forget, a Stockwell takes care of his
own. Please let us help in any way we can.

                                        Jack

Caroline yanked another tissue from the box.
The third card was from Kate.

Well, it's about time somebody finally told me
about you and Rafe. With you two for parents, that
baby's bound to be one gorgeous child. I hope
we'll become good friends soon. The Stockwell
family has needed more women in it for a very
long time.

                            Best wishes, Kate
P.S. We have a quaint saying in our family. A
Stockwell takes care of his own. That includes you
and the munchkin.

Muttering under her breath, Caroline dabbed her eyes
and blew her nose yet again. She sighed, then heard a
discreet cough, looked up and saw Rafe lounging in the
doorway. He grinned at her, and she wanted to hate him
for catching her with her defenses down.

"What are you doing here?" she grumbled.

"Good morning, sugar." He ambled into the room as
if she'd invited him, looking rested and ready for a new
day. "I'm glad to see you looking so much better today.
Are you feeling all right?"

"Fine." She raised her knees and tried to push the
roses under the sheet. She didn't want him to get the
wrong idea about her having them on the bed with her.
"Did you want something, Rafe?"

"How do you like the room?"

"It's lovely. Of course, you didn't have to do this for me. I can well afford it myself."

"I know that," he said with a careless shrug and another grin. "But you're liable to be here quite a while. It's my pleasure to make sure you and the baby are as comfortable as possible."

"Or perhaps you were trying to buy my affection with this VIP treatment?"

His grin faded. Linking his hands together behind his back, he walked over to the wall of windows and looked out over the city. "That thought never crossed my mind."

"Oh, of course not. And your whole family just suddenly got an urge to send me flowers."

He looked over his shoulder at her, his eyebrows arched in a question. "Was I supposed to keep your being in the hospital a secret?"

"I guess not," she said, squirming inside but not sure why she should. "I just feel uncomfortable at the thought that you discussed me with all of them. How much did you tell them?"

"Not much." He came back across the room, stopping to admire the bouquets one at a time. "They'd already figured out the baby was mine. Naturally they were concerned to hear you were having problems with the pregnancy."

"Rafe," she protested.

"Caroline," he said, mimicking her tone with a teasing grin. "That's not just your baby anymore. He's my son and he's my brothers' and my sister's nephew. We're all concerned about you and the baby."

"Are you threatening me with a custody suit?"

He jerked back as if she'd slapped him, and as she

watched his expression go blank of all emotion, she knew she'd gone too far.

"No," he said flatly. "I have no intention of dragging you into court or making life difficult for you in any way. But I also have no intention of letting my son think I don't care about him. He needs to know that I love him no matter what, and I hope you'll do us the courtesy of granting me enough visitation to accomplish that."

"Rafe, please don't take it that way. I didn't mean it the way it sounded."

"What other way is there to mean it?" he asked. "Look, Caroline, I know you don't love me. Hell, after yesterday you probably don't even like me anymore. It'll be a long time before I can forgive myself for not being there when you needed me. I really don't expect you to forgive me, either."

"But last night you said—"

"I said a lot of things last night."

"Did you mean any of them?"

He looked over his shoulder at her, then slowly nodded. "Yeah. I suppose my timing could have been better, but I meant every damn thing I said. So what?"

"So what?" The big idiot knew exactly what she was trying to get at, but he was just standing there, looking at her, and expecting her to—

What, Caroline? her conscience asked. *Take a risk? Fight your own fear and tell Rafe how you really feel about him?*

Her stomach clenched, her breath caught in her lungs and her heartbeat accelerated, and for once, she knew that none of it had anything to do with the baby. Oh, but she couldn't. She just couldn't say those words out loud. Not yet.

Why not? You'd rather go on acting like a coward

and pushing him away? How're you going to feel if he actually does go away? For good?

Horrified at the realization that she really was a coward, she made a quick mental count of all the times she'd pushed Rafe away in the past few weeks.

Think about it, her conscience taunted her. *You've given him every opportunity, every excuse, every good reason to leave you. And he's still here. How do you explain that?*

It was just the baby. The only reason he was still here was that he wanted the baby. Not her.

If that was true, he would've hired other people to help you instead of doing it all himself. He wouldn't have spent so much time and effort wooing Truman. And he'd already have a team of lawyers hammering out a custody agreement.

She covered her mouth with her fingers and shook her head, but she couldn't deny the truth any longer. Rafe's worried voice came to her as if from a long distance.

"Caroline? Sugar, are you all right?"

Rafe watched Caroline's face go pale and her eyes widen in what appeared to be shock. Covering her mouth with her fingers, she shook her head as if in denial, and he just knew something awful was happening to her. He rushed to the bed and frantically dug through the bedclothes for the call button. His fingers encountered something sharp enough to pierce his index finger.

Yelping, he yanked it out, discovered the bouquet of red roses he'd left with her the night before and tossed the whole mess to the floor. Dear God, if she'd started bleeding again...

"Where's the damn call button?" he demanded.

Caroline grabbed his wrists. He tried to shake her off, but his hands were shaking and she hung on like a burr.

"Let go," he said. "We need to get the nurse."

"No, Rafe, we don't," she said softly.

Caught by a new note of warmth in her voice, he looked up at her, his heart still pounding with alarm. She raised one hand to the side of his face and lovingly curved her fingers from his jaw to the outer corner of his eye socket. His heart stuttered around in his chest as if his body couldn't decide whether the situation called for more adrenaline or maybe a shot of testosterone. Her eyes met his and a tentative smile curved her lips, giving him the oddest impression that somehow, she was seeing him for the first time.

"We don't?" Was that his voice, croaking like some big old bullfrog? "You're sure?"

"Uh-huh." She raised her other hand, and with trembling fingers, traced his eyebrows, his ears, his nose, the shape of his lips. Her tentative smile bloomed into a smile of pure delight. It was an incredible turn-on, but he was so blasted confused, he didn't know whether to laugh or cry.

"What the hell's going on, sugar?" Now he sounded like a whiney bullfrog, but it didn't seem to bother Caroline.

"I don't know," she murmured, tracing his features again. "I just had a...revelation, or something."

"Is that good or bad?" he asked.

"I suppose that depends on you."

"What about me?" She was killing him by dragging this out, whatever "this" turned out to be. He desperately wanted to believe—even to hope—that she was finding her courage and her strength, but he didn't know if he could survive the disappointment if he was wrong.

Her smile faded as quickly as it had come. She pulled her arms in close to her sides and twined her fingers together. Suddenly he saw it. There, in the depths of her eyes was her fear, the stark uncertainty that had haunted her for so long. He felt humbled that she could bring herself to allow him to see it with such clarity.

"Do you..." She broke off, swallowed and took a slow, deep breath.

His stomach knotted. He wanted to encourage her, to hold her and tell her that he understood. That everything was going to be all right and she didn't have to do this. But he couldn't do any of it. He wanted the words to come straight from her heart without any prompting from him. And she needed to find out for herself that she could say them to him without having to pay a terrible price.

"Do you think," she murmured, her voice barely above a whisper, "that you could give me one more chance?"

"One more chance for what?" He held his breath, waiting in an agony of suspense for her reply.

"To learn how to fight my fear."

"Your fear about what, sugar?"

"About you. And me. And...us."

"I don't understand what you're saying."

Temper flashed in her eyes. "Yes, you do. You know exactly what I mean."

He shrugged, neither confirming or denying her charge. She glared at him, nearly making him laugh out loud. "Humor me. Just this once. Say the words."

"All right. Maybe I do sort of...love you."

She sounded so cranky and her declaration of love, such as it was, was so grudging, what could he do but believe it? Relief zipped through his system, with a big chaser of happiness following on its tail. But he just couldn't let her get away with that pitiful excuse for an I love you.

"Only maybe? And sort of?" he asked. "Careful there, or you'll bowl me over with your enthusiasm and sincerity."

"It's not easy," she said with an indignant little huff.

"I know, and I'm not tormenting you for the fun of it." Smiling, he clasped his hands around hers, stilling their nervous movements. "I was just as scared last night when I said it to you, as you are now. It would ease my fear a lot if I could hear you say the words like you mean them."

"Oh, Rafe, I do mean them. I mean, I love you. I have since the first time we made love."

The thought of so much lost time made him want to groan, but he held it in. He and Caroline had already wasted too much of their lives rehashing old hurts and mistakes. From now on, he wanted them to focus on the present and the future.

He leaned forward, wrapped his arms around her and held her tight. Snuggling against him, she wrapped her arms around his torso and rested her head on his chest. They both sighed, then chuckled and snuggled even closer.

"Did it hurt?" he asked, kissing the top of her head.

"Did what hurt?"

"Saying you love me."

She pulled back and looked up at him. "No. In fact, I may actually learn to enjoy saying it."

"I sure hope so, because I loved hearing it."

He kissed her then, putting his whole heart and soul into it. She raised her arms and crossed her wrists behind his neck, bringing her belly into contact with his.

Sighing, she opened her mouth to him, just as she'd finally opened her heart to him. He delved inside, tasting her, enjoying the soft sounds of pleasure she made, wanting to absorb her right into himself.

Breaking off the kiss, he gazed down at her face, imprinting every tiny detail on his memory as a way of preserving this moment. "I love you, Caroline. Will you marry me?"

Without the slightest hesitation, she gave him the most beautiful smile he'd ever seen and simply said, "Yes."

Humbled and ecstatic at the same time, he kissed her again, losing himself in the sheer rightness of it. The world narrowed to the hospital bed, the woman in his arms and the child nestled between them. Oh, man, this was it. Everything he needed to be complete, to be happy, to be home finally was within his grasp. He intended to hang on to all of it.

After all, a Stockwell always took care of his own.

Epilogue

One month later, Rafe helped Caroline out of the front seat of their new minivan, then slid open the rear passenger door and unbuckled his two-week-old son's car seat. Douglas yawned, stretched and settled back to sleep, his little mouth making a few suckling motions. Rafe picked him up, car seat and all.

"He's starting to look hungry again," Rafe said, grinning at Caroline.

"Oh, bite your tongue," she said with a chuckle. "All he ever does is eat."

He leaned down and kissed her. "Happy, Mrs. Stockwell?"

She wrinkled her nose at him. "Always, Mr. Stockwell."

The front door of Stockwell Mansion burst open. Cord came out first, followed by Hannah with Becky in her arms, Kate, and Mrs. Emma Hightower, the housekeeper. They all gathered around Rafe and Caroline, jockeying for a good spot to see the new baby.

"Oh, isn't he a darling?" Mrs. Hightower said, dabbing at her eyes with a handkerchief.

Cord slapped Rafe on the back. "Nice-looking boy, you've got there, little brother."

"Look, Becky," Hannah said, "see the little baby? That's little Douglas."

Kate took a glance at the baby, smiled at Caroline and started shooing everyone into the house. "Take the baby inside before he gets a sunburn," she said. "Besides, Jack's call should come through any minute."

"I didn't know Jack was calling," Rafe said.

"Just got an e-mail from him this morning." Cord turned to Caroline. "I hope you don't mind if we turn your first outing into a family meeting. It won't take long."

"I don't mind," she said, "as long as I get to hear all the news."

"Why not?" Kate asked. "You're a Stockwell now, too."

They went into Cord's office. Mrs. Hightower made sure everyone had a soft drink, cooed at Douglas one more time and took her leave. Jack's call came through a moment later. Cord put it on the speaker phone and told Jack who was in the room.

When all the greetings were finished, Jack got down to business. "I've been chasing all over this country, thinking I might eventually catch up to Mom and Uncle Brandon. But yesterday, I found a landlord who swears they went back to the States."

"No kidding?" Cord asked.

"No kidding," Jack said. "He says they were using the LeClaire name when they moved to New England.

Unfortunately he didn't have any more specific information than that, but I think I've found a way to narrow down the search.''

"What's that, Jack?" Rafe asked.

"I'll be home in a few days, and I'll tell you then," Jack replied. "I found something else over here that'll blow you all away. Especially you, Rafe. Bye, everybody."

"You can't leave us all in suspense like that, Jack," Kate protested.

"Want to bet?" Jack said with a laugh. "See you later."

There was a click on the line and everyone groaned in unison. They all speculated about Jack's surprise, but after a few minutes, Cord called them back to order.

"I've got a report, too." Smiling directly at Caroline, he said, "We'll be needing your legal expertise again."

"I'll help any way I can," Caroline said.

"All right. I've been looking into the Johnson situation. That's Madelyn's family," he explained for Caroline's benefit. "We have reason to believe that one of our ancestors cheated the Johnsons out of the land that produced the oil that built the Stockwell fortune. We're still trying to get at the truth there, too."

"What did you find out about the Johnsons?" Kate asked.

"Some of the old-timers around Grandview who remembered when Madelyn's family worked for us, told me that they might've been related to the Johnsons who own a rose farm outside of Tyler. Her mother, Emily, had a brother-in-law named Dabney Johnson. He moved to Tyler years ago and bought a rose farm. When he died, his son Eben took it over."

"Oh, my," Hannah said with a rueful laugh. "Every

time you learn something new about this family, it just gets more and more complicated. Are you going to track down Eben?''

"Probably," Cord agreed.

"I think we need to focus on finding Madelyn and Uncle Brandon first. And we ought to get somebody up to New England right away," Rafe said.

"You might want to bring in a professional investigator at this point," Caroline suggested. "Dad and I have used Brett Larson for a long time now."

Kate groaned and shook her head. "Anybody but him."

"I'm surprised to hear you say that," Caroline said. "Brett's got the best agency in the whole Dallas area."

"It doesn't have anything to do with his competence," Rafe explained. "He's Kate's ex-fiancé."

"Oh, dear, I'm sorry, Kate," Caroline said.

"It's no big deal," Kate assured her. "That happened years ago. I really don't care about him anymore."

"In that case," Cord said, "I vote we hire Brett to find Madelyn and Uncle Brandon."

"I agree," Rafe said.

They both looked at Kate expectantly. She tried her best to ignore them, but finally, the pressure became too great. Tossing her hands into the air in exasperation, she said, "Oh, all right, hire him."

She got up and strolled out of the room with her shoulders back and her head held high. But once she reached the sanctuary of her suite of rooms, she leaned back against the door, closed her eyes and whispered, "Oh, Brett."

* * * * *

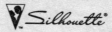

In March 2001,

Silhouette Desire

presents the next book in

DIANA PALMER's

enthralling *Soldiers of Fortune* trilogy:

THE WINTER SOLDIER

Cy Parks had a reputation around Jacobsville for his taciturn and solitary ways. But spirited Lisa Monroe wasn't put off by the mesmerizing mercenary, and drove him to distraction with her sweetly tantalizing kisses. Though he'd never admit it, Cy was getting mighty possessive of the enchanting woman who needed the type of safeguarding only he could provide. But who would protect the beguiling beauty from *him…?*

Soldiers of Fortune…prisoners of love.

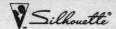

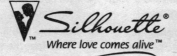

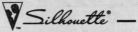

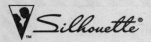

COMING NEXT MONTH

SPECIAL EDITION

#1381 HER UNFORGETTABLE FIANCÉ—Allison Leigh
Stockwells of Texas

To locate her missing mother, Kate Stockwell teamed up with private investigator Brett Larson to masquerade as a married couple. Together they discovered that desire still burned between them. But when former fiancé Brett asked Kate to be his wife for real, she feared that she could never provide all that he wanted...

#1382 A LOVE BEYOND WORDS—Sherryl Woods

Firefighter Enrique Wilder saved Allie Matthews from the rubble of her home and forever changed her silent world. A shared house and an undeniable chemistry caused passion to run high. But would Allie be able to love a man who lived so close to danger?

#1383 WIFE IN DISGUISE—Susan Mallery
Lone Star Canyon

Josie Scott decided it was time to resolve the past and showed up at her ex-husband's door a changed woman. Friendship and closure were all that Josie was after, until she looked into Del Scott's eyes. Finally, with a chance to explore their daunting past, would the two discover that love was still alive?

#1384 STANDING BEAR'S SURRENDER—Peggy Webb

Forlorn former Blue Angel pilot Jim Standing Bear had lost his ambition...until he found gentle beauty Sarah Sloan. She reminded Jim that he was all man. But Sarah—committed to caring for another—would have to choose between loyalty and true love....

#1385 SEPARATE BEDROOMS...?—Carole Halston

All Cara LaCroix wanted was to fulfill her grandmother's final wish—to see her granddaughter marry a good man. So when childhood friend Neil Griffen offered his help, Cara accepted. Could their brief marriage of convenience turn into an everlasting covenant of love?

#1386 HOME AT LAST—Laurie Campbell

Desperate for a detective's help, Kirsten Laurence called old flame J. D. Ryder. She didn't have romance on her mind, but they soon found themselves in each other's arms. Would their embrace withstand the shocking revelation of Kirsten's long-kept secret?